THE SHEPHERD'S HEART - BOOK 4

SPRING ★ MEADOW
Sanctuary

What Readers Think About
The Shepherd's Heart Series

Rocky Mountain Oasis is a delightful step back into the Wild West. Ms. Bonner draws her characters in bold and wonderful strokes that give a portrait of them so tender and convincing you cannot help loving them. I really enjoyed this novel. It is touching and fulfilling. It also includes a very strong message of redemption. I look forward to her next novel.
—Lionel D. Alford
Author of *Aegypt*, and *The Second Mission*.

I love *Rocky Mountain Oasis*. I just couldn't put it down. I kept it in my hands until I was done. The story line was well written and the use of historical facts made the story all the more fascinating for me. Thanks for such a great book! I can't wait for the next one!
—Krista
Amazon Reviewer

Rocky Mountain Oasis is very well written, I really enjoyed every word of it! I really related to Brooke's feelings and emotions. Lynette does an excellent job making you feel each aspect of her life. Plus the suspense part, just really keeps you on the edge of your seat!!! This is a great historical, mail order bride read... I highly recommend it!
—Martha
Amazon Reviewer

Lynnette Bonner has outdone herself with *High Desert Haven*. This action-packed story of life in the Old West just begs to be turned into a movie. It's a powerful tale of hardship and happiness, of loss and love, and most of all, of the power of faith. If you enjoy stories of the way life really was in the nineteenth century, don't miss *High Desert Haven*.
—AMANDA CABOT - Author of *Tomorrow's Garden*

Set in a time when men killed for land and beautiful women, *High Desert Haven* is a sweet romance with enough flying bullets to please any Western fans. The blazing hearts and guns blend well with the faith message, which the author beautifully weaves into the characters' lives. If you're looking for a novel to get you through a sleepless night, this is the one. Then again, it's probably the reason you're still awake.

—April Gardner
Award-winning author of *Wounded Spirits*

High Desert Haven has more than enough action to keep readers' lamps burning into the night. Bonner has shaped a lively romance that shoots straight from the heart.

—Sharon McAnear-
Author of the Jemma series and the Stars in My Crown series

Brimming with endearing flesh-and-blood characters amidst the beautiful high desert mountains, Lynnette Bonner has crafted a heart-tugging story interwoven with enough romance and suspense and spiritual gems to keep readers turning pages far into the night. This second book in The Shepherd's Heart series is worth the wait!

—Laura Frantz
Author of *The Frontiersman's Daughter, Courting Morrow Little*, and *The Colonel's Lady*

Bonner has consistently wowed us with her attention to detail, heart touching characters and hair raising danger. It's a fun ride, one that will make you laugh out loud and then weep. You will never regret the time spent or the sleep lost in reading these books. I have re-read them many times now, and each time is like the first. Her love for Christ shows through every page. I have enjoyed them all immensely and I can't wait for more.

—Anndra
Amazon Reviewer

THE SHEPHERD'S HEART SERIES

Rocky Mountain Oasis
BOOK ONE

High Desert Haven
BOOK TWO

Fair Valley Refuge
BOOK THREE

Spring Meadow Sanctuary
BOOK FOUR

Find other books by Lynnette Bonner at:
www.lynnettebonner.com

THE SHEPHERD'S HEART - BOOK 4

SPRING ★ MEADOW
Sanctuary

Lynnette
BONNER

Serene Lake Publishing

Spring Meadow Sanctuary
THE SHEPHERD'S HEART SERIES, Book 4

Published by Serene Lake Publishing

Cover design by Lynnette Bonner, Indie Cover Design, images ©
www.fotolia.com, File: #18460975_XL
www.bigstockphoto.com, File: #2351853

Author photo © Emily Hinderman, EMH Photography

ISBN: 978-1-942982-04-3

Printed in the U.S.A.

TO THOSE WHO CAME BEFORE:

Our country has been built on the hard work and dedication of many generations and nationalities. Many resided during times when a living was made through hard-scrabble work and a lot of bootstrap pulling. They labored like nobody's business but also put their faith in God for protection and sustenance. I, for one, am thankful, because we wouldn't be where we are today without their endurance and unflinching work ethic.

In my books I attempt to honor that spirit.

Psalm 23
A PSALM OF DAVID

The Lord is my shepherd; I shall not want.
He makes me to lie down in green pastures;
He leads me beside the still waters.
He restores my soul;
He leads me in the paths of righteousness For His name's sake.
Yea, though I walk through the valley of the shadow of death,
I will fear no evil;
For You are with me;
Your rod and Your staff, they comfort me.
You prepare a table before me in the presence of my enemies;
You anoint my head with oil; My cup runs over.
Surely goodness and mercy shall follow me
All the days of my life;
And I will dwell in the house of the Lord Forever.

★

PROLOGUE

Shiloh, Oregon.
September, 1887

Cade Bennett massaged one hand over the muscles of his neck as he stepped out of the bank. He'd just returned from a long trail drive and weariness weighed heavy.

"Cade Bennett! How've you been?"

Cade blinked. Sam Perry was a long ways from home. "Sam! Good to see you." Cade shook his friend's hand, even as a leery uneasiness narrowed his gaze.

The short greenhorn stood in the center of the boardwalk blocking Cade's progress, and his presence here could only mean one thing, more work. And likely the work revolved around some trouble with Sam's conniving sister, Katrina.

He rolled his head stretching tired muscles. "Walk with me, would you?" he said, as he pushed by and headed toward the mercantile. "What can I do for you, Sam?"

Even as Cade asked the question, he dreaded the answer. All he wanted was to drop into a chair out at the ranch, drink a hot cup of coffee, and catch up with Rocky and his wife, Victoria. He hadn't spoken with Rocky, his best friend and partner, for several months, and it would sure be nice to sleep in a real bed for a change. Maybe find out a little information about Rocky's sister, Sharyah. Was she still teaching here in town?

Sam snatched his bowler from his head and hustled to catch up, his snakeskin boots beating a tattoo on the boardwalk and the gold chain from his pocket watch clinking against the buttons of his vest. "Now Cade don't brush me off so fast. You know I wouldn't be here unless I really needed your help."

Cade kept walking. Whatever had brought Sam here, especially if it did revolve around Katrina, smelled like trouble.

And trouble he could do without. Perry, an eastern banker who'd only moved west a few years ago, owned a ranch near Beth Haven where he lived with his sister. Cade had sold Perry horses on a number of occasions, but the man had never come to him – he'd always summoned Cade to his lavish spread, always too busy to leave home. So whatever had broken his pattern must be important. Still…he rolled his shoulders wishing away some of the weariness…the last thing he wanted right now was another cross-country trip.

Knowing Sam would get to the point soon enough, Cade stepped down into the dust of the street, crossing just in front of an oncoming buckboard.

The little man darted after him. "I asked around. And I'm still hearing that if I want to hire an honest hombre to do some lawmen's work, you're the one to talk to."

'Hombre' pronounced with his Yankee twang, was quite the thing to hear. Cade suppressed a grin. "Sam, my friend, I'd like to help, but you're catching me at a bad time. I'm not interested. Sorry." Cade pushed into Halvorson's Mercantile, the bell jangling above his head. He couldn't go out to the ranch without some candy for the three kids Rocky and Victoria had adopted.

Seemingly undeterred Sam darted in front of him and put one hand on his chest.

Cade released a breath of frustration and stopped next to the sacks of chicken feed. Maybe if he just talked to the man for a few minutes he'd go away. "Did Katrina sell another herd of your cattle to that *caballero* for five dollars a head?"

Sam didn't look happy to be reminded of that little incident. "You're just in from a cattle run, correct?" He apparently wasn't going to rise to Cade's bait.

Cade nodded.

"I'm willing to pay you three times what you just made if you'll come to Beth Haven and help me track down some cattle rustlers. They've been plaguing me for months and with my work at the bank, I simply haven't had time to deal with it." The little man folded his arms, his bowler poking out to one side.

Cade arched a brow. Sam could always come up with an elaborate plan, but generally the plan called for someone else to execute it. "I made good money on this run, Sam."

A gleam leapt into Sam's eyes as though he knew he had Cade's attention. "Whatever you made, I'll pay you triple. These rustlers have caused me enough trouble and money. And now Katrina's with them!"

Just as he'd assumed. Cade settled his hands on his hips. Sam's sister had always been peril-in-a-skirt. "Sounds like a job for your local law enforcement."

Sam snorted. "You know old Sheriff Collier would rather fish than track down a clue any day of the week."

Rubbing one hand across his prickly jaw, Cade studied the stack of feed sacks to his right. He didn't have another job lined up yet. And triple what he'd made on this run was certainly good money.

Rocky and Victoria were doing a fine job of running the ranch while he was away. And he hadn't been looking forward to seeing Victoria working in Ma's kitchen, anyhow. With Pa off to who knows where, maybe… His thoughts turned to Sharyah Jordan. If he had any reason to stick around town, she was it. Would sure be nice to see her again. It was certainly time to explain the disaster he'd made of things last summer. Maybe he could make up for it somehow.

Just then Mrs. Halvorson stepped into the aisle. "Why Cade Bennett! It's so good to see you home! When did you get back?"

Cade snatched his hat from his head and nodded. "Mrs. Halvorson." The woman must have heard the bell a moment earlier. She had ears like a fox when it came to her bell and local gossip – but didn't hear much else most of the time. "Good to be home, ma'am. I just rode into town this afternoon. How has everything been around here since I've been gone?"

She cupped one hand to her ear. "What was that?!"

Cade leaned toward her and raised his voice. "I said, 'How has everything been?'"

"Well, it's been downright… different over the last few

months what with the Jordans adopting those three children and moving out to your place after the passing of your—oh listen to me go on, I'm sorry to bring that up. How is your father, dear?"

A wave of sorrow washed over him even as he suppressed a roll of his eyes. The woman could at least try to be subtle as she pried for information to hand on to the next customers to walk through her doors.

He clenched his jaw. Yes, life certainly wouldn't be the same in town for him, now. He had no idea where Pa was, or how he was doing, or if he was even alive. But Mrs. Halvorson waited for an answer so he searched for something truthful to say. "He's fair to middling, ma'am. Getting along as well as can be expected, I suppose." Pa had pulled up every stake he'd ever put down and taken for the hills the very day Ma had passed on. Cade hadn't seen him since and the roll of anger that surged through him threatened to upset his stomach. He swallowed away the bitter taste at the back of his throat, and suddenly realized that Mrs. Halvorson was looking from him to Sam Perry an expectant arc in her brows. "Oh, ah... Mrs. Halvorson," he gestured to Sam with his hat, "Sam Perry. Mr. Perry, meet Mrs. Halvorson."

Sam bowed over her hand. "It's a pleasure to make your acquaintance, ma'am."

"And where do you hail from, Mr. Berry?"

"Uh, Perry, ma'am. I'm from over east of the mountains, a little settlement near Farewell Bend."

"Where was that?"

"Farewell Bend, ma'am." Perry spoke a little louder.

"Really? Well! Our school teacher recently moved east of the mountains to take a school. A town called Madras. Also not too far from Farewell Bend, I believe. I hear tell that it's hot over there this time of year. And the way ol' Mr. Crockett tells it, the outlaws are thick as morning cream out that way." She tsked. "I do hope our young Sharyah makes it back home alive."

Cade's heart tripped over itself. So Sharyah was out of town.

Decision suddenly made, Cade turned to Sam. "Have you had dinner yet, Sam?" He smiled and tipped his head at Mrs.

Halvorson, taking Sam's arm and pulling him toward the candy display.

The man blinked, a little startled. "No. No I haven't." His mouth stretched as he took in the three sticks of peppermint Cade picked up. "Are we having that for dinner?"

Cade grinned and headed for the front. "Why don't you come out to my ranch with me and we can discuss the details of the job you're talking about."

Perry trotted after him. "Certainly. Certainly. Yes, that would be fine. I knew you wouldn't turn me down."

Cade heaved a breath of relief as he placed the sticks of candy on the counter. He hadn't realized until now how much he'd been dreading the thought of living out at the ranch, once again. A few more months on the road wouldn't hurt any. Rocky could certainly be trusted to keep things running smoothly, and the money he'd make on this job would be a nice cushion against any unforeseen expenses in the future.

A certain blond woman came to mind, but he pushed the thought away. Still, Madras was only a crow's hop from Beth Haven....

CHAPTER ONE

Sharyah had just bent over the papers she needed to grade when the small rock landed on her desk with a soft thud. The titter of laugher ceased as she snapped her head up to study her students. Everyone seemed to be in deep concentration and intent on their lessons. She focused her gaze on Brandon McBride, but he looked as innocent as an angel and sat attentively reading his history lesson, just as he should be. Sonja and Sally Weaver both gave her sympathetic glances, from the last row of desks where they were working on their math lesson together.

Sharyah sighed, knowing from past experience that asking the class who had done the deed would prove futile. She'd been here two weeks, now. Two weeks in the God-forsaken little back-water town of Beth Haven and for a solid week-and-a-half she'd been longing to pack her bags and return home.

She had been approached about teaching in Madras, but upon arriving learned that the former teacher had decided to stay on for another year. Disappointed, she'd been all set to go back home when the head of the board told her that Beth Haven had been having trouble keeping a teacher and he thought they might be searching for one again. When she'd arrived and informed the Beth Haven board of her interest in the teaching position, they'd been ecstatic. She could see why, now. No teacher in their right mind would want to stay and deal with this, but she was determined to make it work.

The first week, she'd spent countless hours grilling the students both collectively and individually as to the identity of the trickster, but whoever the little devil was, he had a fierce grip on the loyalty of everyone else in the class. No one would give him up.

For the last several weeks, she'd tried to ignore the incidents in hopes that the prankster would give up out of sheer boredom. Never one to be squeamish, when she'd found the snake in her top desk drawer she'd calmly picked it up and tossed it out the window. A few of the boys had gaped in disappointment, but the next day a tack had appeared on her chair. She'd noticed it before she sat on it, thankfully, and had whisked it out of sight and plunked herself down on the chair with zest. But, even though she'd been watching their faces carefully as she dropped into the seat, she hadn't been able to determine which child was the most disappointed when she didn't cry out in pain.

A couple days ago, she'd actually almost laughed when she'd discovered that all the chalk had been replaced with garden carrots, fuzzy green tops and all. Thankfully she'd had an extra piece in her satchel.

Today however, the large spider in her lunch pail had been almost more than she could bear. She shuddered at the memory and thanked her lucky stars that Papa had never allowed her to luxuriate in a fit of the vapors – because if ever there was a moment when she'd been tempted to, that had been it. The thing had been so large she could see its beady eyes looking right at her! And fuzzy! She rubbed at the goose-flesh on her arms. All afternoon her stomach had been grumbling its complaint. The thought of eating her sandwich and the apple that a spider crawled all over had been more than her fortitude could handle.

Yes, packing up and returning to home would be heaven. But, in a way that would be just like succumbing to the vapors, and she wouldn't allow herself the weakness of retreat. She would get a much-needed break in the spring, just a few short months away, when her entire family came over for Jason and Nicki's March wedding. Tears pressed at the backs of her eyes as longing to see them all welled up inside her. But she blinked hard and reined in her emotions. Until then, she would simply have to forge ahead.

All her life she'd wanted only one thing.

Well, two things if she were honest, but she wasn't going to think about Cascade Bennett today. She sighed and glanced out the window. If she was smart she wouldn't ever again waste another moment of time pondering the way he'd broken her heart. God promised in his Word that goodness and mercy would follow her all the days of her life, so obviously the good things God had for her didn't include Cade Bennett.

Samuel Perry - that's who she should be thinking on. Yes, Sam. If he ever got around to asking her, he would make a very… suitable husband. She could learn to be happy and satisfied with a man like Sam.

Giving herself a shake, she returned her focus to her students. The one thing she'd wanted ever since she could remember was to be a teacher. She loved children, loved to see their eyes light up when understanding dawned. Loved their frank outlook on life and their quickness to forgive and move on. Loved to help them make something of themselves. That love was the reason she was here, and she had to figure out a way to get these children to accept her, or at least respect her.

She glanced at the clock and stood from her desk. "Alright, children. It's time to head home for the day." She gave them all her sunniest smile. "See you bright and early in the morning, and don't forget tomorrow is our day to go leaf collecting, so bring a sack or pillowslip from home to carry with you." She pinned Brandon with a look. "Brandon, if I could have a moment of your time up by my desk, please? Everyone else, you're dismissed."

Purposely she turned her back and began to erase the chalk board, but inwardly she cringed, waiting for some missile or projectile to bombard her. With a determined clench of her jaw, she threw back her shoulders. *Show no fear*!

Amazingly enough nothing happened and soon, other than Brandon shuffling his feet as he waited for her to finish, the room filled with silence.

Finally, she hung the rag on its hook by the board and turned to face her little nemesis. My, but he had the most alluring big chocolate eyes. And right at the moment they were dripping with innocence. *Future women beware! Brandon McBride cometh!* She bit off a grin and folded her hands carefully in front of her.

"Did you need my help, Miss Jordan?" He looked around as though expecting her to ask him to carry something for her.

"No, Brandon. But I want you to know that I'm not going anywhere."

He seemed puzzled. "Not going anywhere, ma'am?"

"No matter the number of tricks played on me, I will finish out the school year. Now," she held up a hand to still his protest, "it can be a good year for both of us, or it can be a miserable year. Your choice."

"But ma'am, I don't…" Suddenly his eyes widened. "You think I'm the one that's been playin' tricks on you?" He shook his head, dark eyes wide and gleaming with sincerity. "It ain't me, ma'am. Honest it's not."

"Isn't. 'It isn't me, ma'am,'" she corrected automatically, then sighed. "You are dismissed, Brandon. See you tomorrow."

"Yes'm." He turned to fetch his lunch pail and slate.

Was that an impish gleam in his eyes? Or simply relief at not being in too much trouble?

She watched him dash out the door, his ever-present slingshot cocked at an angle in the waistband of his pants, and then sighed as she sank down onto her chair.

Wasp-venom-pain stabbed into her backside. With a yelp, she leapt to her feet. And pulled the offending stick pin from her posterior.

Her eyes narrowed. "Why that little—"

The back door crashed in, startling the rest of the thought from her mind.

A man tromped in, black bowler pulled low over his brow, red bandana covering his nose and mouth and a gun leveled at her chest.

Cade Bennett stood in the alley, his heart beating a competition with the tinny piano playing inside the saloon. Judd Rodale and his younger brother Mick had gone in only moments ago. He took a calming breath and checked his weapon one more time, then stepped around the corner and pushed through the bat-wing doors of The Golden Pearl.

The room looked the same as it had the night before when he'd scouted it with Rocky and Sky. Upright piano in the back right corner. Bar along the wall to his left. Stairs leading up to the second floor along the rear wall. And six round tables scattered throughout the room. Judd and Mick sat at a table close to the bar. They'd already been dealt in to the perpetual poker game The Pearl kept running. The dealer wore a white shirt with black armbands and a visor cap, and looked a little nervous as he dealt out a card to Judd. *The other two men in the game must be locals.* Cade didn't recognize them.

He sidled up to the bar and rested his forearms there, lifting a finger to the barkeep.

"What'll it be?" The man wiped his hands on a rag that looked like it would leave more behind than it would clean off.

"Whiskey. Make it a double."

The bartender sloshed the liquid into a glass and slid it his way.

Cade lifted it in a gesture of thanks and turned to face the room, propping his elbows on the bar and one boot on the rail below. He sniffed the whiskey but didn't taste it. He would need all his senses to pull this off.

The poker hand came to an end and Rodale raked in his winnings.

Time to turn on the charm. Lord, a little help here. "You gentlemen care to let a weary traveler in on a bit of the fun?"

Judd Rodale didn't even look at him. "You gonna drink that whiskey, kid? Or just look at it?"

Mick snickered and organized his stacks of coins, taking his brother's lead in not even glancing Cade's way.

Cade chuckled. "Well, I need all my wits about me if I'm going to go up against you Rodales in a poker game. I've heard you're the best."

Judd looked up then, scanning him from head to toe.

Good. He had the man's attention.

"I'm sorry, kid, but I can't say your reputation has spread as far as mine. I have no idea who you are."

Cade grabbed a chair and circled around so that his back would be to the wall when he sat. He turned the chair backwards and straddled it, setting his whiskey on the card table. "Well now, I'm going to ignore the fact that you called me kid in that tone, because basically I'm nobody." He stretched his hand across the table giving Rodale what he hoped was an irritated smile. "Name's Schilling. Cade Schilling."

The dealer fumbled the cards he was shuffling.

Judd's eyes widened a bit as he studied Cade, ignoring his proffered hand.

Cade felt his first moment of ease. So their planning ahead on this one had paid off. These men had definitely heard of Cade Schilling.

One of the locals gathered up his money and stood. "Time for me to call it a night, fellas. Catch you another time."

No one seemed to notice his departure. All attention at the table was fixed on Cade.

Mick cursed. "*You* are Cade Schilling? The Cade Schilling who—"

Judd cleared his throat loudly.

Mick caught himself. "—well, *the* Cade Schilling?"

Cade grinned. "Never met another one of me. So what do you say? We playing cards, or not?" Casually he removed a stack of gold eagles from his jacket pocket and laid them on the table.

Judd flicked a gesture to the dealer. "Deal him in."

"Now you're talking." Cade stood, flipped his chair around the right way, removed his jacket and hung it over the back. He rolled up his sleeves as he sat down again, and grinned at the men who were all staring at him in question. "Had a friend get shot once. Someone thought he had a card up his sleeve. I watched him die, choking on his own blood." He shrugged. "I've made it a point to roll my sleeves up for every poker game since then."

Mick chuckled and picked up his hand of cards.

The kid would be easier to win over than Judd. But if he

could get Judd to like him, the rest of the Rodale Gang would fall in line.

Cade let the first two hands go, cringing inwardly at the amount of money Judd was taking off him. He reminded himself that the money was Sam's anyway – all part of the ruse.

They were halfway into the third round when Rocky and his brother Sky pushed through the doors, their badges plainly visible. Sky sauntered to a table and Rocky eased up to the bar. Cade's heart rate kicked up a notch. The other local folded, snatched his hat from the back of his chair and quickly strode from the room. The only other patron in the room hurriedly followed him out the doors.

Smart men. A little more of the tenseness eased from Cade's shoulders. Less potential for casualties. Less witnesses. The bartender, piano player, and dealer were the only others left now, and they would be easily convinced to keep quiet about the events that were about to unfold.

Cade thought through the plan one more time, making sure he had every detail of what was to happen figured out. Jason had wanted to be here too, but Nicki, the widow Jason had fallen in love with, was due to have her baby any day now and they'd all convinced him they could pull this off without him.

Lord I hope we were right on that count.

He laid a card aside and took another from the dealer. It was time to put everything into play. He lowered his voice and kept his perusal on his cards as he said, "Judd, unless I miss my guess, your dandy of a brother here has been sneaking down to town and has caused a little ruckus. Two lawmen just came in. One at the bar, one at the table near the door." He He

Judd's voice was just as low, barely audible over the plinking of the piano. "I see 'em. We don't have anything to worry about. Sheriff Collier wouldn't know an outlaw from a bread roll. This is his town."

Pretending great interest in his cards, Cade lifted one shoulder. "The barber said they brought in a couple new men. This must be them."

"Well, we ain't done nothing to warrant their attention. They mostly leave us alone so long as we keep to ourselves. I'll handle this." Judd swilled his whiskey and took a gulp then started to stand.

Cade flicked the corner of one of his cards. "I hear tell Judge Green's daughter is sure a pretty little thing."

Mick shifted uncomfortably in his chair.

Judd cursed softly and sank back down. "Mick?"

Mick couldn't seem to meet his brother's gaze.

Judd swore again. "I ought to shoot you, myself! We are just about—" he cut off, tossing Cade a glance before he returned his attention to Mick. "Now I have to figure out a way to get us out of here."

Cade leaned forward. "Maybe I can help you with that."

Judd glowered at him.

Cade pressed on. "I've been needing a place to… hang my hat, for a bit. I get you out of here and…?" He shrugged. Their whole plan hinged on the decision Judd would make right here.

Mick nodded at Cade. "You get us out of here and you can stay with us for as long as you want."

Judd wasn't so quick to take the bait. He lowered his brow. "Why would you do us any favors?"

Cade pushed out his lower lip and eased into a comfortable posture. "Suit yourself. Like I said, I've been needing a place to lie low. Word hereabouts is you have the best hide-out around, and…." He lifted his shoulders and resettled his hat, once again leaving the decision in Judd's hands.

Rocky and Sky stood erect and turned to face their table.

"Judd, just let him help us." Desperation tinged the edges of Mick's tone.

Judd glanced toward the slowly approaching lawmen. Then gave Cade a barely perceptible nod.

Cade suppressed a sigh of relief as he stood and swung his jacket over his shoulder. "Gentlemen," he said loudly, "the game has been fun, but I sense it is time to move on." He tipped his hat to Sky and Rocky as he stepped past them. They were already drawing their guns, right on cue.

"Mick Rodale, you are under arrest for the molestation of Missy Green."

Cade palmed his gun, spun around and swung his coat over Rocky's Colt knocking the aim down and away. He pressed the muzzle of his pistol to Sky's chest. Sky only had enough time to let loose his scripted cry of shock before Cade pulled the trigger. The report was a little loud, but about right.

Sky flew backward and crashed over a table, sliding across the surface and disappearing over the other side as the table toppled onto its edge. His body was concealed, only his legs protruded from one end.

Too bad about that. He couldn't see if the blood packet they'd rigged had worked.

Rocky had recovered from his pretended surprise by this time and had his Colt leveled at Judd's head. "Drop your gun! I will kill him!"

Calmly Cade turned and pressed the muzzle of his pistol under Rocky's chin. "Your friend over there is lying in a pool of his own blood. Do you think I'd hesitate to kill you too? You have five seconds to drop that gun."

Rocky's eyes narrowed.

"Four… three…"

"Alright! Alright!" Rocky's gun thumped onto the table and he raised his hands above his head.

This was the critical moment. Now he had to keep Judd and Mick from shooting Rocky themselves.

He kept his pistol aimed directly at Rocky and his body between him and the Rodales. "Have a seat in that chair behind you. Judd, Mick. I got this. I'll meet you outside of town."

Mick shucked his gun and pushed Cade aside. He stood trembling in excitement before Rocky. "Let me kill this one."

Dear God, give me wisdom. Cade hoped his breathing sounded normal to the others in the room. It rasped ragged and thready in his own ears. He made a quick decision, met Rocky's gaze and then thunked him a good one with the butt of his pistol.

Not hard enough to actually knock him out, but Rocky took the cue and slumped over, toppling to the floor with a low moan.

Cade pierced Mick with a look. "You kill a lawman and it will follow you to your grave. Trust me, I know."

Judd had his pistol free now. He gestured the bartender, piano player, and dealer toward the back wall and they stumbled over themselves to comply. Cade made swift work of tying up Rocky and the bartender while Mick grumbled his way through binding the other two.

Judd stepped over and eyed Sky, then turned to Cade and nodded. "Thanks. We owe you one."

Cade smoothed down his sleeves, buttoned the cuffs, and swung his jacket on. "Best we make ourselves scarce." He wanted to get these two out of here before one of them decided to put an extra bullet into either Sky or Rocky.

Judd snapped his fingers at Mick. "Let's go."

With a sigh of frustration Mick followed them out the doors. They mounted up and galloped toward the foothills.

A tremor of sheer relief coursed through Cade. *First step down. Thank you, Lord.*

CHAPTER TWO

Sharyah blinked at the bandit, her hand still holding the stickpin, frozen in mid air.

It only took her a moment to recognize him.

"Samuel Perry! You nearly startled me right through the Pearly Gates!" She slumped into her chair, resisting the urge to rub her posterior once more, and dropped the tack into her desk drawer. No need for Sam to know the problems she currently faced at the school.

Sam laughed and holstered his pistol. "Aw! You ruined my fun." He pulled the bandana down and winked at her. "I was hoping to rustle me a kiss from the prettiest school teacher ever."

Sharyah knew she should feel flattered by that. Instead her irritation rose. "And what if the gun had accidentally gone off?" Her father would have whipped her brothers good if any of them had ever tried a stunt like that.

Sam lifted his bowler and scooped his fingers through his straight sandy hair. "You're right. I'm sorry." He grinned then. "You should have seen the look on your face, though, Darling."

The "darling" grated. Especially since she knew he didn't really mean it. Sam might find her a passing fancy, but his affections belonged to someone else. The signs of a broken heart were all there. *I should know them well enough.* She just hadn't figured out who the woman was yet. But she had no doubt Sam dallied with her in an attempt to forget someone.

Who was she to talk? Wasn't that the same reason she allowed him to call? So she could forget Cade? She sighed and set to gathering the materials she would need at home tonight. "I'm glad I could be your entertainment for the day, Sam."

He turned serious in an instant. "I'm honestly sorry, Sharyah." He cocked his head to one side. "Is everything alright?"

She shook herself from her melancholy and forced a smile. "Yes, I'm fine. Just tired, I suppose."

"Children giving you trouble?"

"All's well," she quickly assured. Sam was the head of the school board. It wouldn't do for him to think she couldn't handle the children. "The students and I are just… learning to adjust to one another."

"Good." He clasped his hands behind his back and gave her a petulantly pleading look. "Let me take you to dinner, then. You won't have to cook and I'll be able to make up for my little bandito faux pas."

She carefully checked the first window to make sure the lock was secure. "You know my contract stipulates that I can't fraternize with men." Crossing to the other window, she checked it, too.

"Well," he stuck his lower lip out, "I happen to know the banker who is the head of the school board pretty intimately. I know he won't mind. And the other members are eating from the palm of his hand. They won't make a fuss. If they do he'll just call in their loans."

She grinned and slung her satchel over her shoulder. "This head of the school board seems a little arrogant and callous, don't you think?"

He laughed outright at that and reached to take the stack of books from her hands. "It's only arrogant if it isn't true. As for callous…." He shrugged. "Maybe a little." With a grin, he held the door for her. "Mrs. Dougherty down at the boarding house makes a mean pot-roast, what do you say? I'll be a perfect gentleman the whole night. Besides, I have a surprise for you."

A surprise? Surely he wasn't planning to… No. It couldn't be. Sharyah lifted one eyebrow as she pulled the door to and latched it. "Something tells me you aren't used to being told no."

He shrugged. "True. So let's not start now, shall we?" He peered at her over top the stack of books, pleading with his dark eyes.

How could she say no to that? But what if he was planning—

she cut herself off from that thought and picked up the pace toward home. It was too soon. Even though she didn't think she needed to fear him asking for her hand, she really should say no. But she simply didn't want to spend the evening alone. Her little cabin on the edge of town was very nice, but also… solitary. "Well, I would hate to be the one to introduce you to the word no, I suppose."

He grinned. "I was counting on that. How about I pick you up at seven then?"

"Seven sounds fine."

They had arrived at the cut-off she needed to take to get home.

Sam deposited the heavy books back into her arms. One toppled off and sprawled in the dirt. "I'll get it." He picked it up, brushed at the cover and then set it atop the stack and stepped to one side. "Very well, then. I'll be back this evening." He tipped his hat. "I'm very much looking forward to it, Sharyah. Good afternoon." And with that he hurried off toward the livery.

Sharyah rolled her eyes and readjusted her load. Pa would have tanned his hide for leaving her with a pile of books to carry, too.

As she started on toward home she mumbled, "But no man is perfect, right?" A dark-haired visage with alluring blue eyes immediately popped into her mind and she shook it away. "Oh stop it, Sharyah! Not even *he* was perfect." *I'm pathetic.* Still pining for a man who'd made it very clear he was only interested in friendship. But if she didn't find someone to marry soon, she would end up a genuine old maid. God had good in store for her. His Word said so. Obviously the time had come to stop being so picky and accept that she needed to readjust her wants. She would be nineteen on her next birthday.

She had nearly reached her front door when a loud shot rang out from somewhere in town. She paused to listen but there were no responding reports.

Strange. Perhaps someone scaring off a stray dog? Not likely. She wondered what that could have been about? With the Rodale

Gang hanging around, who knew what could be happening. That thought brought Missy to mind and she made a mental note to stop by and see her on the way home tonight. It was a terrible thing to have happened to such a nice girl. Worse yet she felt sure, Missy had been subtly snubbed at church for the past two weeks by the other girls in town. As if the girl was somehow at fault for the monstrous thing that had befallen her. Sometimes society was simply ridiculous!

Smith Bennett squinted his eyes against the Oregon dust filtering over him from the churning of hundreds of hooves. He'd been riding drag for the past hour. Give him lead or flank any day of the week. The constant eating of dust that came with bringing up the rear wore thin, and quick.

He adjusted his bandana and checked the angle of the sun.

Another forty-five minutes and they'd circle up. Tomorrow they'd reach Portland and payday would follow a couple days after that. His boss on these runs had been fair, but this one would be his last. It was time to go back home.

He snapped his whip to the outside of a wandering cow, scaring her back into line.

What was Cade up to these days? Had he sold the ranch?

Smith's jaw clenched. Doubtful he'd sold out. But whether his son would welcome his return, was another thing altogether.

Couldn't say as he blamed him, either. Running off the way he'd done after Brenda's passing wasn't something he was proud of. But time had given him a little distance and a clearer focus. Family ought to stick together. And he aimed to do his part to make that happen.

What Cade decided when he showed up… well, that would be up to him.

Sam arrived at Sharyah's door promptly at seven o'clock wearing a black suit and pulling at his collar. As he helped her up to the wagon seat, she glanced around. Seeing nothing remotely resembling his promised surprise, she teased, "I don't see my *surprise.*"

His brown eyes twinkled. "Patience is a virtue, Miss Jordan."

She smoothed the skirt of her best blue serge and adjusted her gloves as he strode around and hopped up in the driver's seat beside her. She tilted him a smirk. "A virtue best left for times when surprises are not pending."

He guffawed and slapped the reins down. "So patience isn't your strong suit, I see." The team settled into an easy gait and Sam rested his elbows on his knees and looked over at her. "I promise, Miss Impatient, that the surprise will be plainly evident the moment we arrive at the boarding house."

He was good on his word, for when they were still a block from Miss Dougherty's Boarding House Sharyah noticed the two men standing on the porch. "Sky! Rocky! Oh, thank you!" Before she thought better of it, she reached over and squeezed Sam's arm. "Thank you, so much!"

He reined the team to a stop and she didn't even wait for him to come around and help her down but jumped immediately to the ground and rushed up onto the porch. "It's so good to see you!" She pulled first Sky and then Rocky into an embrace. "I've missed you so mu—" She frowned, only at that moment realizing that Sky had winced when she hugged him and a distinct lump bulged on the side of Rocky's head. "—Are you two okay? Rocky what happened?" She reached toward his head.

He jerked away before her fingers could connect with the lump. "We're just fine." He met Sky's gaze briefly. "Nothing a little time won't ease. Now, how about you?" He offered her his arm and indicated the diner. "Shall we?"

"Yeah," Sky chimed in, "how are you liking your new job?"

Sharyah ignored their attempts to change the subject and stood her ground. "That shot I heard earlier? That had something to do with you two, didn't it?"

Both of her brothers looked guilty, but her focus zoomed in on Sam, who was just joining them. "And you? How do you know my brothers?"

Sam's feet shuffled. "Well… they were doing a little work for me today. I've known Cade for years – bought stock from him on a number of occasions, and he introduced me to Rocky and Sky not too long ago. I needed a little job done, so I went and hired them. And Ca—"

"—let's go into dinner."

"—that roast sure smells good."

"Cade? He's here?" Sharyah glanced around. A surge of joy pumped through her, yet a hint of unease at Sky and Rocky's rush to stop Sam from saying his name also niggled at the back of her mind.

Sam's brow furrowed speculatively. He settled his hands into his suit coat pockets, studying Sharyah with a curious lift of his brow.

Sky sighed and folded his arms over his chest, piercing Sam with a glare.

And Rocky attempted to pull her toward the diner's entryway. "Let's go eat, shall we?"

"He wasn't k-killed, was he?" Sharyah couldn't move. The sudden thought had frozen her to the boardwalk, and a wave of light-headedness washed over her.

Sky huffed, rubbed a hand over his chest, and winced. "Cade will most likely outlive us all."

Rocky gingerly touched the lump on his head. "Isn't that the truth." He looked at her. "He's not here, Shar. But he's fine."

The relief nearly took the strength from her legs. "O-okay. Let's go in and eat." She needed to change the subject. "How are Brooke and Sierra, Sky?"

The mention of his wife and daughter brought a smile to Sky's face as he held the door for them all to enter. "They're fine. Sierra's crawling all over the place now. And talk about a chatter box." He whistled. "Can't hardly get her to be quiet now that she's discovered she has a voice."

Sharyah chuckled and sat in the chair Sam held out for her. "I miss her so much." She glanced at Rocky as she settled the blue-and-white-checked napkin in her lap. "And Victoria and the kids? How's everyone?"

"They're good." Rocky's countenance softened. "They miss having you as their teacher, but they like Miss Cooper well enough. Especially Jimmy." He chuckled. "That boy's been studying his lessons like there is no tomorrow."

Sharyah laughed. "Oh good. He's so bright. Well, so are Damera and ChristyAnne."

"Yes, they all are."

The evening passed too quickly and Sharyah was soon blinking away tears as she hugged her brothers goodbye. Their work done, they would be heading home in the early hours of the morning. "Give my love to Ma and Pa."

Sky stepped back from the hug. "We'll do that. You take care of yourself now." His attention paused on Sam and held a hint of appraisal. "Be careful with my little sister."

Sam tipped his hat. "I wouldn't dream of being anything else." He touched Sharyah's elbow, escorting her out onto the boardwalk as Sky and Rocky headed up the stairs to their room.

They rode in silence for a time, the only sounds the soothing rustle of the wind through the junipers, the occasional squeak of wagon wheels, and the jangling of trace chains. The moon, hanging low and perfectly round, highlighted the road with a wash of milky light. She angled her head and studied the sky. Strips of clouds scuttled across the surface alternately concealing and then revealing the pinprick glimmer of the stars. Off to their right a whoosh of wings drew Sharyah's attention to an owl swooping through the moonlight to snatch up a poor, helpless critter.

Sam broke the silence with a soft cough. "So… This Cade… He mean something to you?"

Sharyah felt the heat that climbed into her face, and smoothed an invisible wrinkle in her skirt, thankful for the concealing darkness. "N-no. Not really. Just a childhood friend."

He turned and pierced her with an assessing gaze, the reins draped casually between his knees. "I see."

She couldn't meet his eyes. "I'd like to stop by the Greens' if you don't mind."

"The G-Greens'?" He returned his attention to the road. "Certainly."

Curiosity brought her focus to his face. Surely he wasn't like others in town who didn't want anything to do with the poor girl now, just because of the terrible thing that had happened to her? But Sam's face remained composed. Perhaps she'd only *thought* the name had startled him.

"I'll only be a moment," she said when he pulled to a stop outside the Greens' small farmhouse just a short ways out of town.

"Hold on, I'll come with you."

Was that cold determination she detected in his tone?

Missy herself answered the door and Sharyah gave her a quick hug.

"Miss Green." Sam tipped his hat and shifted from one foot to the other.

"Sam!" Missy's eyes widened and she paled slightly, but she quickly regained her composure. "How is Kat?"

Sam's mouth quirked up. "The same as ever, I'm sorry she hasn't been by to see you. She's… out of town."

Curiosity piqued at Sam's and Missy's reaction to each other. So it was Missy who'd broken Sam's heart? And who was Kat? Sharyah brushed her inquisitiveness away. She could ponder more on that later. "How are you?" She tilted her head, really trying to assess if Missy was alright.

Missy shrugged, then looked down at the floor. "I've had better days."

"I know. I'm so sorry. I brought you something." Sharyah dug through her satchel and pulled out *The Black Arrow* pressing it into her friend's hands. "This is a brand new book. I just finished reading it to the children this week and I thought you might enjoy it. Maybe it will help take your mind off of… things for a few minutes."

Missy took the book without a word. She rubbed her hand across the cover and tears sprang to her eyes.

"Oh Missy, I'm sorry. You don't have to read it. I just thought—"

"No. It's not that." Missy's gaze darted to Sam, before she met Sharyah's eyes, her tears spilling over to course down her cheeks. "The book is wonderful. Very thoughtful. Thank you." She smiled. It looked forced but it was a smile none the less. "You have no idea how much this means to me, Sharyah. Really. You are the only—" She pressed her lips together. "Well," she lifted the book, "thank you. Would you like to come in?"

"I'm sorry I can't. Mr. Perry needs to get me home. My contract stipulates that I must be home by eight thirty. My brothers were in town and he drove me in to have dinner with them. But maybe later this week?"

"Sure. That would be fine."

"Good." Sharyah pulled her into another embrace. *Lord, give her comfort in this trial.* "I'll see you later then."

Sam was silent on the drive home and Sharyah didn't press him for details about the woman who'd obviously broken his heart. Whatever strain lay between him and Missy was really none of her business.

Sam reined the team to a stop outside the teacherage, walked her to the door, and tipped his hat. "Goodnight, Sharyah." He started away.

She touched his arm. "Thank you for dinner with my brothers."

He smiled and tipped his hat. "Anytime. My pleasure."

She watched until he disappeared into the darkness, then bolted the door, made herself a cup of tea, and looked over her lessons for the next day. As she banked the fire and prepared for bed she thought over how truly wonderful it had been to see Sky and Rocky. She missed home so much. She would be teaching there still if she hadn't made the fateful mistake of slapping Cade Bennett that day in Victoria's sitting room.

He never would have realized she had feelings for him, if it wasn't for that. But he had figured it out, and he made it more than clear that he thought of her only as a little sister and nothing more.

And since she hadn't been able to stand the sympathetic

looks she kept getting from everyone around town, here she was. Far, far, far away from Cade Bennett and his brotherly affection. Sam was a good man. She would be happy with him. If he ever decided he could be happy with her too.

With a sigh, she crawled under the covers and blew out the lamp. She had nearly drifted off to sleep when a thought struck her and she bolted upright. Sam had said he'd hired Cade, too. Could Cade be working somewhere in the vicinity?

With a little groan of helplessness she flopped back against the pillows. Why couldn't she simply forget about that man? With a frustrated huff, she flipped over onto one side, mashed her pillow into a compliant lump, and forced herself to close her eyes and breathe normally.

She wouldn't give the man another thought.

CHAPTER THREE

An hour outside of town, Judd turned off the main trail and swung down from his horse at the mouth of a narrow canyon. He glanced over his shoulder, "We'll walk for a time, but from here on in you'll wear a blindfold."

Cade had expected as much. He shrugged and gave a nod of understanding. "A man can never be too careful."

Half an hour later Mick thumped him on the back. "We're here."

Cade pulled the bandana from his head and blinked several times. His eyes readjusted quickly as the sun had set and a dusky gloam had settled over the meadow before them.

Several men sat on logs around a camp fire. A group of horses cropped grass a few paces away, corralled by a make-shift rope strung around three scrawny trees. But it was the woman ladling stew from the blackened pot hung over the fire who caught Cade's attention.

Katrina Perry. So, Sam's deductions had been right. His sister was here. Would she recognize him? He'd sold Sam horses on a number of occasions and eaten at their table just as often.

Katrina glanced their way. She blinked and quickly resumed stirring whatever was in the pot above the fire.

So she did recognize him. Good. That would make it easier to get her to trust him.

Judd and Mick stripped the saddles from their mounts and Cade followed suit. They corralled the animals and then joined the others at the fire.

Judd paused at the edge of the firelight and gestured to Cade. "This here is Cade Schilling." If Katrina was surprised by the strange surname she didn't react. However as the infamous name registered, a murmur of awe rippled through the rest of the men. Thankfully, Judd didn't give it time to build. "And this here," he turned to face Mick, "is the whelp that nearly got us killed in town!" He gut-punched Mick, and as the kid doubled over, brought his knee up into his face, sending him sprawling onto his back, blood streaming from his nose.

"Judd stop!" Katrina snatched up a towel, rushed to Mick's side, and dabbed at the blood on his face. "You okay?"

Fury ignited in Judd's eyes. Two strides and he had Katrina by the hair. "The law came down on us today and you are coming to his defense?! There something I should know about you two, since there isn't a woman Mick's ever seen that he could keep his hands off?"

Cade forced himself to stand still.

"I ain't never touched her!" Mick pulled the towel away from his face and spat to one side. "I swear, Judd, she's only yours. Leave her be."

Vibrant fear radiated from Katrina's eyes. "It's true Judd!" She clutched at the hand he still had wrapped in her hair. "He's never touched me. There's no one for me but you." She left off trying to loose his grasp and rested her palm against his face. "That's the truth."

The taut line of Judd's shoulders eased slightly and Cade released a breath he didn't know he'd been holding. The last thing he needed was for her to get killed before he could get her out of here.

Sensing that the worst of the confrontation was over, Cade sat down next to a large man with a long red beard who shoveled stew into his mouth as though nothing were out of the ordinary.

Leaning forward, Cade rested his elbows on his knees. The sooner he did his job and got out of here the better.

"Good. Now get me some o' that stew. I'm right hungry." Judd shoved Katrina back toward the fire so hard that for one horrific moment Cade thought she would sprawl head long into it.

Katrina stumbled her way to balance and hurried to pick up a bowl and spoon.

By the tremble in her hands as she ladled up the food, this

job should be over by tomorrow. A curl of satisfaction wended through him. This would be some of the easiest money he'd ever made.

As Judd settled onto a log across the fire, the big man next to Cade set his bowl aside and stretched out one hand. "Name's Hendrix. Tom Hendrix. Most just call me Red."

Cade nodded and shook the man's hand even as a chill rushed down his back. Red Hendrix had more bounties on his head than most cabins had shingles. "Schilling. Cade Schilling."

"Fool thing for Judd to bring you here this night."

Judd leapt to his feet in an instant. "What'd you say?"

Red picked his teeth, eyeing Judd with calm confidence. "You heard me."

"Schilling saved our lives today. Shot a lawman clean through. Weren't for him, Mick's neck would be stretching from a hemp-rope noose by now. So don't be telling me who I should or shouldn't trust!"

Red shrugged. "Just sayin' with all we got planned for tomorrow, it weren't such a smart thing to bring a new man in."

Cade's skin prickled. What did he mean, all they had planned for tomorrow?

This job was supposed to be easy. Infiltrate the gang. Get proof of their rustling. Convince Katrina to return home. Deliver her to her brother. Set up a trap to arrest them all. And that was it. But Sam's instructions had been clear. Get Katrina out first. He didn't want her getting hurt during the arrests.

Cade suppressed a sigh. This sounded like a complication. He rubbed a hand over the back of his neck.

"You running this here operation, Red?" Judd's hands hung ready only inches from his guns.

Cade wished he hadn't sat quite so close to Red.

Red shifted uneasily. "No, Judd. That'd be you."

"You forgetting your place then?" The fingers of Judd's right hand flexed restlessly.

The short blond man on the other side of Red stood and stepped to one side. "I think I'll get me some o' that coffee."

Smart man. Cade took his cue and stood, too. Stepping over to his saddle roll, he retrieved his mug. Making sure that his path back to the fire kept him out of the line of any bullets that might start flying, he squatted down by the glowing coals and pulled the coffee pot from its perch on a rock, sloshing the inky black liquid into his cup.

Red still hadn't responded.

"Red?" Judd wasn't going to back down.

Red raised his hands to shoulder height, palms toward Judd. "No, I ain't forgettin' my place." Resignation tinged his tone.

Judd relaxed and resumed his seat on the log behind him. "Red, you'll now be part of the distraction in town, and Schilling, Mick, and I will go in to kidnap the teacher."

Cade's jaw went slack and he covered the lapse with a quick swig of coffee.

Why were they planning to kidnap the teacher? What could they possibly gain from that? Several scenarios came to mind. But none that seemed to make sense.

He glanced at Katrina. She didn't seem fazed by the plot. Maybe she would be harder to turn than he'd first expected. In any case, he couldn't walk away now. Not when an innocent teacher's life was at stake.

He tossed the rest of his coffee to one side and stalked toward his bedroll. This was definitely a complication. He hated complications.

Missy Green laid *The Black Arrow* aside with a sigh. Sharyah Jordan's thoughtfulness still had her blinking away tears. Sharyah, the only one who'd come to visit since that terrible night, seemed to understand her desire for simple normalcy.

Actually... She smoothed a hand over her skirt. Sharyah *wasn't* the only one who had come to see her. Sam had come too. He had called every day for the first week after the incident but she'd always stayed in her room and sent down an excuse that she didn't feel well. There had been truth enough in that statement.

Mother was angry because Sam's status as a banker and a wealthy rancher would keep her comfortable for life. But Missy didn't want anyone marrying her out of sheer pity.

Sam was a smart man. It had only taken that week for him to realize she didn't plan on seeing him any longer. He deserved someone better than her. Someone unsoiled and pure. Someone like Sharyah Jordan.

Besides, his life lay rooted here in Beth Haven and she planned on moving far away as soon as she found a suitable place to live. She couldn't ask a move of him, not when he'd been working so hard to build up his ranch here.

She pulled the hanky from the cuff of her sleeve and stroked the lace along its edge.

Why oh why hadn't she simply stayed at the Sachar's until daylight, that night? After the birthing Mr. Sachar had invited her to stay till he left for his mercantile in the morning. But with the new baby and all, she knew Mr. Sachar would probably sleep better in the spare bedroom than he would in with his wife and the new baby. It was only three blocks, she'd assured him. She would be fine and he needed his rest.

She groaned and leaned her head against the settee. Three blocks that ruined her life. Three blocks and Mick Rodale.

Just the thought of the man made her tremble. A sick feeling coiled in the pit of her stomach and clambered up into her throat. She swallowed hard.

She should have run faster. But by the time she'd noticed him, he'd been only a few paces behind her.

She should have fought harder. But he had been so strong!

She laid a fist against her stomach. A sob escaped and she pressed the hanky first to one eye then the other. *Oh God, what am I going to do?*

Cade unfurled his bedroll a good twenty paces from the nearest man. He laid awake for a long time staring at the stars and trying to determine the best way to handle the fact that he knew the local school teacher was going to be kidnapped tomorrow. His first inclination was to ride out and tell the sheriff, but he'd been blindfolded on the way in, and there had been plenty of twists and turns in that trail. A couple times he'd heard the stirrups on his mount brushing both sides of a narrow path. And if a man got lost in a labyrinth of canyons, he could wander for days and never find the route back to town. Besides, even if he could find his way out, Judd was no dummy. He'd have a guard constantly posted to watch the trail. Anyone fool enough to attempt to get through would be an easy target. And sad to say, a whole heap of distance separated Sheriff Collier from the smart wagon.

Judd would no doubt keep a keen eye on him once they got to town, so there probably wouldn't be time to let the sheriff know then. Besides, he didn't want a shoot out to start where innocent bystanders might be harmed.

He considered and tossed aside idea after idea until he finally came to the conclusion that his surest bet was to simply do his best to make sure the woman didn't get hurt in the exchange. He'd have to figure out a way to help her escape later.

He doubted Judd would blindfold him on the way to town tomorrow. He'd thrown down the gauntlet with Red tonight and would want to prove to the whole gang that he trusted Cade implicitly, even if he didn't.

With a sigh of resignation he turned onto his side and closed his eyes. Tomorrow was sure to be a challenging day and he needed to get some rest.

Someone stepped up by his side.

He came to full alertness in an instant, leaping to his feet as he palmed his gun with practiced ease and jammed it into the intruder's chest.

There was a squeak, then a whisper, "It's me! Don't shoot."

He huffed at her stupidity. "I might have killed you!" It felt like he'd just closed his eyes, but it had to have been several hours because the first pale hint of dawn drew a line against the horizon. "Katrina," He glanced back toward the others. "If Judd catches you here...."

"Cade, you have to help me! I—"

Someone stirred and just that quickly she melted into the darkness.

Cade sighed and reholstered his weapon. Yes. This might just be more complicated than he'd first hoped.

Sharyah ignored the caricature of her that had been scrawled on the chalkboard sometime during recess, and faced the class. "Alright everyone, we are going to do our math lessons now, and then just before lunch we will head out to do our leaf collecting. Raise your hand if you brought a sack."

Every student but Brandon raised their hand.

"Good. Brandon, I have a sack for you but it will cost you two days of washing the black boards after school." She arched a stern eyebrow, hoping to see at least a hint of remorse on the boy's face.

He shrugged. "Yes, ma'am."

Not even a hint. She sighed and stepped over by her desk, choosing not to make more of his forgetfulness this time. "Everyone, open to your math lesson for today. I'm going to do a little work with the second primers at the board. The rest of you work quietly until I can get to you. Second primers join me up front, please." She turned and erased the caricature as though it were any other lesson.

The day progressed as planned until an hour into the leaf gathering when Charlie Conklin rushed over and stopped before her, gasping for breath. "Miss Jordan! I ain't seen Brandon for a long time and I can't find him nowhere."

"What?!" She glanced around. *Don't panic. Don't panic.* "Okay let's think. Everyone, come to me. Quickly please!"

The students gathered around. Everyone but Brandon.

Sharyah took in a quick breath, then another. What if… visions of bears and wolves popped into her head. Or a snake. She closed her eyes, suppressing a little shudder and a moan. *Take hold of yourself.* She snapped her eyes open and that's when she caught the tiny smirk on Charlie's face. The moment he noted her study of him his features composed once more into a somber frown of worry.

Quite the little thespian.

By rights she ought to march everyone back to the school and leave Brandon McBride to his own devices. But somehow she didn't think his parents would appreciate the irony in that punishment.

She thought through her options. He would be hiding somewhere near, because he wouldn't want to miss out on any of the fun. She scanned the bushes nearby. All of them except the laurel only three feet away were too sparse to conceal a boy.

Time to give these little performers a lesson on how to really act.

She injected a good dose of worry into her tone. "When was the last time anyone saw Brandon?"

Everyone looked blank. But Charlie shrugged. "'Bout half an hour ago."

"Half an hour?!" Her screech would have done any actress proud. "Oh." She moaned and wrung her hands. "What if a bear got him?"

The patch of laurel rustled slightly. So that *was* where he'd hidden. She could just imagine Brandon laughing till his sides hurt.

Sally Weaver raised her hand. "Miss Sharyah? I wouldn't worry none too much. Bears ain't round these parts often. And as long as Brandon leaves them alone, they pretty much just lumber off when they see a person."

"Thank you, Sally." *Thanks for ruining my plan to scare the living daylights out of the boy.* "I'm sure you're right. Bears probably didn't get him." She scrabbled for another critter to use giving a couple of moans of worry for good measure. Wolves were probably out of the equation. Sally could probably come up with a reason why it was highly unlikely that Brandon had been carried off by one of them. Not bears. Not wolves. Spiders!

She shuddered. Yes, she could describe a spider in the scariest ways possible, thanks to the torment her brothers had meted out many times after their realization early on that she hated the creepy little things.

"Yes, probably not bears, but… maybe a spider. I didn't want you all to worry so I didn't mention this spider earlier. But there is a spider that is extremely deadly. It was only discovered in these woods quite recently." As she talked, she circled the children, until her back was to the laurel, pulling Charlie around with her so that he wouldn't be able to signal to Brandon that this was all a ruse. Leaning forward slightly, she gave all the children her biggest smile and laid a finger across her lips. Very quietly she whispered, "Class, there's nothing to be afraid of. There is no spider, don't look but Brandon is in the laurel bush just behind me. The one with the shiny dark green leaves. Let's have a little fun with him, shall we?"

The light went on in first Sally, then Sonja Weaver's eyes.

Charlie tumbled to her plan next. "Aw— "

Sharyah clapped one hand over his mouth and held him firmly in front of her.

"I know that spider!" Sonja exclaimed loudly. "It's light green and… and… has eight legs!"

Sally rolled her eyes at her sister's lack of imagination. "I heard that it has fangs that are twice the length of its body – which isn't much since they are so tiny they can hide *anywhere* – but once they bite you, you only have 3 minutes to live!"

The laurel bush gave a satisfactory tremble, behind Sharyah.

Little Hillary Thackary from the first primer whimpered. "Do you think the spider got him, Miss Jordan?"

At the sight of the little girl's big eyes and trembling lower lip, Sharyah felt the first prick of guilt over this little deception. Apparently the little girl hadn't grasped what she wanted to accomplish. But Sonja Weaver bent down and whispered something in Hillary's ear and the little girl's mouth dropped open in sudden understanding.

Sharyah thought back over the last two weeks and all the pranks she'd endured at the hands of this little menace. No she wasn't going to feel guilty. She winked at the younger children and picked up where Sally had left off. "That's right, Sally. And they like to make their nests in bushes, especially ones with shiny leaves, thousands of spiders to each nest! They hide on the underside of the leaves and drop down onto anything that brushes against the bush."

Brandon burst from the laurel, madly slapping at his hair, arms, shirt and shoulders.

Sharyah let Charlie go. "Brandon, there you are! I'm so glad you are alright. We were just talking about a newly discovered spider that—stop! What's that crawling on your back?"

Brandon screeched. "Where is it? Get it off!" He pirouetted in an odd little dance as he tried to see his back, shake off his shirt and not fall over all at the same time.

The class burst into spontaneous laughter.

Brandon stilled. "Wait—" He looked at Sharyah.

She grinned and pinched his ruddy cheek. "Gotcha, Mr. McBride."

He gave a sheepish smile and glanced around at everyone. "You all… this was just a… there's no spider?"

Sharyah shook her head. "But I hope you will learn the lesson that when I ask you to stay with the group, it is for your own safety. There *are* dangerous things out here and we need to be careful. If we all stick together, if something does happen to one of us, we will at least have each other."

He laughed. "You got me a good one!"

Satisfaction threaded through her as she noted the hint of admiration glimmering in his mischievous eyes. "So you forgive me and the class for being a little deceptive with our joke?"

Brandon waved away her concern. "Aw it weren't nothin', Miss Jordan. You're smarter than I figured you was."

Sharyah didn't bother to correct his slaughter of the English language. "Alright class, everyone gather your sacks. It's time to head back to the classroom."

Judd gathered the gang together, just after noon. "Alright, listen up. I want this to go down smooth and easy. The more men we kill the more lawmen and ill will we attract. We're all still alive and I'd like to keep it that way."

Cade resisted a snort of disdain at Judd's magnanimous words and scanned the group.

Besides Judd, Katrina, Red and Mick, several other men stood in the circle with them. Seth Rodale, Judd's youngest brother, was the blonde man who'd been smart enough to vacate his seat on the log beside Red the night before. The other men had kept their distance and their council and Cade didn't know their names.

But rumor abounded that Billy Montell had recently joined up with the Rodale gang and if Cade were a betting man, he'd peg his money on the tall lanky kid across the way. The kid hadn't said a word since Cade's arrival the night before, but he fit the description on the wanted poster hanging in the jail back in Shiloh. Billy's baby-face had come to grace a poster because of a string of bank heists and half a dozen murders, including the death of a woman who'd been in a bank during one of his robberies.

Red Hendrix – also a new member of the gang – was wanted most recently for the murder of two rangers down Texas way. Before that, however he'd had warrants out for everything from horse thieving to arson.

Cade's gut clenched. He hadn't really thought about the risk he was taking when he'd agreed to this job. Until recently, the Rodale brothers were mostly involved in small time crimes – a bar brawl in Portland and suspicion of a mercantile theft over in Farewell Bend. Over the last year, however, they'd upped their ante – a stagecoach robbery and a few horses lifted – and now the men they were associating with were of the all-out criminal variety. If ever these men learned who Cade really was, they'd not hesitate one second to slit his throat while he slept, he was sure of that.

So what had changed? Why were the three Rodale brothers suddenly taking up company with some of the most unsavory characters west of the Mississippi and what were they planning to do?

Other than kidnapping the poor local school teacher.

He pondered on that. Kidnapping was a premeditated crime and generally a set up for something else, something bigger. Something they wanted, or wanted to force someone else to do. So who was the local school teacher and who cared enough about her that the Rodale gang would have power over them once they had her in their clutches?

Cade released a breath of frustration. If only this had been going down in a couple days instead of today. Maybe by then he'd have had time to get close to Katrina and convince her to go back home to her brother. Time to get a message to the Beth Haven sheriff about their plans and time to set up traps to arrest all of them.

As it stood, he thanked God that he'd be around to protect the teacher from this unsavory lot. Hopefully he could complete his investigation quickly and her stay would be short-lived.

Cade returned his attention to Judd who was still lining out their plan.

"I got it on good authority that Sam Perry's been showing up at the school real regular like since this new teacher come to town. Especially after Mick here done soiled his pearly dove." He paused to grin as several of the men chuckled. "Since I want Sam to know this is all about him, we're going to make the grab right before his eyes. He arrives every day right after the kids leave. And today he's gonna get a surprise he won't soon forget."

Cade shouldn't have been surprised, but he was. So they wanted power over Sam Perry. He must have it bad for this school teacher. But what did Sam have that Judd wanted? Something to do with the bank, most likely. He'd have to figure out a way to talk to Sam. Judd already had Sam's sister, but from what Sam had said she'd come of her own free will.

Yet this morning she'd come to him. What had she wanted to tell him? Cade rubbed a hand over his jaw, wishing he'd had more time to talk to her at dawn. Sounded like she was ready to get out. Maybe, if he could get a chance to talk to her, she would know what Judd wanted from Sam.

Sam had an amazing spread. Maybe it had nothing to do with the bank. Maybe they wanted his land? But if that was the case, wouldn't Judd just find a way to remove Sam from the picture and marry Katrina? Cade studied the woman.

Jaw set and eyes glittering, she glowered at Judd.

Unless… Maybe Sam had willed the ranch to someone else? And maybe Judd really meant it when he said he wanted to keep his killing down to a minimum. Or maybe it was something else altogether they wanted from Sam. Could it be that Katrina wasn't here of her own free will?

There were way too many questions. Cade resettled his hat. This job was supposed to be easy.

Katrina folded her arms and huffed audibly. "I've told you, Judd, you can get to my brother other ways than by kidnapping an innocent woman. You should leave her out of it."

Judd spun toward her so fast that Katrina flinched. He grabbed her arm and gave her a little shake. ""Wha—?"

Katrina shifted, but her back was to Cade and he couldn't get a good read on her expression.

Judd stepped closer to her and leaned down to speak into her face. "I don't take advice from nobody, especially not a woman."

Katrina shrugged him off and stalked away, brushing past Cade. "Your loss."

She's got grit. I'll give her that.

Judd growled and started after her. Cade stepped into his path, tugging on the brim of his hat and doing his best to look sympathetic. "Women, you know how they are, Rodale. Can't see the wisdom in a man's thinking, no matter how good it is. Forget about her. Finish telling us the plan so we can ride."

Judd wanted to go after her, Cade could see it in his eyes, but after only a moment's hesitation he turned back to the gathered men. "Alright. So here's what we're going to do. I need the sheriff busy in another part of town so if Perry somehow gets away from us, the law will be occupied and unable to follow us for at least a few minutes."

Seth Rodale scoffed. "Sheriff Collier would have a hard

time finding his own shadow in a desert at three o'clock in the afternoon."

Several of the gang chuckled.

"Perry won't get away from us," Cade assured.

Judd nodded. "Not likely, a pansy like him. But just to be on the safe side Seth, I need you and Billy to start a fight. It needs to draw some attention. You two get arrested, you're on your own, so keep it clean and fair. Likely, he'll just ask you to leave town."

Seth grinned at the young kid Cade had presumed was Billy. He had sandy brown hair and the scraggly beginnings of a beard – the kind Pa had always called kitten whiskers. "I don't know, I sure could use a good night's sleep on a real cot," Seth said.

Billy laughed and nodded.

"Just be careful the Sheriff doesn't oblige you. Or it might be the last night of sleep you'll ever have," Judd said dryly, then turned to the older men. "Mick, you'll keep an eye out from the school yard. I don't want anyone down there catching a glimpse of you, so keep a low profile. You'll come in and let Cade and I know if trouble might be heading our way."

Mick nodded.

"Red, I've decided it's too much of a risk for you to be seen around town yet. You'll stay here with Kat and the extra mounts."

Surprisingly Red didn't make any protest, but he did stalk off, and Judd let him go.

Cade watched Red while Judd explained to the rest of the men where he wanted them staged. Red rolled himself a cigarette and propped one foot up on a stump, studying the horizon, and by the time Cade's attention returned to Judd, the man was finishing up his little planning meeting.

"Alright, let's ride!" Judd called.

Cade's jaw tightened. It was going to be up to him to keep this teacher safe.

Brandon had taken his loving sweet time washing the chalkboards, but had done an admirable job and Sharyah had only needed him to redo one corner before she dismissed him. He snatched up his slingshot and lunch pail and scuttled off for home.

After carefully checking her desk chair and verifying the seat held nothing painful to sit on, Sharyah collapsed into it.

"Oh, I'm exhausted!" She dropped her head back and closed her eyes, propping her feet on the desk in a most unladylike fashion. She needed new shoes and after the long walk through the woods today, her feet were aching something terrible. Just getting them up off the floor relieved some of the pain.

All afternoon she'd felt guilty about the way she'd handled Brandon's prank at the leaf-picking and finally she'd confessed to the whole class that she shouldn't have encouraged them to use deception to lure Brandon out of his hiding place. Despite Brandon's reassurances that all was well, she'd apologized to him and encouraged the class to do the same.

She sighed and massaged circles at her temples. She would have to check for gray hair in the mirror at home tonight. *Lord, I have a feeling this is going to be a long year. Help me to handle anything else that comes up better than I handled this situation today.*

The door creaked open.

Sharyah jolted upright, frantically jerking her feet to the floor and straightening her skirts. Thankfully, the wall that housed several square compartments for lunches, and hooks for coats blocked the outer door from visibility when anyone first entered the schoolhouse.

"Knock, knock." Sam poked his head around the wall, his bowler clutched to his chest.

She smiled, hoping she didn't look as frazzled as she felt. "Hi."

He started down the aisle, then paused. "Rough day?"

Standing, she set to gathering the books she would need at home tonight. "No. No. I'm fine."

"Well you look tired." He paused by her side. "At least come to dinner out at the ranch so you don't have to cook this evening."

Sharyah resisted a groan. The only thing she wanted to do was go home and have a nice long soak in her tub. A refusal danced on the tip of her tongue even as a thought arose. If she kept putting him off, Sam might give up on her. She didn't want that. But neither did she want things to move ahead too quickly. Still, Sam was a good catch. She wasn't likely to find anyone better. She forced a smile, resigned to a few more hours of aching feet.

Laying flat on his belly at the crest of a hill, Cade studied the little clapboard building through his binoculars.

Right on time, Sam Perry climbed the schoolhouse steps. Cade bit back a grin as he imagined the look on Sam's face when Cade busted in to steal his girl right out from under his nose. He liked Sam, and whoever the woman inside was, he wished them all the best at some future date, but Sam was going to be hotter than desert lava when Cade informed him that he hadn't yet had time to convince Katrina to come home, that something big was about to go down but he didn't know what yet, and that his girl was going to have to live in the hills with a gang of outlaws for a couple days until he could figure things out.

"Sure is strange – Judd's horse throwing a shoe like that." Mick shifted by his side.

Cade nodded. "Well, he'll get it fixed and be ready to ride in no time. Meanwhile, let's not let him down." He clapped a hand to Mick's shoulder and nodded that he should take his spot in the school yard.

As Mick slunk away to his assigned post, Cade smirked. *Mysteriously* – thanks to his knife and a few minutes alone with the horses – Judd's horse had thrown a shoe five minutes out of town. Cade had hoped it would fall off sooner. But it would still take Judd a couple minutes extra to walk her into town and several more minutes to get the blacksmith to nail it back on. He'd bought himself some time.

Judd had cursed and kicked at a rock. "Five minutes! I want you in and out in five minutes, you hear? You double cross me, Schilling, and I will hunt you till I die."

"What would I have to gain by a double cross?"

Judd snatched up his horse's reins and set off walking. "Nothing. Just see that you remember it. You got five minutes in there and if you ain't out by then, I'm coming in after you."

"Five minutes will be more than enough."

Now he pulled his bandana up over his nose, more for Mick's benefit than anyone. Carefully, he made his way down the hill toward the schoolhouse. The little white building was separated from town by a copse of Poplar trees, so little fear of anyone seeing him existed. Besides he could hear the uproar Seth and Billy were apparently making in front of the saloon right this minute. All attention would soon be focused that way, if it wasn't already.

Sam had left the door open slightly when he went in, and Cade slipped inside without making a noise. As soon as he stepped through the door and out of sight of Mick, he pulled the bandana down. Sam would recognize him the minute he saw him anyhow, and he didn't want to scare the teacher half to death. It was going to be hard enough to tell her she had to come with him into the hills and live with outlaws for a few days.

A wall just a pace ahead separated the entry from the main part of the schoolhouse, hooks for coats on one side and a set of cubby holes for lunches and what-not on the other.

From the other side a woman spoke quietly. "Yes, I'd be happy to come to dinner at your place this evening, Sam."

Cade jolted to a standstill, his spine pressed to the grid of cubby holes. That voice. It couldn't be! They'd said she was teaching in Madras, over thirty miles from here. His heart thumped hard in his chest.

A vision of blonde curls and brown eyes a man could drown in leapt to his mind. A woman he'd walked away from and tried to forget. She'd been like a little sister to him all her life, until there right at the end when he'd noticed what a beautiful woman she'd become. If Ma hadn't been so sick at the time he might have… well… He gave himself a shake. Nothing had come of it and then after Ma's death everything had been a blur, what with Pa up and running off. Then he'd taken that herd down to Frisco and by the time he got home she'd moved away.

He glanced down at his trembling hands. There was no way he could kidnap Sharyah Jordan and take her up into the hills with the Rodale gang!

But… Sky and Rocky had been in town with him just yesterday and hadn't said a word about Sharyah being here too. Needing to make sure it really was her, he held his breath and listened.

"Great. I'll pick you up at six." Sam replied, more than a little flirtation coloring his tone.

The hackles rose on the back of Cade's neck.

Sam chuckled softly as his lilting words continued. "And maybe I could talk you into taking a moonlit stroll with me, afterward?"

"Sam… you helped write my contract, remember? You know that even dinner is pushing the limits."

There was the rustle of fabric and the woman gave a soft gasp.

"Yes, but you'll also remember that I told you I know the head of the school board very well and he thinks I'm doing the right thing, courting you." Sam's words were lower, more intimate this time.

She gave a breathy laugh. "Is that what you're doing? Courting me?" A tremor laced her voice.

Cade's breath came fast and shallow now. Definitely Sharyah. And flirting with Sam, of all people. He rubbed one hand over his face. His time was running out. He had to think.

Sam mumbled something too low to understand and without another thought Cade lurched around the corner.

At the front of the classroom, Sam stood, body tilting forward, about to kiss Sharyah. She had her eyes closed and her chin lifted in expectation.

Cade scanned her in a swift assessment.

She looked better than any woman had a right to. Several blonde curls had escaped her pins to caress flushed cheeks. Her small hands fluttered in apparent nervous anticipation then settled on Sam's shoulders. The green material of her skirt splayed out from her tiny waist. A waist currently wrapped in Sam's grasp.

Sam shouldn't be anywhere near her. He was the president of the school board for crying out loud! Talk about taking advantage of a woman.

Anger, hot and ugly, surged up inside him.

"Hope I'm not interrupting anything." He folded his arms and leaned into his heels, proud of the calm his voice portrayed.

CHAPTER FOUR

Sharyah squeaked and spun toward the voice. A voice she would still have recognized a hundred years from now. "Cade!"

Sam leapt back as though stung by a bee.

How much had Cade seen? A hot wave flooded her face and she smoothed at the fabric of her skirt.

Shoving his hat back on his head, Cade glowered at Sam. "Yes. Cade."

"B-Bennett!" Sam stuttered, smoothing trembling hands down the front of his coat.

Sharyah clenched her own quaking fists, knowing just how he felt.

With swift strides, Cade devoured the distance between them. "Don't use that name! You want to get me killed?"

Sharyah frowned. What did he mean? She glanced down and blinked. Cade held a gun in his hand, but he had it pointed off to one side. "Wha-What are you doing, Cade?"

Heaven help her, he looked good. She followed the sinewy forearm behind the gun to the broad expanse of shoulders stretching tight the fabric of his blue shirt, then slid to where his gun belt emphasized trim hips, and continued down the denim expanse of firmly splayed legs to the black hand-tooled leather of his boots. But it was when her gaze rebounded to his eyes that her knees went weak.

Eyes as blue as the sky and studying her with decided disappointment.

"Good grief man, put that thing away," Sam demanded. "What's gotten into you?"

Cade ignored Sam and held her gaze. He scanned every line

of her face, a heat in his expression that made her pulse thrum. The air in the room grew thin and inadequate.

One of his eyebrows cocked. "Didn't expect to find you here." His mouth quirked up on one side as he nodded his head toward Sam. "I see you aren't pining away for lost love."

She couldn't have spoken if her life depended on it. She swallowed, hating herself for the blank slate that filled her mind, giving her no quip of reply.

Suddenly his expression turned serious and he glanced toward the back door. "Sam, I don't have a whole lot of time to explain." He gestured with the gun and pulled a long strand of rawhide from his back pocket. "Sit down in that desk."

Sam looked aghast. "Have you gone mad?"

With an exasperated grunt, Cade grabbed him by the forearm and jerked him into the desk.

Sharyah gasped. "Cade! What are you doing?"

"Shut-up and listen." Cade holstered his gun and glowered at Sam. Then set to tying Sam's hands with sure swift strokes as if she'd never spoken. "Sam, I haven't had time to talk to Katrina yet, but something big is about to go down and I think it has something to do with you. I'm here to kidnap the school teacher—"

Sharyah took a step back. "Kidnap me! You'll do no such thing!"

"—because Rodale noticed your interest in her. He wants something from you. What is it?"

Sam stared at Cade, jaw slack, face paling.

Cade bent down and spoke in Sam's ear, his voice remained low but he slammed his palm against the desk. "What is it?!"

Sam jumped. "I don't—I don't—I don't know! I don't have anything he would want."

"Cade, stop it!" Sharyah plucked at his sleeve.

He pointed a finger in her face. "Be quiet and sit down a minute."

A wash of light-headedness swept over her even as she stumbled a few steps and sank into her chair. She'd never seen him like this before. He always joked and teased. Laughed. Winked. This focused intensity was new, and she wasn't sure she liked it. Not even a little.

Cade returned his attention to Sam. "Rodale will be here any minute. And," he jabbed a finger in her direction, "she's in danger because of you. So you better start thinking and figure out what he wants from you because," he lowered his voice even more and stepped around to meet Sam eye to eye, "I'm not going to put her in danger. She and I are going to walk out that back door and go to someplace where she'll be safe. In a few minutes, Rodale is going to come storming in that door," he pointed toward the main entrance, "and you'd better be ready with either the information he wants or your gun, otherwise he'll kill you."

Sharyah couldn't believe this was happening. She leapt to her feet. "Kill him! Cade, you can't let that happen."

Cade's jaw clenched and he paced two steps down the aisle and then returned. With a low growl he slapped one of the desks then continued pacing. He rubbed the back of his neck in thought as his gaze stopped on Sharyah. "No, I won't take you into a situation like that." His attention returned to Sam and he bent until they were face to face. "You had to have known something when you hired me."

Fear bulged in Sam's eyes and he couldn't seem to meet Cade's gaze. "I'm telling you I have no idea what they could want from me!"

"So help me… If something happens to her, I won't be responsible for what I do." A tremble coursed through the edges of Cade's words.

Sharyah's insides went all soft. He cared that much for her?

Cade straightened and tossed her a glance then returned his attention to Sam. "She's like the sister I never had, and you've put me in an untenable position here."

Her eyes narrowed and the softness hardened to granite anger. Again with *the sister he never had* nonsense.

Cade took her arm. "Sharyah we have to—"

The back door crashed in with a shuddering clamor.

She squeaked and spun to face the entrance.

Cade jolted and jerked the bandana around his throat up over his nose.

"Schilling! You coming? Judd's horse is just about ready and he said he'd meet us at the top of the hill." A blond man appeared at the rear of the room, a pistol in his hand. He scanned the space, but stopped when he noticed Sharyah. His gaze slithered over her and a leering light leapt into his eyes. "Well! What have we here?"

Her heart hammered in her ears and she looked down at her desk, hands fluttering to straighten books that were already straight.

Cade hesitated as though trying to decide what to do.

Sam sat still, his hands resting in plain sight on the desk.

Sharyah felt more than saw Cade's attention hone in on the pistol the man held. Cade's own gun was still in its holster.

After only a split second Cade said, "I'm getting there." He stepped between her and the man's continued perusal. "Just give me a couple minutes to finish up."

Footsteps sounded coming nearer up the aisle. "Well hurry it along. The fight just broke up and the Sheriff is giving them the boot now. We've only got minutes to get out of town. I'll keep an eye on the lady and the door." Several swift strides and the man stepped around Cade and took her by the upper arm. "Hello, darlin'." He leered as he started to pull her toward the door of the schoolhouse.

Stark fear coursed through her.

She scrabbled a hand across the top of the desk as he dragged her by, searching for anything to use as a weapon. The Webster's Dictionary! Snatching it up, she swung with all her might and slammed it into the man's head with a satisfying *thunk*.

His hat fell to the floor and he grabbed at his head. A string of violent curses darkened the air. Just as quickly he spun around and reached for her, one hand balled into a fist and anger blazing from his eyes. "Why you little—"

Cade knocked his hand away and scooped Sharyah behind

him with one arm. "Mick, we need the lady in one piece if she's to be of any use to us." He bent and picked up the man's hat, shoving it into his chest as he gestured toward Sam. "You finish up with Perry, and I'll deal with the lady. We'll wait for you by the door."

He presented his back to the man, slipped his gun from his holster, and led her several steps down the aisle. "Ma'am, if you just give us your cooperation I'm sure you'll find we really are reasonable folks." He kept his gun carefully trained to one side, pulling some leather thongs from a pocket. Lower he added, "I need you to trust me, Shar. There's a lot more to this than I have time to explain right now. But there are others whose lives I have to consider."

She shook her head and backed away, gaping at him. "Are you crazy?" she whispered. "I'm not going to some outlaw hideout with you!" She nodded her head to where Mick was busy gagging Sam and mouthed, "There's only one. You can take him."

He shook his head, his gaze darting to the windows before returning to capture hers.

She gritted her teeth. "No." She trembled perceptibly, hating herself for the show of weakness even as she slid a step away from him.

His eyes above the bandana narrowed, darkening to the color of an ocean storm as he advanced a step. "You'll be with me. I promise to keep you safe." He straightened and added loudly, "Don't make me hogtie you and carry you out of here over my shoulder like a gunny sack, ma'am."

She lifted her chin and backed up some more. "You wouldn't dare!"

Was that a crinkle of humor at the corners of his eyes? If so he hid it quickly.

His shoulders drooped wearily and he muttered something indecipherable before he said, "Suit yourself." He sheathed the gun once more and snatched a hold of her wrist. His voice lowered again, "On second thought it's probably better this way. I wouldn't want you trying anything that would buy you a bullet from one of the gang."

Her free hand shot out of its own volition, her palm itching to connect with the side of his face.

With a lightning-quick move, he caught her wrist while her hand was still a good six inches from its destination. Slowly his thumb stroked her pulse, his eyes never leaving her face. The red cloth of the bandana moved in and out with each breath he took, the movement growing more pronounced the longer they stood there.

Cade seemed to shake himself and took a step back. Dropping one lid in a quick wink, he tipped his head toward her still itching palm and whispered, "I saw that coming." His eyes did crinkle at the corners this time. "Wonder how I knew you would be slap happy?" Calmly, he slid a slip-knot in one end of the leather down to her wrist.

"You're laughing at me!" She made sure to keep her voice down. "How could you find anything in this situation even remotely humorous?" She lifted her chin, refusing to meet his gaze for even a moment longer. "Besides, I've never slapped any man but you." Her eyes betrayed her and darted his way before she jerked them back into proper alignment with her chin.

He laughed outright then. "Well, maybe I should take that as a compliment." He pulled her other hand over, wrapping the cord several times firmly around and tying it off. "There that should keep your hands under—"

There was a loud hollow *thunk* and a short grunt from Sam in the child's desk.

Sharyah's eyes widened. Mick had just knocked Sam out!

"Schilling, pony up! What's taking you so long?" Mick stalked past, slapping Cade on the shoulder and gesturing with his gun that he should hurry up.

"I'm coming, Mick. Just some women make it harder to be a gentleman than others if you catch my meaning."

The man chuckled, lifted his hat, and gingerly rubbed his head. "Sure do."

Cade grinned. "I'll be along directly. I think she's coming around to my way of thinking now."

A slow leer stretched Mick's mouth. "Want I should help you with that? I think between the two of us we could make quick work of teaching her a lesson."

A muscle bunched in Cade's jaw. But all he said was, "Take a look outside and make sure all's clear, would you?"

Mick sighed and disappeared behind the partitioning wall, presumably to make sure their escape route was unobstructed.

Cade turned back to face her. "Now, if you'll pardon me…" He swept his hat from his head, bent forward and planted his shoulder in her middle, swinging her up and over before she could even cry out in surprise.

"Sam is hurt! You put me down this instant, Cade Bennett!" she whispered fiercely.

He dropped her to her feet, gripped her shoulders, and gave her a firm shake. "Don't call me that or you'll get us both killed. The name's Schilling. Cade Schilling. Sam will be fine. I tied his hands loosely. As soon as he regains consciousness he'll be able to get free." Another swoop and she was back up on his shoulder.

She felt more than saw Cade glance in Sam's direction and then she was watching the schoolhouse steps disappear from sight.

Cade trucked up the hill behind Mick and deposited Sharyah on her feet before Judd. He steadied her and clamped his jaw shut tight, angry with himself. He never should have taken the time to question Perry. He should have just grabbed Sharyah and helped her escape the first moment he recognized her voice. Once Mick had busted in, it was too dangerous to try and get away. Any strange sounds coming from the schoolhouse would have brought Judd and his whole team on the run and there would have been too much danger of her getting hurt.

"You made it. I was beginning to wonder." Judd eyed him warily, then after a long moment turned to Mick. "*WhooEee* you should've seen the fight that Seth and Billy put on out in the street. That little brother of ours should've gone into boxing, I tell ya." He chuckled and clapped a hand on his brother's shoulder.

"I seen it." There was a hint of pride in Mick's voice. "We'll make something of that young pup, yet."

Judd nodded then paused as he noticed Sharyah. "Well…" His eyes slipped over her from head to toe. "The teacher's a looker, isn't she?"

Mick laughed. "She sure is!"

Cade pushed down the terror clawing at his chest. The predatory expression on Judd's face made him want to pull his gun and arrest the men right here and be done with it. The thought of what might happen to Sharyah in the fracas was the only thing that kept him from acting on the desire.

Sharyah swallowed and stepped closer to him.

Think. He had to play his cards right to keep her from molestation. He swiped one side of his face against his shoulder considering his options. There was only one way. The same thing he'd told Mick inside. "I'd have to concur," he pinched her cheek and slid one hand down her arm, hating the look of shock that crossed her face. He forced a laugh. "Too bad none of us will be able to have any fun with her."

Sharyah's eyes widened and the sudden fearful realization drained her face of all color.

Cade hated that it was his fault she was here. He willed a message into the arch of his brows and the dip of his chin. *Trust me.*

A flash of understanding lit her countenance and eased the tense line of her shoulders. But the anger emanating from every square inch of her did not lessen.

Judd frowned. "What do you mean?"

Cade lifted one of Sharyah's curls and wrapped it around his finger. "Well, just that, if this was my woman, I'd want her returned all in one piece, if you get my meaning. If we're gonna use her as a bargaining chip, then we'd best keep the merchandise in good condition."

"Merchan—" Sharyah gasped and stomped one foot. "Good condition or not, my brothers will kill you all!"

That's my girl. He laughed as he resettled his hat. "Aw, but they'll have to find us first, and by then we'll have gotten all we need from you and be long gone, darlin'."

Judd grunted and gave him a punch in the arm. "That's some right smart thinking." He stalked off in the direction where they'd left their horses. "Best we get back. The others are already headed out. The sheriff just escorted Billy and Seth to the edge of town and sent them on their way. So come on, saddle up."

Relief washed through him even as he prodded Sharyah to follow Judd. Just a couple days. He'd get the information he needed as quickly as possible, convince Katrina to return home and then he'd get Sharyah out of here. He swallowed. *Lord, keep her safe, please.*

Sharyah shifted in the saddle, working her bound wrists and wishing Cade hadn't wrapped them quite so tight. At least he'd tied them in front of her. Still, he hadn't needed to tie her up at all! He'd done all of that for show. She clenched her teeth, wishing for the umpteenth time that she could catch even a glimmer of light through the blind-fold they'd put on her.

They were stopped again. Probably brushing out their trail. Papa had told stories on numerous occasions of the various ways criminals hid their tracks so they couldn't be tailed. But a good tracker should still be able to follow the sign. Maybe Sam would hire someone and come to her rescue. These men were despicable!

And Cade was helping them. What was he doing with them? He was obviously working for Sam. But why would Sam need Cade to be involved with outlaws? And why had the outlaws knocked Sam out if they were all working together?

She shuddered at the memory of the way the two blond men had looked at her. Just wait until she got Cade Bennett alone! She planned to give him a piece of her mind up one side and down the other that would leave him begging for mercy. The man was a living breathing definition of the word impossible!

"We're starting up again." Cade leaned over and took her arm and she heard him cluck to the horses. He walked his along beside her. She'd never considered how hard it would be to maintain her balance on a moving creature with no saddle and blinded eyes. But after her horse had taken its first steps and she'd nearly fallen to the ground, Cade had taken the precaution to hold her steady each time. "The trail narrows just ahead and we'll have to dismount and walk."

Great. Just what she wanted to do. Her feet already ached like nobody's business and all she wanted was wake up in her own little teacher's cabin and take a nice long hot bath. She bit back a smart reply and forced the incoming tears away. She would not give him the satisfaction of seeing her cry! But the harder she tried to keep them at bay, the more intensely the tears pressed, until finally they squeezed out and soaked into the bandana blindfolding her.

A few moments later, Cade pulled her horse to a stop and she could hear the men dismounting.

Her nose was runny and she had nothing to wipe it with, which only made the tears come faster. She held her breath lest a sob escape and give her away.

"This is the place." Cade spoke from her side as his hands settled at her waist and he lifted her down. He stilled. "Hey." His fingers touched the underside of her jaw.

She jerked away from the soft caress, lifting her chin. Her horse was still at her back and the jangle of a bit sounded from just behind Cade. Otherwise all remained silent. The others must have gone on ahead. A fresh surge of anger suddenly dried up all the tears.

"Sharyah." His voice was soft. "I'm sorry." He pressed a cloth into her hands.

She put it to good use but kept her silence with gritted teeth.

"Listen," he stepped closer, "if this was at all avoidable, I'd never have brought you here. But I'm going to keep you safe. I need you to trust me." One hand settled on her shoulder and his thumb stroked a path along her jaw.

She tipped her face away again.

He sighed and took her arm. "We need to get going or they will be suspicious. Just trust me."

She ground her teeth but was unable to suppress a low mutter. She'd trust him about as far as she could throw him.

"What was that?" he stilled.

"I said, I'd trust you about as far as I could throw you." *Probably not far. But I'd sure like to give it a try.*

"Oh, well, at least you're speaking to me now."

He led her forward, carefully guiding her around boulders and lifting her over rocks. Soon she could hear the others ahead of them. It wasn't long until they topped out on a flat area. A breeze cooled her hot cheeks, and grass softened the ground and rustled beneath her feet.

"Well little lady..."

The voice of the man the others had been calling Judd stopped before her. She felt Cade tense slightly, but after only a moment he let go of her elbow and she heard him step away. Her heart thundered as she tilted her head straining to listen. Surely he wasn't leaving her with this man!

Judd gave her blindfold a tug. She squinted and cringed. The sun hung low in the sky, painfully bright.

Sweeping a gesture around the meadow they stood in, Judd gave a little bow. "Welcome to our humble abode, miss."

The others laughed, everyone except Cade, who she now noticed stood only two steps from her side.

Hands resting on his hips, he studied her intently, a question in his eyes.

She worked her lower lip with her teeth. He did seem worried about her. Maybe she shouldn't be so hard on him.

A woman bustled up to them then. A beautiful woman with assessing green eyes. She shot Cade a withering glare then turned back and cupped Sharyah's shoulders. "I told them to leave you be, hon. But I have no authority over what goes on around here. As soon as they get you untied, you come on and sit down and I'll give you a nice hot bowl of rabbit stew."

"Now, Kat…" Judd shooed the woman away and followed her back toward the fire leaving Cade to guard Sharyah.

Cade stepped over and worked at the rawhide around her wrists.

"Who's that?"

"Sam's sister."

Sam has a sister? She glanced over at the woman and felt a prick of irritation to find those alluring green eyes fastened on Cade. As the last knot released and fresh blood surged into her hands, prickles of pain zinged down her fingers with each beat of her heart. She hissed and shook her hands.

Cade reached for them, seemingly unaware of the woman watching him from across the camp. "You should have told me it was too tight." He massaged her palms, and stroked her arms firmly, frowning and looking none too pleased.

She sniffed. He had tied her up and hauled her up into the mountains with a gang of outlaws, yet *he* was frustrated with *her*? And still the only thing she wanted to do was collapse against him and feel the safety of his arms around her. How pathetic was that? Refusing the impulse, she glowered at him, "Like you would have cared."

He froze for just an instant and she saw a spark of anger ignite the blue of his eyes before he returned his attention to her wrists and rubbed at the indentations left there by the rawhide. "This is not the time or the place for me to deal with that comment."

"I don't suppose it would do any good to tell you I needed… well, that I needed—" her face heated as she bumbled to a lame stop.

His jaw bunched and he glanced over his shoulder toward the fire. "The lady needs to use the necessary."

Judd waved his permission and Cade took her hand, pulling her after him down a slightly worn trail.

Something had obviously made him hotter than a pan full of sizzling bacon. He stormed ahead of her so fast she was hard-put to keep up, especially since she had to take three steps for every one of his. As they rushed over the rough terrain, she did her best to remain on her feet and hurried after him.

He rounded a corner in the trail where a huge boulder jutted out of the ground and a hillside climbed to their left.

She leapt over a log that Cade strode across without seeming to notice, landing hard on the other side. "If you think I'm going to use the… privy with you standing guard over me, you've gone out of your head, Cascade Bennett!"

He jolted to a sudden stop and spun toward her. She crashed into his chest with a squawk of surprise, clamoring to regain her balance.

Cade's hands settled firmly around her waist, lifting her a quarter turn until her back was pressed against the large boulder by the side of the narrow trail. His gaze never left her face as he stepped closer.

Taking in the icy fire glimmering in his eyes, she swallowed and tried to step away, but the boulder wouldn't budge. She had nowhere to go.

He scanned her face, one hand coming up to touch her cheek. "You're determined to kill me, aren't you?"

"What?" She frowned, trying to will away the rapid breathing that had nothing to do with the hurried walk they'd just taken. Summoning every ounce of self control to the fore, she refused the desire to lean her cheek into the secure warmth of his palm. Instead, gritting her teeth, she remained aloof, as though his gentle touch had no effect on her whatsoever.

"What are you doing in Beth Haven? You're supposed to be in Madras."

One shoulder lifted. "They gave the Madras position back to last year's teacher. But Beth Haven was open and they were happy to have me."

A short puff of breath flared his nostrils. "I bet they were. Tell me about you and Sam."

Her throat worked. *Sam who?* Out loud she said, "Sam is a wonderful gentleman who cares for me very much." *Or at least might learn to with time.*

"So you're settling for a man who cares for you, instead of love, is that it?"

An angry little laugh escaped before she could stop it. "You wouldn't know the first thing about love if it slapped you in the face!" *Oh, that was a terrible analogy to use.* Her eyes dropped closed for just a moment and when she opened them a hint of humor glimmered in his eyes.

"You can't say that name."

Confusion furrowed her brow. "What?"

"Bennett. Up here, I'm not that man, understand?" His hand lingered and his thumb caressed short strokes at the corner of her mouth, his perusal pausing on her lips.

She swallowed hard and nodded. "Sorry. I forgot. You just make me feel… so… angry."

The corners of his eyes crinkled. He leaned closer and she could feel the brush of his breath feathering across her lips. "Only angry?"

He's just toying with you! She planted her palms firmly against his chest, scrabbling for anything to put a little distance between them. "I really do need to…"

A lazy grin filled his face and slowly, after what seemed an eternity, he stepped back. "Fine, I'll send Mick down here to stand guard."

"No!" she grasped his arm before he could take another step.

His eyebrows arched. "Oh? So you do want me to stand as your protector then?"

She gave a very unladylike growl and glanced both ways before she whispered, "Just stay put and *maybe* I'll keep your real name to myself!"

With a parting glare, she flounced into the bushes doing her best to ignore his laughter.

★

CHAPTER FIVE

Cade lay in his bedroll, once again having a hard time falling asleep. Tonight, however, he wasn't worrying about how to report that the teacher was going to be kidnapped, but about the fact that if he fell asleep, she would be at the mercy of the rest of the Rodale gang. Forget that Judd had warned all the men to stay away from her. Cade had seen the looks Mick kept giving her all evening.

She slept only a few feet away on a make-shift pallet Judd had forced Seth to put together. Cade had placed his bedroll between her and the rest of the men. Still, this was no way for a lady to spend even one evening.

Flipping onto his side, he snatched a blade of grass and methodically broke it into tiny pieces. What a mess this job had turned into.

Tomorrow... Tomorrow he would get the evidence he needed, get Kat and Sharyah and make an escape with them. He'd seen several horses that would do. He only needed to bring back one and that would be enough to hang the entire gang.

He just had to find a way to talk to Kat without arousing the others' suspicions. Maybe she would try and talk to him again. A man could hope. It would certainly be nice if something went right on this job. She had come to Judd of her own free will, but unless he missed his guess, she wasn't remaining because of it.

Who knew that the teacher he didn't want to kidnap in the first place would end up being none other than the woman he'd spent the better part of the last few months trying to forget?

He released a long breath. Sky and Rocky were going to kill him. To say nothing of Mr. Jordan.

As morning light kissed the snowy caps of the Three Sisters, Sharyah seated herself on a log just down from Cade.

Foot propped up on a rock, arms folded over his knee, and his black Stetson pushed far back on his head, he stared into the flames, lost in thought. He barely acknowledged her with a dip of his head when she sat down. He looked grumpy and disheveled.

And more tired than he had before he went to sleep last night. Like maybe he hadn't slept at all.

When Katrina sashayed his way with a steaming cup of coffee and pressed it into his hands with a coy lift of her brow, he perked up, though. He lifted the cup in a small salute and downed a gulp.

The woman's pendulum gait carried her back to the chuck wagon.

Sharyah blew a little gust of air through her nose and turned to study the dance of the flames. She might have known. Could she ever remember a time that Cade didn't have another woman in his life? She should be used to it by now. But still the pain of it stabbed deeply.

Well, she was moving on. She had Sam now. He would be here with the law for her any minute.

She glanced toward the horizon, searching for any little puff of dust that might indicate someone was riding this way. Nothing.

Cade took a slow sip of his coffee. Then turned to look at her, his mouth flattening into a wry grin. "He won't come for you."

She lifted her chin. It didn't look like Katrina was going to bother bringing her a cup of coffee, so she stood, strode over to Cade and took his. "Don't worry. She'll bring you another one just as soon as she notices this one's gone, I'm sure." And with that, she walked away from him, out into the meadow to where she could enjoy the sunrise over the Three Sisters. She cupped the mug in both hands, taking in the heady aroma with a long appreciative inhale.

Off to her left, the horses cropped grass. The horse she'd ridden yesterday lifted its head with a quiet nicker and she stepped over to it and patted the side of its neck. The horse whuffed her coffee and then shook its head and backed up a step.

Sharyah chuckled. "What? Not your idea of a tasty breakfast, huh?"

She returned her attention to the mountains then, drawn further into the field by the sheer beauty of the magenta sky streaked with peach and yellow hues. Her feet moved of their own accord as in breathless awe she studied the arc of the vast creator-painted canvas stretched before her. Each snow-capped Sister loomed a color-kissed blue-gray shadow against the vivid sky.

Sharyah took a sip of coffee then tipped her head back and closed her eyes. If such beauty existed here, what must heaven be like?

The grass to her right rustled as someone stepped up beside her.

"Go away, Cade."

A man chuckled. "Well ain't you a testy little thing. Pretty though. Right pretty."

Cade had just started after Sharyah, when Judd walked up to the fire and called for all the men to join him. Cade hesitated, torn. He didn't want to leave Sharyah alone. But if he went after her he might miss out on an important piece of information. His fists clenched and he glanced over his shoulder. The men would all need to be at Judd's little meeting. And based on the fact that Judd was throwing his saddle on his mount, this shouldn't take long.

She'll be fine.

Reluctantly, he decided he'd best find out what Judd was up to.

Judd stepped over to the fire, rubbed his hands and warmed them, then glanced up as Katrina handed Cade a second cup. Even though she didn't have the same saucy air as she'd had when she placed the first cup into his hands, Judd frowned thoughtfully as he watched Katrina resume her place by the chuck wagon.

When Judd looked back with a curled lip and an assessing

glower, Cade studied his coffee, making sure to keep a bland expression. He wanted no part in that fight, this morning. He bit back a chuckle. Or any other morning for that matter. Judd could have the woman. She had calamity scrawled from the top of her head to the bottoms of her feet.

The other men moseyed on over to the fire in Judd's wake. Several horses stood saddled and ready.

Hurry it along, gents. Cade glanced out toward the field. Still no sign of Shar.

He looked around at the others. Everyone accounted for except Red and Mick.

His stomach clenched. On watch, maybe?

He took a swig of coffee and swept his gaze around the area. *Shouldn't have ribbed her about Sam.* This wasn't good, her being out of sight.

Cade plunked his coffee cup onto the rock beside him and strode in the direction he'd last seen her.

"Schilling! You going somewhere?"

Cade thought fast. "That teacher. She wandered off. Figured I'd best go bring her back." His heart beat as though to race a galloping stallion.

Judd waved a hand of dismissal. "She can't go far. Red's standing guard at the only path outta here. We'll only be a jiffy."

That still left Mick unaccounted for. Sweat dampened Cade's palms. "I'll just—"

"Sit!" Judd glowered and touched a hand to the butt of his gun.

Cade tossed one more glace out over the field. "Where's Mick?"

Anger glittered in Judd's eyes. "He went out early this morning to see if he could wrangle us up some meat."

That brought a slight relief. Likely they wouldn't run into each other, but the longer Cade kept Judd waiting, the longer she would be out there on her own and the more likely it was that Mick might find her. He gritted his teeth, but complied with Judd's request. *Dear Jesus, keep her safe.* He picked up his coffee.

"Alright, listen up." Judd rubbed his palms together,

apparently satisfied with Cade's acquiescence, because he turned away and scanned the group. "Today we ride for Farewell Bend. Everyone could use a little break and a reward for a job well done. Schilling, you'll stay here and guard the women. Red is on watch and Mick," he waved a hand, "is off rustling grub, like I said. When he gets back he'll help you... *guard* the women."

Several of the men chuckled.

Even as the hair stood up along Cade's neck, he felt his attention sharpen. This was exactly the break he needed. Still he was surprised that Judd would leave him here. But then Rodale had no reason to distrust him. He'd done nothing wrong, yet. And he'd come through for the man yesterday. But so help him, if he could work it out, by the time Judd returned this evening he would have every reason to hate Cade.

He was careful to keep his eyes off Katrina, but in his peripheral vision he saw her straighten and glance his way. He fixed his attention on the black liquid in his cup, noticed the reflection of the vivid morning sky, gave it a swirl, then met Judd's gaze with a frank arch of his own brow. "Fine by me."

Judd nodded. "Alright men, let's ride."

They couldn't ride out of camp fast enough to suit Cade. As soon as they turned the corner out of sight, Cade leapt to his feet and ran.

Sharyah snapped open her eyes and leapt around to face the man, her coffee arching out in a spray as the cup slid from her fingers and landed a few feet away. It wasn't Cade. It was Mr. Dictionary, himself. Mick Rodale. The one who'd looked at her like she was a delicious side-dish yesterday. The same way he looked at her now. The same man that Missy Green had accused of... unspeakable things.

Sharyah glanced back toward the fire where she'd left Cade. But she'd wandered further than she intended over a slight hill and she couldn't even see the fire anymore. The field between her and the hilltop stretched silent and empty.

Her legs felt like they might give out from under her at any moment. She forced a smile praying her terror didn't show in her eyes. "Oh, hello."

Mick grinned and folded his arms. "A little jumpy this morning, are we?" Stepping between her and the way back to the camp, he planted his feet wide. "Don't worry, I won't hold that whole book incident against you."

She laughed, and even to her own ears it sounded high pitched and strained. "You startled me is all." Skirting around him, she started back toward safety. "Did you sleep well? I actually did. I was surprised, under the circumstances." She couldn't seem to stop prattling. "The sunrise is beautiful, don't you think?" Why oh why had she walked out this far alone? She hadn't realized she'd wandered so far from the fire, from Cade's protective presence.

After only a few steps Mick took her elbow in a firm grasp and pulled her to a stop. "Let's not be in such an all-fired hurry to run off, shall we? The sky *is* right pretty this morning." But he wasn't looking at the sunrise. His eyes had wandered to places that no decent man would…

Every limb quavered. She worked her mouth, but it was as dry as the tangle of tumbleweeds piled up against the sage brush just a few feet away. She glanced over her shoulder, hoping against hope to see someone else.

With a tug, she tried to free her arm. "Just the same, I'd rather get back."

"Naw." He grinned. "You wouldn't. 'Cause I'm about to show you a real good time, Darlin.'"

The blood drained from her head so fast she thought she might faint right on the spot. The scenery circled around her in a blurry swirl of greens, browns, pinks and yellows. But Mick's leering face remained rock steady at the center of it.

She closed her eyes and inhaled, willing herself with every fiber of her being not to give in to the hysteria clamoring for release. After two purposeful breaths, she regained control. Anger surged up inside to take the place of the hysteria. "Let go of my arm this instant."

He only laughed and pulled her closer.

Just the action she'd been hoping for. As he drew her nearer, she used her momentum to bring her knee up swift and hard. With Pa, Sky, Rocky and Cade all serving as lawmen, she'd learned a few things through the years. They'd made sure of it.

Mick cried out and doubled over and she brought her elbow down on the back of his head, just like she'd been taught. Then she turned to run and crashed into a firm hard chest. She did scream then, flailing her arms with all her might and striking out with everything in her. This was too much. She couldn't fight two of them.

The man grunted. "Sharyah, it's me! Cade! Stop. Shhhhh." He gave her a gentle shake. "It's me, Shar. Just me."

"Cade!" She spun back around, clutching him to ensure he didn't leave her, but not wanting to let her attention wander from her attacker for even a moment.

Mick groaned and clambered to his feet, rubbing the back of his head and seemingly unable to stand to full height.

"He—he—he was going to—he said—" It was no use. She couldn't form a coherent thought to save her life.

But Cade seemed to understand. Slowly he stepped forward and set her firmly behind him. Feeling instantly safe shielded by his bulk, she clutched his shirt and pressed up close to him.

She heard Mick's boots slither through the field grass as he shuffled a few steps. "Aw, come on, Schilling. I was just gonna have me a little fun with the lady, is all."

"Yeah? Just a little fun, huh?"

"That's right." Mick sounded like he thought Cade might be coming around to his way of thinking.

Sharyah shuddered and leaned her forehead into Cade's broad back.

"Well, I'm just going to have me a little fun, right now. What do you think about that?"

Mick chuckled. "Hey if you want the first—wait, what are you doing man?"

Sharyah realized Cade had quietly palmed his gun.

"Whoa, whoa, whoa!" Mick's voice cracked. "Let's just slow this train on down. If it means that much to you, I won't touch her, I swear."

A tremor rippled through Cade. "It means that much to me. Now you pull that gun out nice and slow and don't get any ideas because I won't hesitate to shoot you." Authority rang through his words. After a stretch of silence he said, "Good. Now toss it over to the side and get down on your knees."

Mick huffed and the gun thudded off to their left. "Judd's not going to like you getting all high and mighty like this."

"There'll be a site o' things Judd won't like when he gets home this evening. Now all the way to your belly and lock your hands behind your neck." Cade angled his head, then, and spoke to her over his shoulder, but kept his gun and his eyes focused on Mick. "Shar, I'm going to step away for just a minute, I need you to let go of me."

She suddenly realized both her hands were fisted so tightly in the softness of his shirt that her knuckles had turned white. She blinked and slowly released her grip.

He stepped forward to tie Mick up and, as his warmth left her, a wash of cold terror swept in. She folded her arms and glanced around to make sure no one else was coming their way. Her legs trembled and threatened to give out from under her, pain clenched a tight knot in her stomach, and her arms felt like she'd just done a full day's washing with Grandma Eltha's washboard. She forced herself to draw in a long inhale of air, then another. But the trembling persisted.

"Hey," Cade cupped her shoulders and bent down to peer into her face, "I'm so sorry. Everything's going to be alright now."

She leaned to one side to see Mick on his belly with his hands tied behind him and a gag around his head. "Wh-what are you going to do?"

Cade touched her face and returned her attention to him. "I need you to go on up to the fire. To Kat. Can you do that?"

She nodded. "Yes, but…" she scanned the field again, "do you think… are the others…?"

Again, he pulled her attention back to him. "Everyone's gone but Red, and he's on watch. Tell you what, I'll walk with you to the fire, but we have to hurry, alright?"

Relief coursed through her and she nodded.

Cade stepped over and grabbed Mick by one arm, pulling him to his feet. "Let's go."

Cade cursed himself every which way for a fool as he dragged Mick back to the fire with one hand, and with the other gently prodded Sharyah to keep moving. Her whole body shivered periodically, and her face held about as much color as a bed sheet flapping from the clothes-line in bright sunlight.

He clenched his jaw. This whole sorry mess ended today. If only he hadn't let Sam talk him into taking this job. But if he wasn't here, maybe she would have been kidnapped anyway. Maybe God had brought him here to protect her?

Katrina, leaning over a pot at the fire, glanced up in surprise as they approached.

Cade shoved Mick down onto a log. "Kat, be ready to ride in ten minutes. Get five horses saddled for me, would you?" He glanced over at the remaining horses. "Make sure to saddle the paint and the dun."

Wide-eyed, she nodded, lifted her skirts and hurried toward the horses.

As he stripped off Mick's boots, Cade glanced at Sharyah.

She stood quietly, her fingers fiddling with each other, staring into the fire.

That was so unlike her. Normally she pitched right in and did what needed to be done.

As though she had heard his thoughts, she suddenly straightened and glanced around. Walking purposefully toward the chuck wagon, she began to put things in order, preparing it to be moved.

They wouldn't take the wagon, but he didn't tell her that. Right now she needed to be busy, but the sooner he got her to a safe place the better.

Movement at the corner of his eye caught his attention. Mick launched toward him, but Cade jerked out of the way just enough to avoid the full force of skull against skull. Still, shard's of pain burst to life at his temple, and light danced before his eyes. Mick landed partially across him, and Cade rammed his elbow into the man's rib cage.

Cade kicked him off and lurched to his feet, ready to finish the fight.

Mick grunted, but hampered by his bound hands, he didn't seem to have much brawl left in him. And it only took Cade a moment to wrestle him back onto the log.

He strapped Mick's feet together and then tied them to the log. Standing, he gave the man's face a couple of gentle slaps. "Don't go anywhere while I'm gone, you hear?"

Mick glowered and grunted a protest.

Pulling the derringer he always carried in his boot from its hiding place, Cade walked over to Sharyah. "Here." He pressed it into her palm. "If he tries anything, shoot him." He knew she could handle the gun. He'd been with her many times when she'd gone out to target practice, much to her mother's dismay.

She didn't say anything, but she put the gun into the pocket of her skirt and smoothed her hands over the fabric studying the ground.

He wished he had time to talk with her. He could tell from the gesture that she felt disturbed. Of course she did. What woman wouldn't after what had almost happened to her. But talking would have to come later. Right now he needed to get Red. He touched her elbow. "I'll be back in just a few minutes, alright?"

Sharyah nodded and watched him hurry toward his horse then resumed her task of packing up the chuck wagon. She reached for the whisk broom and her arm brushed a tin canister and knocked the top from it. The round lid clanged and clattered and warbled until she reached out and stopped its circular rotation with one hand. She frowned. The canister held a folded piece of paper. Some ink had bled thru, so there was writing on the inside.

She picked up the lid and started to replace it. Whatever was on the paper was none of her concern. However, a quick glance over her shoulder revealed Katrina quietly talking to Mick. Sharyah reached out and deftly slipped the paper free of its hiding place, smoothing it open on the flat of the gate.

Her brow puckered. It was a letter. A letter addressed to Judge Green. And from the De Beers Mining Company, with a South African address.

She tossed another glance over her shoulder. Katrina was walking purposefully her way. Quickly, she stuffed the letter back into the canister and reached for the cover.

Katrina appeared by her side, clapping one hand over the top of the container and holding her other out for the lid. "I can finish up here."

Sharyah shrugged. "Alright." She handed over the cover. "I'll see to the fire." She hoped the woman hadn't noticed her hand trembling. The letter was obviously something Katrina didn't want her to see. Could it have something to do with why she was kidnapped in the first place? But why would Katrina have it? Cade seemed to trust her. Yet why was she up here with these men? Was she really trustworthy? She sighed and made a note to mention the letter to Cade when they had a moment together.

CHAPTER SIX

After shucking his rifle from the scabbard of his saddle, Cade hurried in the direction where Red would be standing watch. The man had to have heard Sharyah's screams earlier. Cade had halfway expected him to come running to help her and discover him tying up Mick. But he'd forgotten the caliber of men he was dealing with here, and for once he was thankful for it. If Red had come upon them out in the meadow, who knew how things would have gone down. This way, he would at least have the jump on the man.

Easing into a low crouch he studied the ground. He didn't know where the men stood guard exactly. Finding Red might be a little tricky. It only took him a few moments, however, to discover the path to the watch site. And no one had bothered to hide it, of course. Cade followed as quickly as he could, yet still kept a careful watch ahead so that he wouldn't come upon Red unexpectedly while his eyes were on the trail.

A few moments later the tracks came to an abrupt end at the edge of a cliff. The scent of tobacco floated on the air. Cade dropped to his belly and scooted forward to peer down on the man. He stood on a ledge just below Cade overlooking the main trail. Already several cigarette butts littered the ground at his feet. Red's rifle leaned against a rock at the far end of the ledge, but his pistol hung low and tied down at his side. Cade took a deep breath. Red was said to be very fast with his guns. Well, he didn't plan on giving the man a chance to prove his speed.

He stood and raised his rifle to his shoulder. "Red, put your hands up." He cocked the Winchester as he spoke.

Red tensed, started to move, then hesitated, his hands hanging just by his sides.

"Don't do it! Hands on your head. Now. I won't hesitate to

shoot you and lest you question my aim, I can bring down a duck mid-flight without ever ruining any of the meat."

Slowly, Red raised his hands and clasped them on his head, turning to look up at Cade. "I knew you was trouble the minute I laid eyes on you." A cigarette still dangled from his lips.

Cade didn't acknowledge that comment. "You keep your eyes on me and move slowly, you hear? Any sudden movement and I pull this trigger."

Red gave an almost imperceptible nod.

"Good. Now with your left hand, you reach over nice and slow and pull your pistol out with two fingers."

Red did.

"Drop it by your side."

The gun hit the ground, raising a small puff of dust when it landed.

"Now take the knife out of the sheath hanging down your back."

Red sighed, but slowly moved to comply. He apparently hadn't expected Cade to have noticed the weapon concealed by his shirt, but many years of helping Sean Jordan on cases had made the knife obvious the first time he'd laid eyes on the man. The eight-inch blade joined the pistol on the ground.

"Now the blade in your boot." Cade gestured with the muzzle of the rifle.

Red's lips pressed together grimly even as he moved to comply.

"Now take the path up here, moving nice and slow. And if your hands so much as twitch when you walk past that rifle it will be the last move you make."

Hands on his hat, Red sauntered the length of the ledge. He passed the rifle leaning against the rock, and started up the narrow little sloping path.

Cade switched from the rifle to his Colt as Red slowly took the incline. Once Red stood before him, he said, "Down on your knees."

"You're making a big mistake, son." Red spoke around the still-smoking cigarette.

Cade plucked it from his lips and crushed it beneath his boot. "Oh yeah, how's that?" He kept the muzzle of his pistol pressed to Red's head, as he stepped behind him and slipped a loop of rawhide over one of his hands.

"If you betray him, Judd won't let you live."

Cade made quick work of binding the man's hands behind his back. "By this time tomorrow, Judd won't be in any position to give me any worries. And neither will you. Now on your feet."

Cade glanced down at Red's weapons on the ledge below. He hated to leave them lying around for just anyone to find, but after he considered his options he decided to simply leave them there. Going down for them was too risky.

When they arrived back at the camp, Katrina had all five horses saddled and ready to go. Sharyah had finished packing up the wagon, and had pulled the logs in the fire apart so that only a few glowing coals remained. Smart girl not to douse the fire with water. The sudden cloud of smoke kicked up by a dousing of water, and then its immediate disappearance would be a sign to anyone paying attention that something was amiss. This way the smoke would peter out slowly, but the fire wouldn't be in any danger of spreading unless a drastic wind developed.

Katrina blinked at Red as Cade walked him toward one of the horses. "I didn't expect you to go down without at least a shot being fired."

Red shrugged. "Judd's going to kill you, you know. You betraying him like this."

Katrina paled slightly, but she lifted one shoulder. "He's not the man I thought he was when he begged me to come with him." She tossed Mick a quick glance.

Mick growled and tried to speak but his words were indecipherable through the gag.

"Sharyah, bring me that rope on the chuck wagon," Cade called. He boosted Red up onto a horse.

Sharyah handed him the length of rope and he passed her the pistol. "Hold this on him while I tie him."

Red chuckled. "That little slip of a gal wouldn't have the guts to shoot me even if she knew how to handle that gun."

He kicked out, his boot connecting solidly with Cade's sternum and Cade felt a jolt of surprise as he stumbled backwards trying to catch his balance.

Red swung his far leg over the horse and leapt after Cade, his boot narrowly missing crushing his ribcage as Cade rolled away to one side. "And I could take you even with both my hands tied behind my back."

The report from the forty-four caliber crashed through the glade and Red's hat flew from his head landing a few paces away.

Everyone froze.

A large hole, jagged and black, marred the crown of the ten gallon's leather.

"Next time, I won't miss." Sharyah's voice was as calm as could be. She thumbed the hammer back with a loud click and Red turned whiter than pancake batter above the line of his beard.

Cade clambered to his feet the rush of adrenaline sending tremors all through him. That was too close for comfort. *Lord, I just want Sharyah safe.* Scooping up his own Stetson, he dusted his pants with it giving himself time to suppress the shuddering. Then he stepped over and took Red by the arm once more. "Never judge a dog's bite by the shine of her coat. Now get up on that horse and sit quiet." He snatched up the rope as Red grumbled and moved to comply. "Sharyah, if he tries anything else shoot to kill."

Her face paled and he knew she'd never be able to obey that command. But he figured Red was in a much more compliant mood right now than he had been a moment ago, thanks to her smart thinking and he wanted to keep him scared. This time he was able to get Red's feet tied to the stirrups without incident and after he did the same to Mick, Cade put Katrina at the front of the string, followed by the two outlaws, and they all headed for Beth Haven with Sharyah bringing up the rear. He wanted as much distance between her and the two men as possible.

The main street of Beth Haven lay silent as they all rode into town. Sharyah sighed in relief, feeling tears prick the backs of her eyes as tension released from her shoulders. The whole way here she'd only been able to think what might happen to Cade if the other outlaws had decided to return early and they met them on the trail.

Cade directed them all toward the sheriff's office.

From everything she'd heard from Sam and the other locals, Sheriff Collier left a lot to be desired when it came to being a lawman. The man was nicer than hot tea in a china cup, and had the tendency to be too trusting and easily deceived. He'd originally been elected because everyone thought so well of him, and only after he'd been Sheriff for a while had people realized the same characteristics that made him so likable made him a terrible lawman.

Sheriff Collier stepped out onto the boardwalk as they rode up in front of the jail and Cade swung down. "Sheriff."

Collier nodded and eyed the two trussed up men. "What have we here?"

"Two members of the Rodale gang." Cade reached to help her down from the saddle.

Sharyah wanted nothing more than to step close and feel the strength of his protective arms surround her. But as soon as her feet touched the ground he turned away to help Katrina down, all the while holding the reins of the two outlaws' horses in one hand. "You have a deputy?"

Collier shook his head. "Nope. Can't rightly say that I do."

"Well you're going to need one. This is Mick Rodale and that there is Red Hendrix. I know for a fact you've been wanting a meet up with Rodale here in regard to the incident with Miss Green. And I believe you'll find a long sheet of grievances on a poster somewhere with Red's name and handsome mug on it."

Collier pulled at his beard with a low whistle. "Well, I'll be. I been Sheriff several years now and haven't seen hide nor hair of any o' that gang. And here you been 'round these parts, what, two days?"

Glancing up and down the street, Cade apparently didn't recognize the awe in the man's voice. Either that or he was simply ignoring it. He asked, "When's the next time a judge is supposed to come through?"

"Well now we have Judge Green here most o' the time, but since it were his daughter Mick is accused o—," the sheriff glanced her way, snapped his mouth shut, then opened it and continued, "well, I don't think the Judge would be the best man to preside at Mick here's trial. But, as luck would have it, Judge Thatcher, a traveling judge who stops by to take care of any cases Green needs help on, is due to ride through tomorrow or the next day."

Relief eased some of Sharyah's tension. At least the man's justice would be swift. That was something that didn't happen too often these days with judges spread so thin.

Cade nodded and set to untying the knots in the rawhide strips around one of Red's feet. Pure hatred glittered from Red's eyes.

Sharyah couldn't stop a shiver at the memory of those boots almost crushing the life from Cade earlier. Thank God her aim had been true.

Cade moved around the horse to loose Red's other leg and said, "You'll need a deputy to help you stand guard over these two until the trial's over."

Collier grinned. "Well I think I know just the man for the job."

Cade glanced up, a question on his face, but then apparently realized Collier was referring to him. His eyes flicked Sharyah's way and then back to the knots again so quickly that if she hadn't been paying attention she would have missed it entirely. "Sure, I'll hang around for a couple days. No problem. But we need to take a posse and ride back to the Rodale hideout right away. They should all traipse in half-drunk about midnight tonight." Cade stepped back, drew his gun, and motioned Red down from the saddle.

Red complied. Rather stiffly, but without incident.

So Cade Bennett would be in town for a few days. Sharyah pressed one hand to her chest, willing away the double-time beating of her heart and looked at Katrina. The woman's eyes held a gleam of decided excitement and her focus was fixed solely on Cade. With a disgusted sniff, Sharyah returned her attention to the men.

Collier escorted Red inside at gunpoint and came back a moment later as Cade was pulling Mick down off his horse. Cade handed the young disgruntled outlaw off to him, and Collier thrust something into Cade's hands. "Pin that on. You're deputized." He disappeared back into the jail with Mick and a moment later Sharyah heard the satisfactory clang of the jail gate locking into place.

Cade pinned the star to the shoulder of his shirt and stepped over in front of her. The blue of his eyes was as dark as sapphire. His black Stetson, pushed back on his head, had allowed several curls to escape across his forehead and the dark stubble from several days of missed shaving accentuated the sharp angles of his jaw. Sharyah swallowed and forced her gaze away. She was a hopeless case.

He shifted. "Come with me out to the Perry's to take Kat home, and then I'll bring you to your place before I ride out with the posse to the hideout."

She pressed her lips together and nodded.

"I'm sure she simply wants to get home to rest." Katrina's expression had turned decidedly cool.

"No. No. I'll ride with you, I'm fine." She forced a smile. Tired as she was, she wasn't ready to face her little cabin alone, just yet.

Besides maybe seeing Sam again would help her regain her determination to finally and completely forget about Cade Bennett and his alluring blue eyes.

"You're sure?"

She nodded. "Yes. Let's go. It will be good to see Sam again."

A muscle ticked at the corner of his eye, and he pressed his lips into a firm line, giving a concise nod and holding out his hand toward her horse in indication that he would help her mount now. She kept her eyes averted from his as he lifted her into place, but Katrina had no such qualms.

As Cade attempted to help her into her saddle, the woman rested her hands much too far around his shoulders for propriety, and at one point she contrived to slip and crash forward into his chest. Cade grunted and caught her to him. "You okay?"

Katrina somehow insinuated herself even closer to him and tilted her head, batting her eye lashes, as she looked up at him. "Yes, thanks to you." She ran the tip of a long fingernail across his chin.

Cade grinned.

Sharyah's mouth turned dry and she felt a familiar wave of jealousy cramp her stomach. The woman was obviously another of Cade's female friends. He had one in just about every town. Each one of them smitten and hoping that some day he would make them his wife. Not that she thought he'd ever done anything improper with any of them. But he certainly had never discouraged them from thinking he might be in love with them. Well... had never discouraged anyone but *her*.

The humiliation of the day he'd told her there could never be anything but friendship between them, crashed over her in an all-too-familiar wave. She glanced down and smoothed the material of her skirt. What did she care what Cade felt for this woman? It was nothing to her. She'd moved on, and she wouldn't give him the satisfaction of getting angry that right at this moment he had another woman in his arms and was grinning about it. She clenched her teeth, lifted her chin, swallowed her mortification, and forced her gaze down the street, waiting in silence for their little tête-à-tête to finish.

Cade glanced past Katrina to where Sharyah sat on her horse. If her nose lifted any higher it would be pointed at the sky and her hands clutched the reins so tightly that her horse sidled a step backwards. *Well, well.* His grin widened. Maybe he hadn't shot his chances with her all to pieces that day at the church picnic, after all.

He let Katrina go so abruptly that she had to scramble to keep from falling onto her backside. She cast him a glower of annoyance, then caught herself and quickly tried to hide her displeasure with another round of fluttering lashes.

He did his best not to laugh. "You get some dust in your eye, there?" He handed her the bandana from his back pocket. Whatever the woman wanted with him it couldn't be anything good and her flattery and flirting would get her nowhere. "I'll be right back." He needed to let Collier know he would come later this evening to lead the posse to the hideout.

Collier agreed to the arrangement and when he came out onto the walk again Sharyah still stared toward the other end of the street as though her very life depended on it. She'd had a hard day. He really should just get both ladies home and let them rest, yet he couldn't help but feel a tad giddy at the evidence that she still cared for him, at least a little, even if Sam might be a slight complication.

He walked over to Katrina. "We really should be going. Here let me help you up." He grabbed her and tossed her up onto the saddle so quickly that she didn't have time to do anything but grab onto the reins out of sheer surprise. The bandana he'd given her fluttered to the ground and he retrieved it.

Swinging onto his own horse, he clucked to the animal and set it into motion, leaving a sputtering Katrina and a silent Sharyah to follow in his wake.

As Cade reined up at the hitching rail in front of the main house out at the ranch, Sam stepped onto the porch.

"Sammy, darling!" Katrina leapt from her horse and threw herself into her brother's arms. "I'm so sorry. Do forgive me and let me come back home."

Sam patted her, doing his best to maintain his balance. "There, there, Kat. All is forgiven and you've learned your lesson, I hope?"

Katrina sobbed against her brother's neck. "I certainly have! It was most dreadful! Most!"

Cade had to stop himself from rolling his eyes. He turned instead to focus on Sharyah. Her big brown eyes were shimmering with a soft glow and focused directly on Sam. Cade's stomach bucked in protest as a wave of jealousy rolled over him. Disgusted with himself he swung to the ground and strode to her side. "Here let me help you down."

She leaned toward him and as his hands settled around her waist and he lifted her down, he couldn't help but linger over the task.

Her small hands resting on his shoulders, she carefully kept her attention fixed on the center of his shirt and tried to step away the moment her feet touched the ground.

He tightened his hold and her gaze flew to his before darting away.

Sam was still busy with his sister so he kept her where she stood. "You alright?"

"Yes. I'm fine. Thank you." She tried to take a step back, but her horse didn't take kindly to being crowded and bumped her back toward him. A little gasp of surprise escaped her, and as he steadied her in his arms crimson tinged her cheeks.

He suppressed a smile. He'd have to give the beast an apple later. A man could stand looking down at this woman all day and never tire of the view.

"Cade I'm fine." She pushed at him. "You can let go of me now."

"Maybe I just like where I'm standing."

She cleared her throat and gave a little shake of her head. "Don't."

He bent down to interrupt her line of vision. "Don't what?"

"Please, Cade don—"

"Sharyah?" Sam strode around the tail end of her horse.

Cade rolled his eyes. Lucky for Sam Sharyah's mount was as docile as a kitten or he could have been kicked to kingdom come.

"Are you alright?" Sam glanced from Sharyah to Cade and back.

Relief etched her face and she stepped away, smiling at Sam. "Yes, Sam, I'm fine."

Cade let her go and she went willingly into Sam's arms for an embrace. Clenching his fists, he shoved them into his armpits and, as Sam dallied over the hug, reminded himself that Sam was his friend.

Finally after interminable moments Sam stepped away. "So Katrina tells me that Red and Mick are down at the jail and Cade here has been deputized."

Sharyah nodded. "Yes. And Cade is taking a group of men back for the rest of them tonight. If the judge arrives tomorrow as scheduled, the trial will be held then. I'm sure Missy will be so relieved."

At the mention of Missy's name an odd look crossed Sam's face and he shuffled his feet. Cade felt a prick of curiosity. *Interesting.*

"Well," Sam recovered quickly, "Did you gather any evidence about my rustling problem?"

Cade gestured to the two horses he and Sharyah had ridden. "I'm fairly certain I sold you both of these horses, but their brands have been reworked."

Sam glanced at the brand on the haunch of the nearest horse and then bent to look at something on the animal's inner foreleg. He stood with a grin. "But they missed the second brand I always tag my animals with.

Cade squatted down to peer under the animal. Sure enough there was Sam's Rocking P brand, way up high on the left front foreleg. He stood and nodded. "Well there's your evidence." That would save them from having to slaughter and skin one of the animals to see the original brand on the inside of the hide.

Sam shook his hand. "Thank you. I'll have your money for you tomorrow."

"All of them aren't caught yet."

Sam shrugged. "I hired you to get me evidence and you've done that."

Cade rested one hand on his horse's saddle and the other on his hip. "I like to finish what I start." He didn't add that he wouldn't feel safe leaving Sharyah here until Rodale and his entire gang were either behind bars or strung up.

Poking out his lip, Sam cocked his head to the side. "Suit yourself. And I appreciate it."

He nodded.

Sam motioned Sharyah toward the door. "Come into the house. Millicent just about has dinner ready and I want to hear all about your adventures."

Sharyah's face paled at that. "Oh, I'll have to tell you another time. I really should let Cade take me home. Could you pass the word to the school families that lessons will resume tomorrow?"

Sam cocked his head to one side. "Are you sure you want to do that?"

She nodded. "We might make it a short day if the judge arrives and the trial begins, but the children need the discipline and structure of daily studies."

Cade held his silence for the moment, but he would have to talk to her about that. The last thing she needed to be doing right now was going back to teaching. She needed to give herself time to rest from the whole ordeal, but mostly from the terror of what had nearly happened to her this morning.

"Alright." Sam stepped back. "Well if you are sure… I'll drop by the school tomorrow afternoon then?"

Sharyah smiled. "Yes, that would be fine. I'll look forward to it."

A muscle in Cade's jaw flinched. Maybe he *didn't* stand a chance with her.

Sam helped her up into the saddle and it was a moment before he realized that he still stood on the ground and she was waiting for him to take her home. Mounting up he led the way back to town.

They were nearly there when he realized he had no idea where she lived. "Where's your place?"

She gestured in the direction of the school. "There's a little cabin not too far from the schoolhouse."

He pulled to an abrupt stop. "Wait a minute. You live alone?" He'd pictured her living with a family, or at a boarding house. Somewhere with people around to protect her.

She nodded.

There was no chance he was leaving her alone tonight of all nights. If something went wrong and one of the gang escaped back at camp who knew what the man might do. He turned in the direction of town. "Come on, you can sleep in my room at the hotel. It's paid up for two weeks."

"Cade!" She kept her horse reined to a firm stand-still, exasperation coating her tone.

"Just… in my room. Where you'll be safe. I won't even be there." His heart pounded a rhythm against the wall of his chest. What would he do if she said no? He wouldn't be able to concentrate on anything with her out here all by herself.

"No, absolutely not!" She jerked her horse toward the school and kicked it into a trot.

He spurred his mount after her and reached out, taking her reins and pulling her to a stop. "Shar, please, I can't have you staying someplace all alone tonight."

"I have spent the last two days in the hills with a band of outlaws." Her voice warbled on a tremor. She shuddered and wrapped her arms around herself. "The way he—he looked at me just—just—" Tears spilled down her cheeks and she turned her face away from him.

"Shar," He dismounted and helped her down, pulling her into a comforting embrace and simply letting her cry. He cupped the back of her head, pressing the side of her face into his chest and stroking the curls away from her damp cheeks.

She buried herself against him, covered her face with her hands and heaved great shuddering sobs.

For a moment he closed his eyes and turned his face to the

sky. *God, forgive me. This is my fault.* "It's alright. I'm not going to let anything happen to you, now. I'm so sorry." He threaded his fingers into her hair and rested his cheek atop her head. "He's gone. He won't ever be able to hurt you again, I promise."

After a few torturous minutes, she drew in a long thready breath. "I was so scared."

"I know."

"But all I can think of is that you came to my rescue."

He chuckled softly, attempting to lighten the mood. "I don't know. You looked like you were doing alright for yourself when I got there." He leaned away and lifted her face so he could look into her eyes. Big brown eyes in which a man could lose himself forever, eyes now magnified by terror and tears.

"And Missy Green didn't have anyone to come to her rescue. That man… he… Oh Cade it must have been so awful for her."

Okay, there was no lightening this mood. "I know, Shar. I'm so sorry."

She leaned in again, tucking her head under his chin and clutching fistfuls of his shirt.

He rested his mouth against the top of her head swaying slightly in a comforting rhythm and simply letting her relax in safety. His eyes fell shut as thankfulness that she hadn't been hurt more severely than she had washed over him. It could have been worse. Much worse.

He could stand here holding her forever, but time was running short and he needed to get back to the jail and meet up with the posse Sheriff Collier was putting together. He eased back slightly and rested one palm against her cheek, rubbing away the moisture with his thumb. "Come to town. I'll drop you by the hotel. I can't have you staying at your place all alone."

"Cade please…" She trembled all over. "It will be a strange place. With strange men walking the hallways. We're almost to my house."

Her pleading was almost his undoing. Then a thought occurred. "Maybe you could stay out at Sam's place? Katrina's there."

Her face turned crimson in an instant. "No! No I can't stay out at Sam's. Especially not… no, it wouldn't be proper."

Frustration welled up inside him and he knew it had to do with more than simply finding her a place to stay tonight. She'd told him in no uncertain terms out at Sam's ranch to back off and now it was quite obvious she really did have feelings for the man. He studied the pink of her cheeks and took a deliberate step back, dropping his hands to his hips. If Sam was the man she wanted, far be it from him to stand in her way. "Fine, if not at Sam's it will have to be the hotel."

"Cade please can't I just stay at home? I'll lock the doors and won't open them for anyone." Her head tilted over to one side, a curl falling to rest against her shoulder.

His fingers itched to reach out and feel the softness of it. He swallowed. "I'm sorry." He shoved his hands deep into his pockets where he could be sure they would behave themselves. "The only place I can be certain of your safety is somewhere close to other people. Your pa and brothers would have my hide nailed to the nearest wall if I let something happen to you."

Sharyah sighed and wrapped her arms around herself, closing her eyes. She missed the feel of Cade's arms already and wished he hadn't backed away. And then immediately wished that she would stop wishing things about him.

No more tears. She couldn't let this one incident turn her into a spring filly, shy and startling at the drop of a hat.

She lifted her chin. "Fine."

The line of Cade's shoulders eased perceptibly. "I know that was a hard decision to make, but it was the right one. I'm proud of you."

There he was back to being her brother again. Oh! She wanted to slap that brotherly affection right off his face. The man could get under her skin faster than anyone she knew. She spun toward her horse and mounted up without waiting for him to help her. He seemed fine with that and, from his own mount, led the way toward the heart of town at an easy lope.

He reined up at the hitching rail in front of the hotel and just as they were headed through the door to the lobby, Sheriff Collier rounded the corner from the alley.

Cade hesitated.

The man seemed lost in thought his eyes fixed to the boardwalk at his feet, and he didn't even notice them until he'd nearly bumped into Cade. He jolted to a stop and blinked slowly, as though returning from far away.

"You have a posse together, yet?"

"Oh, yes, yes. They are waiting for you down at the jail, as we speak."

"They? You aren't coming with us?"

Collier laughed. "Naw. The town will be much better served by my presence here."

"I see." Cade folded his arms, a thoughtful furrow creasing his brow. "I'll be along in a moment. I'm just seeing Miss Jordan safely to a room in the hotel."

"About that…" The sheriff glanced up at the hotel sign swaying over their head and then down at her, scratching under his chin. "I'm afraid I've just come from a hastily assembled meeting of the school board, Miss Jordan."

Nausea rolled through her at that.

Cade planted his shoulder into the wall and rested the toe of one foot against the boardwalk. She recognized the action as something Cade did when he was holding off his anger. Eyes narrowed, he studied Collier. "That's interesting, because we just left Sam Perry's place only a bit ago. He's the head of the school board, isn't he? I know he couldn't have had time to make it to the meeting."

Collier tugged at the loose skin under his jaw. "Well, in this instance we didn't feel like Perry would be the best one to give a… fair vote on the situation. He's obviously developed an… interest in Miss Jordan, and the rest of us felt that might… mar his judgmental abilities."

Sharyah forced herself to breathe slowly as she straightened her sleeves. "What was the meeting about, Sheriff?"

She knew what it was about. She'd spent the night up in the hills with a gang of outlaws. Her virtue had come into question. They were doing to her the same thing they'd done to poor Missy Green, only in this case nothing had actually happened.

Realizing she was fidgeting, she folded her arms in despair. She'd wanted so badly for this job to work out, for Mama and Papa to be proud of her. What would it do to them if she was sent home on suspicion of having her virtue stolen? How would Sky and Rocky and their families feel? She suppressed a moan. Forget what it would do to her family. What would it do to her?

"Well… uh… last night, you see… with you up…" Collier rolled his hand in the general direction of the hills surrounding Beth Haven and stumbled to a stop. He shuffled his feet, smoothed his vest and then took hold of the support post by the stairs with both hands. Still not looking her way, he continued, "Well, some of the parents have expressed a concern about you teaching their children, now."

Cade stood erect and Sharyah stepped closer to him, afraid that he might take a swing at the older man. "I'll stand as a witness that nothing happened, Sheriff. I made sure she was safe the whole time she was there."

Collier cleared his throat. "I'm afraid Mick Rodale is telling another story." The sheriff looked at her, then. "Did he compromise you, ma'am?"

Sharyah's eyes dropped shut and a shudder coursed through her.

Cade muttered something low and menacing. "She was out of my sight for five minutes. The man approached her, but he never… no."

"I see." Collier's feet shuffled. "Well, I'd be inclined to believe you, but… for now the board has asked that classes not resume until a final decision can be made. I'll take her mount on over to the livery for you."

Neither one of them commented as the man ambled down the steps and led her horse away.

Stunned and numb, Sharyah couldn't seem to make her feet

move. She simply stood and stared across the street at the way the paint peeled from the walls of The Golden Pearl saloon.

This might be the end of her teaching career. This story would follow her wherever she went looking for a position. Not that she wanted to be a teacher for the rest of her life. Some day she'd like to be a wife and mother. But even that… What man would want her now? What would this do to her chances at a relationship with Sam? Her eyes narrowed. This was all so unfair!

Cade touched her elbow. "Sharyah, I'm sorry. Let's go inside, shall we?"

She jerked her arm from his grasp. "I suppose, if we must."

His brow arched in surprise and he stepped to the side, folding his arms and keeping his silence.

With a huff she hoisted her hem and stepped into the lobby ahead of him.

He removed a key from his pocket as they climbed the stairs and opened the third door on the right down the hall, holding it open for her to precede him.

He hadn't said a word since she'd snapped at him out on the boardwalk. He started to turn down the hall and she laid a hand on his arm, stopping him. "I'm sorry, I shouldn't have—"

His finger rested across her lips, and she stilled.

"I'm the one who should be sorry." Dark chips of anger glimmered sapphire in his gaze. "If I could have figured a way to keep you safe *and* leave you out of it…." He massaged the muscles along his neck. "For what it's worth, I only wanted to protect you."

Sharyah glanced at her fingers. He *had* been ready to leave Sam on his own until Mick had busted in with his gun. "You did the best you could. I know that."

A grim smile flattened his lips. "Sometimes that's not good enough. Get some sleep." Defeat inflated his tone and exhaustion weighted the plains of his face.

He started away again and once more she stopped him.

"Sometimes it's not until we come to the end of ourselves that God can take over and work out what He wants to accomplish.

And I want to say thank you." She meant it as thank you for everything, for taking care of her, for protecting her from Mick, for caring enough to make sure she rested in safety tonight, for understanding when she snapped at him. The two little words didn't sound like enough to convey what was in her heart.

But when he nodded again and walked away, this time she let him go. She shut and locked the door and sank down on the bed, pulling the blanket up over her, skirt and all.

Exhaustion begged her to release the day, yet sleep evaded her and she tossed and turned. After several minutes she heard a noise at the door. Flipping around, she glanced at the portal. It remained closed, but a paper lay on the floor just inside the door.

She frowned and threw off the covers, crossing the room to pick it up.

The note held no address. Just a sloping scrawl that pricked Sharyah with curiosity. *If you care anything for Cade Bennett you won't mention the letter about the diamonds, or this note, to him. It would be a shame if he was killed.*

A cold chill sluiced down Sharyah's back. She crushed the note in her palm and jerked the door open to look both ways down the hall. Not a soul in sight.

Stepping back into the room she bolted the door once more and stared at the wall next to the window. She'd forgotten to tell Cade about the letter she'd seen at the chuck wagon. The crumpled paper trembled in her hand. A death threat? Who would have written it? The only person who had seen her reading the letter was Katrina Perry. Well, Maybe Mick had noticed, too. But Mick was in jail and Katrina was out at her ranch with her brother… so who would have slipped this note under her door? And how would they have known she'd seen the letter from the mining company in Africa?

She slipped the note into the pocket of her skirt then sank onto the edge of the bed and massaged circles at her temples. What should she do? If someone didn't want her talking about it, the letter was obviously something important.

With a groan she slumped over onto her side and pulled

the covers over herself once more. "I just want to go home," she mumbled as her eyes slipped shut and exhaustion overtook her. Perhaps she would be able to think more clearly once she'd gotten some rest.

CHAPTER SEVEN

Sam allowed Katrina to eat her dinner in peace, but as soon as he'd finished his after-meal coffee, he stalked through the house and barged into the parlor where she sat writing on a piece of parchment.

She jumped, glancing up from her place at the desk. "Sam! You nearly startled me to death!"

"What aren't you telling me, Katrina, dear?"

Blinking large round doe eyes, she picked up her peacock feather fan and set it into action. "Why, I simply have no idea what you are talking about."

"I saw you send Millicent's boy off on an errand before you'd been home five minutes. Where did you send him?"

"Really, Sam. A woman has to have some privacy." The fan swished so fast that a stack of papers flitted off her desk and fluttered to the floor. She bent quickly, gathering them back into a neat little pile before her.

He crossed the room and leaned one hand on the papers, stilling her movements. Bending down he glowered in her face. "You haven't given up on your little scheme, have you? I told you, I won't help you!"

"Sam, your part will be easy. Judd and I are making all the preparations. No one will know you are even involved."

"I'm not involved!" He slammed his palm down, rattling the desk and everything on it, before he turned and stalked over to the window. Clasping his hands behind his back, he rocked on his heels. "Judd's been rustling our cattle and horses, Kat. I have the proof I need, now. I don't want you seeing him anymore, understand?"

"So that's what you were doing. I nearly dropped my jaw when Cade Bennett rode into camp posing as an outlaw." She leaned into the slats of her chair and crossed her legs. "You could have sent me a message. I would have checked into the situation."

He faced her. "Katrina, honestly, I'm not sure if I can trust you anymore."

"Sam dear, everything I've ever done, I've done for us. For this ranch." She cursed. "You'd think I'd get a little gratitude! Do you think I enjoy being with that man?" Her eyes sparked and she pointed a finger outside. "Do you think I'm with Judd Rodale because he means so much to me?" With a disgusted snort, she leaned back in her chair and rubbed one hand over her face. "You really are a croaker, Sam. I'm doing all of that for *us*. And what do I get when I ask you to pitch in and help a little? Nothing but whine, whine, whine."

"That's all well and good, Kat. But in trying to *help* us, you are throwing in your lot with a man who is robbing us blind! Sanderson says we've lost fifty head over the last two weeks alone."

Kat jutted her jaw forward, working her lower teeth over her upper lip. Her eyes narrowed. "Are you sure it's him?"

He threw his hands up. "Who else would it be?" Swinging one arm toward the door he finished, "And Cade brought the proof with him. You saw that."

She tapped out a rhythm on the desk with her fingernails. "Fine. We can use that. We just have to get past this situation with Missy, and then we'll turn Judd and the gang in with the evidence we have on them. That will mean more for us."

Cold terror washed through him. "You had Judd kidnap Sharyah, didn't you?"

She blinked and straightened the stack of papers again. "Why on earth would I do that?"

To force my cooperation. He felt the blood drain from his face and spun to look out the window once more. His eyes narrowed. "You're playing a dangerous game, here, Katrina."

"Sam, darling. I'd never do anything to hurt you! I need you to trust me."

"Allowing Judd to keep rustling our stock is hurting me. Both of us."

Her laughter tinkled like sleigh bells. "You just leave Judd to me. If there's one thing I know about it's manipulating men. Father saw to that, now didn't he?" He held his silence and after a moment she moved on. "You just worry about getting that date out of Missy."

He sighed. "She trusted me with private information, Katrina. What kind of man would I be to take advantage of that for my own gain?"

"A smart one." Soft footsteps approached and then she put one arm around his back and leaned her head against his shoulder, looking out the window with him. "Just think of all we could do with that kind of money. You've never liked it here. Maybe we could travel to Paris, or New York." She squeezed him. "Just a few more days, Sammy. And she's very easy on the eyes, don't you think? You have to keep courting her, wooing her. And get her to tell you when the shipment is due to arrive. Judd and I are all set up to take care of everything else."

Sam rolled his shoulders to dislodge her embrace and glanced down at the fringe of the carpet beneath his feet. "People might be killed." *Not to mention the stealing.*

Katrina sighed and turned him to face her, gripping his shoulders gently. "If everyone does their job there will be no need to worry about anyone getting killed."

"Katrina, we don't even need the money! I can't help you. I won't."

"Yes. You can. And you will! *She* doesn't need the money! Look at that fancy house she lives in with her parents."

"They don't live in much nicer of a place than we do."

Katrina growled. "But they aren't barely scraping by like we are."

"We'd be doing just fine if Judd quit rustling our cattle!"

She touched his face. "Judd will get what's coming to him. For now, he's useful to us. You just have to keep your focus on the reason for it all. Just think of you and me strolling down the streets of Paris, France. Or dining with senators in New York. You could run for office! Or simply fritter away your days doing whatever it is you feel like doing at the moment. Just think of the theatres, operas, and galas we could attend!"

He sighed. That did sound good. All except the part where the money wasn't really theirs.

Apparently thinking it was resignation in his eyes, Katrina gave a firm nod. "Good. Stay focused. Oh, and forget about this school teacher! She's not for you, Sammy. Besides, I think she saw something she shouldn't have. However, Mick should be taking care of that for me as we speak."

"Kat! If he hurts her…"

"Would I do something like that? Of course not. She just won't be teaching here ever again."

So she'd concocted some lie about Sharyah. Sam despaired of ever getting his sister to see the error of her ways. "Mick is the one who messed up the plan in the first place. If he'd have kept away from Missy, she wouldn't have shunned me." Not that that meant he would have gone along with Katrina's plan.

Katrina sighed. "Mick is young and restless with a lot to learn, yes. In fact, I'm planning on leaving him in jail to think about it for a few days. But he's a good young man."

Sam glanced at her. Sometimes he worried about Katrina. "Good young men don't go around raping women, Katrina Perry."

She gasped. "Such language! You shouldn't speak of such things in front of a lady."

Sam pretended to search the room. "A lady? I'm sorry. I didn't realize there was one present."

Lifting her skirts she tilted up her nose and stormed from the room.

He watched her go, then turned to face the windows.

Good young men didn't go around stealing money, either. And he'd come to genuinely care for Missy during their talks. He clenched his fists. What was he going to do?

Cade hunkered down under the chuck wagon, which still sat in the exact place they'd left it that morning, with his Winchester by his side. Collier had put together a crew of twelve competent men and Cade had stationed them at various hiding places and now they waited.

Rodale and his men should be back any moment now. Cade had instructed that they would take the men the moment they rode into the glen, before they had time to realize that Mick and Red weren't here and something was wrong.

But as the hours stretched on past midnight, he realized Judd wasn't coming. Finally he stood, summoning the men to him. "Let's call it a night, men. If Rodale was coming back, he would have been here by now." Cade picked up a rock and heaved it into the darkness, frustration coursing through him.

Someone had tipped the man off. Could nothing about this job be easy?

She must have been much more tired than she realized because the next thing Sharyah knew, someone gently called her to wake.

"Sharyah." Whoever it was stood just on the other side of the door, knocking.

She stretched and sat up, pushing her cascade of curls back from her face. The sun was already up and streaming through the lace curtains at the window creating a mottled pattern on the floor. "I can't believe I slept so late!" Or that she'd slept at all after that note had been shoved under the door.

Wondering what had happened the night before she bolted to her feet and opened the door. Cade, stood there holding a steaming cup of coffee out to her.

"Thank you. How did it go last night?" She tried to step out into the hallway to talk to him, but he didn't budge. She stilled and looked at him. He seemed a little dazed. Weariness lined his face and she suddenly realized he was staring at her hair which must be in its usual wild morning disarray. Quickly she set the coffee on a shelf, scooped her hair up and twisted it into a semi-disciplined style.

He cleared his throat and gave himself a little shake. "Someone must have tipped them off. They never came back."

A tremor of fear raced through her. What if they had set up an ambush of their own and she'd lost him? How easily they would have been able to harm him. He'd made some fierce enemies when he arrested Red and Mick.

In that instant she made her decision. She would not tell him about the letter she'd seen or the note that had been shoved under the door the night before. At least not yet. She needed to think some things through before she brought it up. Slipping one hand into her pocket to insure the note remained hidden, she said, "You look exhausted."

He blinked slowly and nodded.

Purposefully, she placed one hand on his chest and pushed him backwards. She grabbed up her reticule and stepped out into the hallway gesturing him into the room. "You need to get some sleep."

The fact that he didn't argue with her proved her point. He stepped into the room, but as she started down the hallway, he reached out to grab her arm. His fingers tangled in the strings of her reticule and it tumbled to the ground, spilling its contents across the hallway.

Her handkerchief, the last letter she'd received from Mama. The tintype of Cade that she carried with her everywhere. She gasped and snatched for it, but he beat her to it.

Lifting the image, he stared down at it for a long moment.

If ever there was a moment she'd have liked to disappear, that was it.

He flicked the corner of it, as he angled her a measured look, then without comment he handed it back to her. "Two hours." He cleared his throat. "Give me two hours and then come back and wake me. And Sharyah," he reached into his boot and pulled out the derringer, "please, stay around places where there are other people. Carry this with you and don't go anywhere without it for the next several days. Put it in your little bag there with your other... treasures."

Flames licked at her cheeks as her gaze flew to his.

He winked.

And she couldn't help a sheepish smile. She'd wanted to go to the schoolhouse and look over some lessons. Even if she wasn't allowed to teach right away she would still need to have plans if she was ever reinstated. But despite his teasing, there was real concern in his eyes, and the memory of Mick Rodale's lecherous hands grabbing her made her nod her head in agreement. She folded her arms and rubbed them. "I will."

With a curt nod, he disappeared behind the door and it clicked shut.

Missy Green had just finished her morning toilette when a knock sounded at the front door. Staring blankly into the mirror at her dressing table, she listened closely to see who it would be at their door at this hour of the day.

Papa's footsteps echoed on the foyer floor and the door creaked open.

Someone spoke low words, too muffled for her to understand. Only a moment later, Papa tapped at her room with his signature *rat-tat, tat, tat*.

"Come," she called.

Papa poked his head in, a worried look on his face, hair mussed and protruding at odd angles from his head. "Join me in the parlor for a moment, would you dear?" A furrow puckered his brow.

She pressed away the wave of fear that surged, threatening to send her straight back to bed to cower under the covers for the rest of the day. "Certainly, Papa. Who was at the door?"

Papa cleared his throat and polished his glasses, avoiding the question with, "Just join us in the parlor if you would, dear."

"Alright." She rose and followed on his heels to the parlor.

Sam Perry paced the carpet at the center of the large room, his bowler twirling from one finger.

She halted at the threshold.

Papa always forgot to use the hat-tree when guests arrived. Mama would give him what-for about it later.

The moment he noticed her standing there, Sam froze to one spot, pressing his hat to his chest with both hands.

"Missy," his eyes darted to her father standing off to one side of the room, "ah, Miss Green." He nodded and gave a small bow to complete the greeting.

She dropped a faint curtsy. "Mr. Perry." Then she waited with suspended breath.

Mama floated into the room, her skirts swaying around her ankles. "Mr. Perry." She curtsied. "What a pleasant surprise. May I take your hat?" She tossed Papa a quick glance of disapproval.

Sam didn't seem to notice. "Ah, I'll only be a moment, ma'am. It's fine, thank you."

"Very well." She started to turn, and Missy knew she would be headed toward the kitchen to fetch refreshments, but she paused. "Would you prefer coffee or tea, Mr. Perry." Mama was always willing to go out of her way, even when someone showed up for a visit unexpectedly.

"Neither, thank you. I'm fine, really. I'll only be a moment."

Sam seemed a little put-out. Like he simply wanted to get to the point of the matter and be gone. He hadn't been comfortable around her since... well, since that very dreadful night.

Apparently taking his cue, Mama sank onto the settee and clasped trembling hands in her lap.

Papa was the first to speak after that. "Please, Mr. Perry, have a seat. Missy, dear, why don't you sit as well. Mr. Perry has news. News about a trial for Mick Rodale."

That man's name took the strength from her legs and she needed no more prompting to sink into the settee next to Mama. She glanced back and forth from Sam to Papa, waiting expectantly.

Sam sat on the wing-backed chair, his hat dangling between his legs as he leaned toward her. "Missy—" He closed his eyes in a quick gesture of frustration at his repeated blunder, then pressed on— "Miss Green, Mick Rodale was brought into the jail last night. Judge Thatcher is due to ride through town today, and the trial will begin right away." He paused, his eyes softening. "I'm afraid we'll need you to testify."

She swallowed. She'd prayed the day would come, but she'd never ever dreamed how difficult it would be when it happened. Pressing her lips together, she glanced down at her hands folded properly in her lap and nodded. "I can do that."

Could she really? Get up in front of the whole town and tell the indescribable things that man had done to her? Just imagining the gasps that would ensue from all the local families sure to be in attendance made her lightheaded and woozy. She closed her eyes. Then there was the guilt of knowing that the truth once spoken would most probably send the man to the gallows. Did she want that on her conscience for the rest of her life? He wasn't very old.

She shuddered. Then again, if he was old enough to do to her what he had done, she supposed he was old enough to dangle from the end of a rope.

Sam stood, tucking his hat under his arm. "Alright then, someone will be by to get you a little later."

Missy nodded but couldn't meet his gaze.

"I know it won't be easy."

She didn't respond and after a long moment Papa escorted him from the room.

"She'll be ready," Papa said.

But deep inside Missy knew she would never be ready, no matter how long it took them to come for her.

Two hours after leaving the hotel, Sharyah returned and glanced both ways as she walked down the hallway toward Cade's room. She didn't want anyone to see her going to knock on a man's door. She already had enough problems with her reputation.

No one was in sight so she timidly tapped the wood, calling softly, "Cade?"

No response.

She knocked a little louder. "Cade?"

Still nothing. Her heart thumped hard in her chest. What if something had happened to him? She could almost feel burning heat emanating from the threatening note in her pocket.

She glanced up and down the hall once more. Still no one in sight. Turning the knob, she opened it a spare inch and called again. This time she could hear his deep even breathing. Relief eased the tension in her shoulders. She should just back away and let him sleep, but she knew if he missed the trial which she'd learned was indeed going to proceed today, he would never let her hear the end of it. Judge Thatcher had ridden in just a few moments earlier and announced the trial for ten that morning.

Making a quick decision after one more assessment of the hallway, she pushed through the door and shut it behind her. Leaning back against her hands, her pulse hammering in her ears, she scanned the man. He looked like he hadn't moved from the moment he'd fallen onto the bed.

Her heart stirred.

Fully clothed, he must have lain down and then remembered that he still had his boots on and removed them, because one boot lay beside him on the bed, while the other lay on its side on the floor near the brass headboard. His hat lay across his face to block out the sunlight, and even with her entering the room he was still breathing evenly.

She walked over beside him and touched his shoulder, giving him a little shake. "Cade."

With a jolt he sat up, grabbed her arm, and before she could even think to cry out he had her flipped onto the bed. The metal barrel of a pistol that had magically appeared in his hand chilled the skin of her throat.

"Cade it's just me!" She swallowed and did her best to suppress her trembling.

He blinked down at her slowly, his tousled black curls poking from his head in unruly abandon. "Sharyah?" He squinched his eyes shut and when they opened again they were wide awake. "Sharyah!" He jerked the gun away from her and let the hammer down, clambering to his feet and reaching out one hand to help her up. "Sorry. What are you doing here?"

"You told me to wake you up."

He glanced around the room, obviously still trying to shake off the weight of sleep. "I meant to call to me from the hallway."

"I tried."

"I see." He blinked slowly again. "Uh. Give me a second and I'll be right out."

She nodded. Yes, that was a very good idea. Because right at this moment she wanted nothing more than to run her hands through those disheveled curls and kiss away the sleepy confusion in his eyes. She clasped her hands behind her. "I'll, just be in the hallway."

A few minutes later, Cade escorted her down the boardwalk toward the diner. The back of her neck prickled, and she glance behind them. Could someone be watching them, even now? Maybe even thinking she'd told Cade about the diamonds? What if she didn't tell him and they killed him anyway?

He glanced at her sideways. "You alright?"

"What?" She frowned and only then realized that she'd been scanning the street nervously. "Yes. It's nothing." She composed her features to reflect calm assurance.

He touched her elbow and pulled her to a stop. "Something happened, didn't it? What's the matter?"

She worked her lower lip with her teeth. She should just tell him. It would be a relief, really. But then she reminded herself that Cade's trap from the night before had been compromised. Whoever these people were, they were powerful and she couldn't risk Cade's life simply because she couldn't handle the pressure of a little secret. She forced a smile. "Really. I'm well. Just tired and maybe a little jumpy from all that's happened over the last couple days."

He looked skeptical but didn't press the issue and fell in beside her as she continued down the boardwalk.

They passed the millinery shop and Sharyah admired the way Mrs. Haversham had covered her half of the alley between her building and the boarding house next door with a lattice fence. Pots of morning glories, planted just in front of the lattice, climbed through and around the fence, hiding the dingy alley behind. A movement down the alley caught her attention and she stopped mid-stride, leaning closer to the lattice to get a better view through one of the holes.

Just down the alley, crouched behind a barrel which sat against the wall by a door she presumed led to the kitchen of the boarding house, sat a small child. The child seemed familiar, but his back was to her.

Cade looked at her, then leaned forward and followed her gaze down the alley.

The door opened and someone tossed a bucket of garbage into the burn barrel the child hid behind. As soon as the door closed, the boy stood and filtered through the fresh offerings.

Her heart clenched in pity. Brandon McBride was hungrily chomping down scraps from the garbage for breakfast. "Cade?"

"I see him."

"He's one of my students." The boy had told her he lived several miles from town and that his Ma and Pa worked real hard and it wouldn't be likely she would ever get to meet them. She'd taken him at his word and felt no offense when all the other families in the area had her over to dinner, except the McBrides. The boy brought a lunch pail to school every day, always carefully draped with a cloth. Now she wondered what was under that cloth each day, and why had she never paid attention before?

Cade squeezed her elbow. "Wait here." Bending down he pulled the knife in his boot from its sheath.

"Cade? He's just a boy!" She reached out to stop him, but he waved her off and gestured again for her to wait.

Halfway down the alley he dropped the knife into the dirt and continued on. A few more paces and Cade started mumbling to himself and searching the ground like he was looking for something. Sharyah frowned. What in the world was he up to?

Brandon heard him and spun toward him, a half eaten roll in one hand and a piece of something unrecognizable in the other.

Brandon's eyes widened as he saw that Cade was nearly to him and he turned and darted down the alley.

"Wait!" Cade called to him, still searching the ground around his feet.

The boy paused and glanced over his shoulder, waiting for Cade to go on.

"I seem to have dropped my knife. You haven't seen it have you? I know it's in this alley somewhere. It means a lot to me. Pearl handle, blade sharp enough to split a hair three ways. My father gave it to me." Cade glanced up at the boy. "Could you help me look for it? There would be a reward in it for you if you help me find it."

Brandon's brows lowered in suspicion. "What kind of reward?"

Cade shrugged and rested his hands on his hips. "Oh… I don't know. How about I buy you breakfast for the next week?"

Brandon's eyes widened. "For a whole week?"

Tears pricked the backs of Sharyah's eyes.

Cade nodded.

"You ain't funnin' me?"

Cade shook his head.

"Mister, you got yourself a deal, but if I help you look and you're the one to find the blade, you still have to buy the meals, 'kay?"

Cade stretched out his hand and they shook on the agreement. "I really appreciate your help. This knife means a lot to me, like I said." He glanced down the alley to where she waited behind the lattice and tossed her a wink.

Brandon was already busy searching the ground at his feet.

Sharyah stepped over to the display window of the millinery shop, and blinked the moisture from her eyes. Cade Bennett was a wonderful man. She had no doubt who would be the one to find the blade in the alley. If it took all day, Cade would let the boy be the one to discover it.

It was only moments however, before Brandon bounded from the alley followed by Cade, who swiped the dust from his knife onto his denims.

He glanced up. "Sharyah, thanks for waiting. This lad here helped me find my knife. Would it be alright with you if he joined us for breakfast?"

Brandon turned to see who Cade was talking to and his eyes widened. "Miss Jordan!" He grinned, the familiar sparkle leaping to life in his brown eyes.

"Well, hello, Brandon." To Cade she said, "Certainly he can join us." She laid a hand on Brandon's shoulder. "Mr. McBride is one of my students."

"Is he now?" Cade sheathed his knife. "He and I haven't yet had the pleasure of a proper introduction."

"Well then, this is Brandon McBride. And Brandon, this is Mr. Bennett. Mr. Bennett is... I've known Mr. Bennett... Ah, Mr. Bennett is... a new deputy in town."

Brandon didn't seem to notice her discomfort on how to introduce Cade. He stretched out his hand and shook Cade's with a firm little nod. "It's a pleasure to make your acquaintance, sir."

Cade grinned, apparently amused by the boy's impeccable manners. "Likewise, young man. Well," Cade stretched a hand toward the diner, "shall we?"

Brandon eagerly headed for the door and Cade winked at her once more, offering her his elbow. "Cute little guy," he murmured.

She nodded and replied in a low tone, "When he's not putting spiders in my lunch pail."

Cade threw back his head on a laugh. "Now that is a look I would have loved to see on your face."

She arched her brows in mock offense. "Oh there was no look, Mr. Bennett. I was as calm as a summer breeze."

He grinned and held the door open for her. Brandon had already disappeared inside. "That wouldn't be a tornado you're referring to, would it?"

She chuckled and held two fingers a spare half inch apart. "Well, maybe just a little one."

He laughed again, but they'd caught up to Brandon now and both paused to watch him. The little boy stood with his dusty cap in his hands, jaw hanging open, as he gaped at the contents of the pastry shelf, and then up at the menu, and around the room at several patrons with plates full of food.

Sharyah swallowed and pressed one hand to her throat. *Father, forgive me for not noticing his hunger earlier.*

Cade touched a hand to the middle of her back and guided Brandon by one shoulder. "Let's sit at that table in the corner over there."

Brandon plopped into a chair across the table as Cade held one out for her and then sat beside her.

Sharyah felt true contentment as she watched the little boy wolf down the food Mrs. Shane placed before them a moment later. She was hungry herself since she hadn't eaten all day the day before, but she purposely left half a roll and a good portion of hash on her plate and offered her leftovers to Brandon when he'd finished his.

"Don't mind if I do." He grinned and swapped the plates setting into the second portion as though it might be his last meal.

What was Brandon doing in town all alone? Where were his parents? She had to find out. A boy as young as he shouldn't be running about town all alone. Could it be he'd been living on his own all this time? She cleared her throat. "Ah, Brandon? Where are your Ma and Pa?"

His fork stopped half way to his mouth and he met her gaze. She could see the cogs whirring in his little head.

She put on the sternest face she could muster. "Be honest."

His shoulders sagged and he dropped the fork onto the plate. "Truth is…" He looked across the room at the diner's door. "I don't got none." He spoke so quietly she barely heard his words.

Her worst fears registered like a mule-kick to her stomach. "Oh Brandon." She tilted her head and studied him. "How long have you been on your own?"

He hesitated for a long moment, then finally met her scrutiny with a shrug. "Awhile now."

"Where have you been staying?"

Another heft of his shoulders. "Around."

She met Cade's glance. What was she to do with a homeless child? He certainly couldn't go on living as he was.

Cade's hand settled at the back of her neck with a gentle squeeze. "Tell you what, son. I have a room at the hotel that has a nice bear-skin rug on the floor and an extra pillow on the bed. Why don't you bunk with me for the next couple nights?"

Warmth coursed through her and she had to clench her hands in her lap to keep from reaching out in thankfulness to touch Cade's arm. At least she now had a few days to figure out what she needed to do about the poor child.

Brandon's eyes lit with excitement. "You mean it, mister?"

A smile softened Cade's face. "You bet I do."

"Sure as shootin'! I'll be there!" The boy leaned over his plate and shoveled in two more mouthfuls of potatoes, before he threw back his shoulders, his face turning serious. Two chomps and he tried to swallow, then had to work to get the unchewed food to go all the way down. But finally he was able to add, "I'm much obliged." He stretched his hand across the table to shake like a little gentleman.

"Sure." Cade gave his hand a firm shake. "We men have to stick together."

As Brandon set to finishing his breakfast, Sharyah sighed softly.

This wonderful man by her side, and a child across the table. Yes, this was something she could get used to. The impact of that thought hit her square in the stomach and she turned to look at Cade.

He was already studying her, a contemplative look on his face.

The corners of his blue eyes crinkled in a warm smile. "You sure you don't want to tell me what's bothering you?"

She blinked, knowing he wasn't referring to the fact that she'd just discovered one of her students had no parents. She opened her mouth, wanting to confide in him, but instead all she whispered was, "I can't." If she told him, he would try to investigate the issue and there was no telling what might happen to him if whoever wrote that note learned that she hadn't listened to them.

He leaned toward her, his eyes flickering blue flame. "Can't? Or won't?"

"It-it's for your own good." She pressed her lips together and studied the grain on the table.

Cade reached out and tilted up her chin. "What's for my own good is that the woman I care about confides in me."

She cleared her throat and looked down, smoothing at the material of her skirt. *Brotherly affection. All he feels for you is brotherly affection. And don't you forget it.* "When you find her, I'm sure she will."

His mouth dropped open to reply, but before he could voice an objection, she leapt up from the table. "Brandon? Are you ready? We should get going."

Brandon, glanced back and forth between them, then gave a little shrug and nodded his head.

Spinning on her heel, she led the way out the door.

CHAPTER EIGHT

Sharyah glanced down at Brandon as they emerged from the diner. "Since there's no school today, what do you plan to do with yourself, Brandon?" She needed to keep the conversation in safe waters.

His eyes sparkled. "I'm gonna go watch the trials. I might be a lawyer when I grow up."

Sharyah glanced at Cade. The last place the boy needed to be was in watching the trials. There would be some very unpleasant things discussed, she felt sure.

Cade didn't look happy with her, but he apparently decided to drop the matter for a few moments because he sat on the bench just outside the diner and propped his arms along the back of it. "Too bad you're so set on being at the trials. I have a chore I was hoping I could pay you to do for me."

"You do?" The sparkle expanded into radiant beams. "Well, you know, a man's gotta work when he can find it. I suppose I could do a chore for you."

Sharyah caught a slight twitch at the corner of Cade's mouth.

"You sure? I'd really appreciate it and would make it worth your time, but I don't want to take you away from watching the trials if that's what you'd rather do."

"I don't mind. I could do the work. I've watched other trials and I'm sure there will be more another time."

"Alright then." Cade slapped his hands down on his knees and stood to his feet. "Let's escort Miss Jordan to the court house and then I'll take you on to the livery and show you what I have in mind." He tossed Sharyah a smile over the boy's head, and she knew whatever chore he asked Brandon to do would be good and long to ensure he kept busy for the bulk of the day.

Sharyah followed Cade across the street. "Brandon. You be sure to get to school tomorrow, alright?"

Cade frowned, but she didn't meet his gaze. Just because they wouldn't let her teach didn't mean someone wouldn't be there teaching, and she didn't want the boy to miss out. She just hoped whoever took her place would be kind to him.

"Miss Jordan," the boy hooked his thumbs into his belt loops in imitation of Cade's stance, "I don't know about school. I might be working for Mr. Bennett here tomorrow too. He might need me. Us men have to help each other out."

She bent to ensure she had Brandon's full attention. "I'm sure Mr. Bennett knows the importance of school for a young man. He went to school too, you know, and loved every minute of it. He studied very hard and he never, ever, played tricks on his teacher."

Cade coughed as they reached the court house entrance and she didn't dare meet his gaze. She remembered the time he and her brother Rocky had somehow managed to hoist Miss Vandermeer's desk three feet off the floor.

Brandon apparently caught her sarcasm. He tilted his head to squint up at Cade. "You played tricks on your teachers?"

Cade settled a hand at the base of the boy's neck. "Sure did. Come on, I'll tell you all about it." They sauntered off down the boardwalk as he continued, "Sure were some pretty girls in my school. What about yours?" As the boy replied, Cade turned and walked backwards a couple steps grinning at her.

A hot wash of color shot up past her collar and she spun away. Sam and Katrina were just coming down the walk.

"Sharyah," Sam greeted. "We were just heading inside. Would you care to join us?"

She glanced back toward Cade, but his attention had returned to the boy.

"Thank you, Sam. I would." She took his arm, refusing the desire to look and see if Cade had even noticed she was on another man's arm.

The trial started right on time. Judge Thatcher was a fair man and it only took him an hour to determine that there wasn't enough concrete evidence to convict Red of any of the things he'd been accused of. There hadn't been enough time for any witnesses to arrive.

"That being said, however, Mr. Hendrix will be held over and transferred to Prineville where a more thorough trial will be held two weeks hence." His gavel banged down with an authoritative thump that made Sharyah jump. "Next case."

Cade stood from where he'd been sitting at the front of the room and escorted Red to the jail across the street and brought Mick Rodale back with him.

Mick's trial was a different story altogether. During Missy's testimony, Sharyah could only close her eyes and pray for the woman to have strength as she described what had happened to her.

"And where is the man who did these things to you?" The judge asked in a sympathetic tone.

Missy held out a trembling finger pointed directly at Mick.

"And is there any doubt in your mind that he is the man who attacked you?"

She shook her head. "None, your honor."

Mick Rodale clasped his hands behind his head and tossed Missy a bold unrepentant wink.

Sam, sitting beside Sharyah, tensed and shifted.

"Very well, you may resume your seat." The judge glanced to Mr. Hanson, the lawyer.

"Your honor, at this time I would like to call Miss Jordan, to the stand."

Sharyah's stomach dropped nearly to her toes, but she'd known this would happen.

Cade met her gaze and gave her a reassuring nod as she lifted her skirt and made her way to the stand.

As Mr. Hanson questioned her, she did her best to simply present the facts without exaggeration and to keep her eyes off of Mick. She didn't want to see his leering grin.

"So Mr. Rodale attacked you, but Mr. Bennett stopped him before… anything unsavory happened?" the judge asked.

She pressed her lips together and nodded.

When Cade was called on for his testimony, the Judge pinned him with a look. "And why was it you were party to kidnapping the school teacher, young man?"

Cade squirmed like a little boy, for a moment. "I was working undercover, Your Honor. I had planned to help Miss Jordan escape, but then Mick came in with his gun drawn. I didn't want her to be hurt, and I figured she'd be fairly safe as long as I didn't let her out of my sight."

"Surely there was a better way to handle this, Mr. Bennett."

"There probably was, Your Honor, but at the time with lives at stake I felt like I was making the best decision for all involved."

The Judge arched a skeptical brow, but after confirming Sharyah's account of Mick's attack, dismissed Cade without further questions and turned to look at the lawyer over the top of his spectacles.

"Your honor, I would also like to present testimony from one Samuel Perry, with regard to this kidnapping business and also about some horses found in Mr. Rodale's presence."

"Very well." The judge nodded for him to proceed and Sam took the stand.

Sam gave his version of what had happened in the schoolhouse.

"So, Mr. Bennett did step in to rescue Miss Jordan when Mr. Rodale got rough with her?"

Sam nodded. "Yes, Your Honor."

"Well, perhaps chivalry isn't totally dead, as I had feared." The judge gave Cade a withering look.

And Cade shifted uncomfortably in his seat.

The judge sighed and waved a hand at Sam. "Get on with the horse story."

Sam twisted his bowler around by the rim. "Mr. Bennett brought back two horses with him. Horses that the Rodale gang had in their possession. Horses that bear my brand. The brand has been reworked."

Mick Rodale jumped to his feet. "That's a lie! Those horses

are ours. I may be a lot of things, Your Honor, but I'm not a horse thief."

Sharyah pressed her lips together. Horse thieving was a hanging offense. Not that attacking a woman wasn't, but if convicted of stealing horses he would most certainly be hung.

Judge Thatcher banged his gavel on the desk and leveled Mick with a glare. "Another outburst like that, young man, and I will have you gagged."

Sam cleared his throat. "Your Honor, if I may?"

After making sure that Mick resumed his seat and his lawyer was taking him in hand, the judged nodded.

"I always brand my horses twice. A little trick I learned when I first started ranching – once on the haunch as normal, and then another time with a smaller brand on the upper inner part of their front left leg."

A murmur traversed the room.

Mick paled and scooped a hand through his hair. Rubbing the base of his neck, he tossed a glance at Katrina over his shoulder.

Katrina shifted uneasily and Sharyah frowned.

Judge Thatcher simply kept his eyes on Sam.

"The second brand is still there, Your Honor. Untouched."

The judge sighed, pulled his spectacles from his face and set to polishing them. "You have the horses here in town, I presume?"

"Yes sir, Your Honor. Right outside."

It only took a few minutes for the judge to walk outside with several of the men to view the evidence. When he came back in he wore a pinched-lip look of determination. He sat down behind his desk and rubbed his eyes for a moment, then resettled his spectacles. "Mick Rodale, please stand."

Mick did and Sharyah couldn't help but notice the trembling in his hands.

"Mick Rodale, in light of all the evidence that has been presented to me this day, I find you guilty of all charges. I sentence you to be hung by the neck until dead. Your sentence will be carried out tomorrow at sundown. Case dismissed." The gavel banged down.

Mick plummeted back into his seat as pandemonium broke loose in the courtroom.

Sharyah's stomach felt hollow. Some were laughing and shaking hands. Some shook their heads and talked in low tones. Missy Green looked pale and sorrowful as her mother took her elbow and hurried her from the room. Sharyah's gaze flitted over Katrina Perry, who sat just on the other side of Sam, and then paused. The woman was jotting a note of some sort onto a piece of paper. It seemed an odd thing to be doing in the midst of the chaos surrounding them. Maybe she kept a diary and was marking down something she didn't want to forget about the trial. Sharyah's eyes dropped to the paper. Her handwriting had a distinct slope to it. Her mouth went dry and she felt the blood drain from her head. *It was Katrina!* The handwriting on the note in her pocket… well, she couldn't be certain, but it sure looked the same.

Katrina glanced up and her eyes narrowed before she angled her body away and wrote some more.

Dazed Sharyah glanced around the room.

Cade pulled Mick to his feet and led him out a side door to await his fate at the jail and Sharyah couldn't help but feel sorry for the man. He was a monster, yes. He'd done some terrible things, yes. Still she felt compassion for him. And worry for what would happen when Judd learned that his little brother had been sentenced to hang. But more pressing, she needed to decide what she would do about Katrina.

She glanced back to Sam and Katrina. *She's gone!*

"Where's Katrina?"

Sam shrugged. "She saw someone she wanted to talk to. Said she'd be back momentarily." He looked uneasy and frustrated.

Sharyah felt dizzy from the weight of the decision before her. What had she really seen? Similar handwriting was all. Could she accuse the woman of such a terrible thing, merely on that thin thread of suspicion?

Sighing, she accepted Sam's proffered arm and walked with him toward the rear of the room. What she needed was a nice hot bath and a good night's sleep. Then she would consider this dilemma again.

Katrina Perry pushed through the doorway, her heart hammering in her chest and the note clutched in her hand. Judd would never forgive her if Mick hung. She'd known the minute Cade sauntered into camp like he owned the place that their plans might fall to pieces, and she'd been scrambling ever since to prepare a backup. If Sam would just trust her and do as he was told, everything would be going as planned.

She'd thought if she just let Cade bring her home to Sam and laid low for a bit, that things would calm down and they could all continue as intended. She hadn't wanted to get Cade killed – she'd known him for several years and genuinely liked the man – so she'd kept the fact that he was working for her brother to herself. And, in the end, he may have proven useful in ridding her of the Rodales when she was done with them. But all had changed now.

She gritted her teeth. If Sam would just quit sticking his nose into her business, things would go a lot smoother!

Of course, Mick had to go and attack the school teacher. And Cade took it upon himself to arrest Mick and Red. Katrina had figured to use that to her advantage to get Cade out of the camp before he learned of their plans and just how deeply she was involved. But then that woman had stumbled onto the letter.

And now this! Had she recognized her handwriting? Was that what the shocked look on her face had been? Or had she been able to read the missive from her place on the other side of Sam? *I should have been more careful!*

When Mick attacked the teacher, she'd decided to let him lounge in jail for a few days to teach him a lesson before they broke him out. He was always dallying with women, and this time with more than one, and just before they had an important job to do! The man needed a reminder to get himself under control.

She hadn't counted on the judge coming through town right

away, nor on such a final and rapid sentence. And sadly since the little teacher had seen the letter, and now most likely recognized her hand writing, she would have to be dispensed with, but she didn't dare tell Sam that. His pitying heart wouldn't be able to keep it quiet.

Katrina pressed her lips into a grim line. She doubted the woman even knew exactly what she'd been looking at when she found that letter, but it never hurt to be extra careful. Cade would certainly know what it was, if she breathed a word of it to him.

The sun beat down on the roadway, glinting off particles of dust that filtered up as people and horses disbursed from the area. A little boy with big brown eyes fidgeted on a bench just to the left of the door.

Perfect. "Hey there young man." She gave him her sunniest smile. "How would you like to earn a little money?"

His eyes brightened. "Today must be my lucky day."

"What?"

He shook his head. "Nothin'. Sure, I could use some money. Whadya want me to do?"

She pressed her note into his palm. "I need you to head east of town. There's a tree about half a mile out that was struck by lightning awhile back. The top's all burnt. You'll find a hollow in the trunk. I need you to put this paper in there."

The boy nodded. "I can do that."

She cocked her head. "It's sort of a private letter, so no reading it, you understand?"

The boy grinned. "I never did go in much for readin' anyhow."

Relief eased the tension in her chest. "Alright then. Go do it right away now, you hear?" She pressed the note and two bits into his palm.

"Yes'm. Right away."

She watched him scamper off and disappear between two buildings on the east side of the road, before she turned and made her way toward the livery where she and Sam had left their horses. She couldn't do anything about any of this until later tonight, so she might as well head home to rest.

Judd watched through a pair of field glasses as a kid placed a note in the hollow of the tree. The boy spun in a full circle studying the area. Apparently satisfied that he was alone, he trotted off back in the direction of town.

Several minutes ticked by as Judd scanned the scrub brush around the tree for any movement. He didn't want to walk into a trap. He wasn't sure what Katrina was up to, but if she'd really double-crossed him, she would regret it. He could guarantee that.

Finally, after he felt confident the area was safe, he nodded to Seth. "Get on down there and bring me that note."

Seth grumbled, but complied and returned a few moments later.

Judd snatched the paper from him and spread it open.

Mick sentenced to hang tomorrow at sundown.

Judd cursed and his hands trembled.

Must liberate quickly. Distraction set for tonight. Be ready at midnight. All my love, K.

So Kat was still with him. Hang it all, but she was good. There wasn't a soul in town that had any idea what that little woman was capable of.

He grinned. "Boys, let's ride. We've got plans to make."

Cade was dog tired. He hadn't slept for more than a few hours at a time in the last three days and all he wanted was to fall into bed at the hotel and not come out until breakfast the next day. But he couldn't.

The school board had come to Sharyah, with Sam this time he'd noted, and reinstated her as the teacher without so much as an apology. But the smile on her face had shown she didn't care whether they apologized or not.

She had gone home to her little cabin on the edge of town behind the school, and he hadn't protested this time. He couldn't keep her sleeping in his hotel room forever.

But neither did he want her out here without some protection, so when Collier asked him if he could stand watch at the jail tonight he'd insisted Collier hire someone else to guard Hendrix and Rodale so he could get some sleep. Collier had a local rancher who needed a little extra money doing the job and Cade now spread his bedroll under some trees just a few yards from Sharyah's place. He would doze a little but still be right here to keep an eye on her.

Judd and the rest of the Rodale gang would be gunning for revenge. Who knew where they would strike and even though he doubted it would be at Sharyah, he wanted to be nearby just in case.

There was still the question of what had been bothering her earlier today. Tomorrow he would make it a point to find out. For now, his body begged for sleep.

Wearily he sank down and closed his eyes.

Sharyah heated water for a bath and pulled the wooden tub into the middle of the one room cabin. With a soft groan she sank into the heavenly, steamy water scented with her favorite splash of lilac. She scooted down until her shoulders sank beneath the warmth, even though doing that forced her knees to poke up at the other end.

She rested back against the lip and angled her head both ways to stretch out weary muscles.

Whoever had invented baths deserved a double portion of blessing in heaven.

She sighed, closed her eyes, and let the water wash away the tension of the last few days. Sorrow for Mick's impending doom welled up, but she tried not to think about it. He'd made his choices.

Instead, her thoughts turned to Brandon. Where had he been sleeping at night? They hadn't been able to find him after the trial today. *I hope he's safe, wherever he is.*

She and Cade had searched everywhere they could think of.

And no one they'd asked recalled seeing him anywhere around town. Finally, Cade had reminded her that the boy seemed to have been doing fine on his own until now, and insisted they would look for him again tomorrow. "I owe him breakfast, and you can bet he'll show up to collect," he'd grinned.

He was probably right. *Lord, watch over that young one wherever he is tonight and please help me to know whether I should tell Cade about the note and the letter, or not. I really don't want to get him hurt, but I think they might be planning something bad and I don't know what to do about that.* A groan escaped. This was all too much!

She forced her thoughts to move on and sent up a little prayer for Missy Green, too. She couldn't imagine what the woman might be feeling about now, but was sure it had to be a muddled up mixture of emotions.

Her consciousness drifted and when she came to she realized sleep must have gained the upper hand. The water was barely even tepid. She ducked her head under and rinsed her hair, then stood and reached for the towel.

That was when the smell of smoke registered.

Slowly rubbing her hair dry, she sniffed the air.

Yes, definitely smoke from a rather large fire. It must be coming from outside.

She hurried into petticoat and camisole, and then noticed a thick drift of smoke waft under the door! "Dear Jesus!" Lurching toward the pile of clothes negligently left in a heap, she snatched skirt, hat, and blouse. *My reticule!* She grabbed that up too, and then rushed over to the door. "Ouch!" The handle was too hot to touch. Pressing down the panic, she looked around the room searching for a means of escape. She was about to burn alive in her own house! She rushed to the window, but flames already engulfed that wall.

"Sharyah!" The faint call seemed to echo all around her, and she spun in a circle trying to determine where it had come from.

"I'm here!" Smoke crawled through her nostrils in a choking invasion and infiltrated her lungs. She coughed hard, gagging as she pressed the cloth of the skirt over her nose and mouth. Tears streamed so that she could barely see.

Suddenly the door splintered inward scattering shards of wood everywhere. "Sharyah!" Cade was by her side in an instant, his bandana pulled up over his mouth and nose, but a wall of fire already engulfed the hole he'd just smashed through.

"Come on!" He grabbed her arm and dragged her toward the door. "We have to get out of here now. Two steps through the fire and off the porch, alright?"

She couldn't seem to move.

"Shar," he gave her a little shake, "we have to move now! Come on."

"Wait! The water."

He frowned at her.

She gestured to the bath. "The tub!"

The roof crackled and shifted above their heads.

Cade hoisted the small tub and sloshed the water out the door and they chased the path it made across the porch and down the steps.

Cade pulled her along and didn't let her stop until they were a good twenty yards from the house, then he turned and jerked her into a fierce embrace. He huffed two breaths in her ear and then set her back from him at arm's length. "Are you hurt? Are you burnt?" He scanned her, a look of near panic on his face.

Just her hand and it wasn't serious. Even as she shook her head a coughing fit set in. Wheezing, gagging, and doubled over, she couldn't seem to breathe, much less speak.

Cade scooped the curls away from her face, holding them in one hand and rubbing the other over her back, his own breathing ragged and loud. "You're okay, now. You're going to be fine."

In town someone clanged the fire gong, and shouts arose.

Cade pulled her further into the shadows and brush under the trees.

Sharyah looked out toward the cabin, still coughing.

Orange flames licked hungrily at the planks and even as

they watched, the north wall fell inward sending up a shower of orange sparks. There would be no saving the place.

Finally after several long moments she straightened and pulled sweet refreshing air into her lungs.

Cade touched her cheek. "You going to be okay?"

She nodded.

He took hold of both her shoulders and leaned forward to look directly into her eyes. "Listen to me. I need to get out there and help fight the fire, but I want you to stay here."

Sharyah stared past him dazedly, hearing his words but as though they were coming from a long distance away.

Several people came running from the direction of the town carrying buckets and gunny sacks. Sharyah brushed past him and started out of the trees. They would need to know she was alright.

"Sharyah, you can't go out there." Cade laid a hand on one arm, stopping her. His gaze skittered over her, and he gestured to the darkness behind him. "Get dressed."

A glance down, jolted her back to reality. Yes, that would probably be best. If she ever wanted to teach in this town again, it was best not to appear out of the shadows with Cade Bennett dressed only in her unmentionables.

Stepping deeper into the trees, and hurriedly pulling blouse and skirt over camisole and petticoats, she stuffed the green hat into her reticule. Her hair was still wet and tangled all about her face, anyhow.

She couldn't believe she'd been in his arms dressed like that! She suppressed a groan. The man would never see her as anything more than a little waif he needed to keep rescuing.

The task done, she stepped up beside him. His attention was fixed on the burning building and the people fighting the blaze, a hard angry line to his stance.

He scanned her then pointed to a tree. "Sit right there and don't move until I come back."

She blinked. "But people need to know I'm okay."

"That's exactly what I'm trying to avoid. Listen, I don't have time to explain right now, but I need you to trust me. Can you do that?"

A loud roar rent the air and the ground shook beneath her feet.

Cade dropped into a crouch, pulling her down with him. "Sharyah, I have to go. I need you to stay right here and don't move until I come for you. If it starts to get light before I get back, I need you to hide. You can't let *anyone* see you." He touched her face with his palm. "Understand?"

She didn't understand, but nodded anyhow.

"Good." He pressed a chaste kiss to her forehead. "Your life depends on it. I'll be back, I promise."

And with that he took off at a run through the trees, heading in the direction of town. Within moments his lithe form blended into the darkness and she sat shivering and alone.

CHAPTER NINE

Cade leapt a fallen log and slapped aside a branch that loomed out of the darkness. He glanced toward the fire through the trees. Thankfully the blaze seemed content to stick to the cabin and there was no wind to pick it up and carry it to the trees. It didn't look like they would have to worry about it spreading to the nearby poplars or the schoolhouse. The cabin, a charred mound of smoldering ash, had burnt clean to the ground now.

Only a few minutes more and she wouldn't have made it out of there alive. Anger, cold and hard, clenched a fist in the middle of his belly.

He should be over there helping to beat down any sparks that tried to flame up in the grass. But that blast had to have been dynamite. Judd was breaking Mick and Red out of jail at this very moment, with Collier probably snoring away at home.

Cade's lungs burned for oxygen as he surged out of the trees and sprinted down First Street. The rear of the jail bumped up against First and all the outlaws would have to do would be cross it, run down the alley between the Chinese laundry and the butcher shop, and they'd be home free to make a run into the hills. There would be no way to track them until morning and by then they'd be long gone.

Shucking his Colt, he swung around the corner at the back of the jail, hoping against hope to see them still trying to extract Mick and Red from the rubble.

Too late.

He sagged against one wall and sucked in air.

The alley was empty. Empty except for the mound of bricks and mortar-dust where the wall of the jail had once stood. With no more need to hurry, he gave himself a moment more to catch his breath. He tipped his head back. Stars winked from the night sky as though all were right with the world. A disgusted growl escaped. Holstering the gun, he jammed his hands onto his hips and strode toward the disaster, kicking scattered bricks aside.

Bending down, he peered through the gaping hole into the jail. They had placed the dynamite in the exact right place to break through the walls in both men's cells. The inner bars that separated the middle two cells where the men had been held were mangled into an odd braid, but the outer two cells seemed to be unscathed.

The man Collier had hired to stand guard groaned from under the upturned desk in the front. The woman who ran the millinery shop, was trying to lift it off of him.

"I'm coming!" Cade leapt over the pile of bricks at his feet and rushed through the front of the building to lift the desk off the man's torso. Blood pulsed from a gash on his upper arm. Cade pressed the heel of his hand against the flow. "Get the doc. Quickly."

The woman lifted her skirts and ran from the building, screeching at the top of her lungs for the doctor.

The rancher groaned and Cade realized he didn't even know the man's name. "You're going to be alright. The doctor is on his way. Did you see what happened?"

The man only moaned, apparently too concussed to be able to respond.

Collier stumbled into the room. "Holy—" He turned in a full circle assessing the damage to his domain. "Sweet mother, they did it. They really did it." He rubbed one hand over his belly. "I'll put a posse together. We'll head after them right away."

"Going out after them at night would be suicide. They have all the advantage in the dark and besides that you'll only obliterate any trail there is to follow if you head out now." He motioned the man his way. "I need you to come here for a minute."

Collier did.

"Bend down and put your hand right here." He traded his hand for Collier's. "Keep the pressure on. He'll bleed out if you don't."

Cade headed for the door. There was nothing more to do here.

"Did that little teacher really die in the fire?"

Cade hesitated. How should he respond to that? He wanted to be honest. He rubbed his thumb at a rough spot on the door. "That's what they're saying, I guess." With that he turned his back on the man and hurried down the street.

"Wait! Where are you going?"

He paused.

Collier still wore a look of dazed befuddlement.

"I have to be gone for a day or two but I'll be back. Put your posse together in the morning, with your best tracker out front."

Likely they'd never find them, but one could always hope. Right now his priority was to get Sharyah as far away from danger as possible. And if he had to shake it out of her he would find out what had been bothering her.

Something rustled in the brush to Sharyah's right. Cade had said not to let any people see her. He hadn't said what to do if a wild animal snuck up on her. She scrabbled her fingers across the ground, searching for something to use as a weapon. When her fingers closed around a stout stick she breathed a little easier. *Thank you, Lord.* She strained to see into the thick darkness, listening intently.

The sound came again, a little closer this time.

She pulled her feet under her and stood slowly, keeping her back to the tree and gripping her stick with both hands like a baseball bat. She'd played the game often with the boys on the playground and she didn't have a bad swing, even if she did say so herself. She took in a fortifying breath and pressed her head back against the bark. Whatever prowling creature ambled her way would soon wish it had chosen another path for its little midnight foray. She swallowed hard and replayed Papa's advice. *Just remember animals are more scared of you than you are of them. Please let it be true.*

"Sharyah?"

With a squeak of surprise she swung the makeshift bat toward the sound with all her might.

Someone grunted. "Ow! Give me that!" he whispered, wrenching the weapon from her hands.

"Cade?" The tremor in her voice said more than she'd intended.

"Who else did you think would know you were hiding out here by this exact tree?" Irritation mixed with humor traced the edges of his whisper.

"I'm sorry. I heard a noise over there," she motioned behind her, "and then you startled me. Are you hurt?" She reached out to touch the side of his face in the darkness. From the sound of the whack, she had a feeling she'd connected with his skull.

He brushed her hand away and captured her fingers. "I'm fine." Without letting her hand go, he turned to look at the last smoking embers of what had been her cabin only a short hour ago. A few people still lingered to make sure the fire didn't spread. But most had gone home now.

"They think I'm dead." She'd heard them talking about it. A tremor coursed through her at the thought of how close she'd actually come to that being true.

Cade shifted and studied her for a long moment. His fingers tightened around hers and he glanced down. "If I had lost you..." His words emerged tattered and thready.

She fidgeted. "You didn't though. I'm right here." She should pull away this minute. Being near him when she felt this vulnerable was dangerous.

But when he slowly pulled her to him, his gaze roving over her face and one hand sliding back into her damp hair as his thumb skimmed across her cheek, she could no more have moved than a stone.

He drew in a ragged breath and released it on her name as he leaned down toward her.

The moonlight behind his head left his face in shadow, but she could feel a quaver in his arms that made her knees weak.

She closed her eyes, tipped her face up, and leaned against the strength of him.

"Shar."

She felt the brush of the word against her cheek, just before he dropped a kiss there. He pulled her in tighter and pressed another just below her earlobe, and then eased back to study her, his trembling hands cupping both sides of her face.

"Cade." How long had she wanted this? Dreamed of the day Cade Bennett would finally kiss her?

She thought of Sam, and swallowed. She didn't dare let Cade kiss her, or all her resolve to be happy and satisfied with Sam, or another man if Sam worked things out with Missy, would vanish like so much smoke.

He tilted his head toward her.

She spoke quickly before she lost her resolve. "Cade, wait."

A low sound escaped him and his breathing sounded frayed, but he did pause. His gaze bored into hers. "What?"

She forced herself to take a step backwards and folded her arms in a shield of protection. "You were right earlier today. I do have something I should tell you."

Cade stepped after her, tucking his chin into his chest and resting his forehead against hers he rubbed her arms from shoulder to elbow and back. "Please tell me it isn't something worth killing you over."

She shivered. "M-maybe…." The catch in her voice said more than a thousand words ever could.

Frustration swelled through him. How was he to protect her if she didn't confide in him?

Swift on the heels of frustration came thankfulness that he hadn't lost her. This wasn't just any woman he was with, here. When he'd woken and seen the flames engulfing the house, he'd thought his heart would stop on the spot. Pure terror had carried him through the blaze already engulfing her porch to crash down the door.

Behind them, two of the men decided they should call it a night and, buckets clanking, headed back toward town.

He pulled away just a fraction, allowing his eyes to take in every detail of her face. The wisps of damp hair that clung to her forehead, begging to be brushed back. The smattering of moonlight-kissed freckles across the bridge of her nose. The shadows that undercut each cheekbone, angling down to full trembling lips. She smelled like smoke and … something floral that he couldn't place. Grandma Jordan grew whatever it was in her garden back in Shiloh and the scent lured him like a siren.

"Shar…" he leaned toward her.

She stiffened. "Cade…please."

He stilled once more, but did give in to the temptation to finger the curl fluttering at her temple. "Please kiss you?" he whispered with a quick wink.

Humor softened the corners of her eyes, but she made no response.

With resolve, he lifted her by her waist and set her at arm's length. He supposed he deserved that. He'd waited too long. Right now she was going through enough emotional upheaval. But so help him, he wasn't about to let her get away from him without at least letting her know he realized what a mistake it had been to let her walk away. "I'm sorry. I shouldn't have …" He backed up a step. "I'm glad you're okay." Rubbing the knuckles of his hand across his lips, he steadied his breathing and studied the darkness, stepping further from temptation. "What was it?"

Her feet shuffled. "What was…?"

He studied her, shoving his hands deep into his pockets to ensure their obedience. "What did you see that you should have told me about?"

Her hands shook as she focused on them. "A letter. Addressed to Judge Green from a mining company in South Africa. Something about diamonds. I didn't have time to read the whole thing."

He clenched his fists and looked at the ash-heap that had been her home only moments ago. "I was thinking this had to be revenge for Mick. But you're right. If you saw something about diamonds, that could very well be the reason for the fire. Whose diamonds?"

Lower lip trembling, she shrugged. "I'm not sure. I just caught a glimpse of the letter." Stark fear etched her features. "They would really want to burn me alive?"

It took all his willpower not to step forward and pull her into an embrace. Instead, he shrugged. "I fell asleep, so I didn't see what happened, but they had a plank propped to hold the front door shut and had jammed the window. Someone was definitely trying to kill you."

"Why try with a fire I might escape? Why not just sh-shoot me at his convenience?"

"As a diversion while they broke Mick and Red out of the jail."

She made a short little gesture and huffed her frustration. "I'm so glad my death could be their little distraction!"

"Hey." His hands moved without permission and he brushed the tangle of curls back from her face, his fingers lingering on the softness of her cheek. "He didn't succeed. That's all that matters. And we know to be on the lookout now." He tilted his head and made sure she focused on him before he continued, "And from now on you're going to tell me about anything suspicious, so I can keep you safe, right?"

Her eyes were luminous and large in the moonlight. She looked at him silently, her lips pressed into a firm little line. Rapid puffs from her nostrils fogged the chilly night air around them with little clouds. But after a long moment, she gave a quick nod of her head and stepped back.

Somewhere in the bushes something rustled and he jolted to attention scanning the brush for intruders. He took her arm, lowering his voice and drawing her further into the shadows. "Listen, I told you to hide because I think it would be good if whoever set this fire thinks that it… killed you."

"You want me to play dead?"

He nodded. "Just for a few days. Especially after what you just told me."

Leaves rustled again.

He grunted. "I have to get you out of here."

"I don't have anywhere to go, Cade."

"I know exactly where to take you. Your cousin Jason lives not too far from here, but far enough that it will be a safe place."

She squeezed the bridge of her nose. "Okay. But don't you think we should go see Judge Green before we leave town? To tell him?"

Cade frowned. It would be best if no one knew she was alive, however the Greens needed to know if someone was planning a robbery of some sort. He hadn't heard anything about the Judge being invested in diamonds, but that would be something the man would keep to himself. Still, Sharyah's safety needed to come first. "I think my plan would work best if only you and I know what's going on."

"Please, they would have no reason to hurt me, or tell anyone that I'm alive. It will only take a few minutes. And they've been through enough recently. What we know could spare them another tragedy."

He gritted his teeth and scanned the darkness above their heads. She was right that if any family around these parts was safe to trust, it would be the Greens. "Alright. We can do that on our way out of town, but we need to be quick about it."

She sighed. "Thank you."

"You have a horse here, right?"

She nodded. "I board it at the livery."

"Good. Mine's there, too. Follow me." He turned and started through the darkness and tripped over a soft warm body. He stumbled forward, crashing into the underbrush. "Sharyah get down!" He flipped onto his back and leveled his gun at the person. "Don't move or it will be the last thing you do."

"I ain't moving!" A young voice squeaked. "And I swear I won't tell no one that Miss Jordan is alive."

Cade grunted, rolled to his feet and lifted Brandon McBride up by the nape of his shirt. "That's right you won't, because you are coming with us!"

The reality that someone had just tried to kill her, slammed through Sharyah like a full speed locomotive. She folded her arms and rubbed at her shoulders, tossing one last look at the smoldering vestiges of her home only a clearing away before following Cade through the trees.

What if someone was watching and decided to shoot her to finish the job? Fear crawled along her spine but she pressed it down, refusing to give it headway. She would think of something else.

Like Cade Bennett.

The man was an enigma. She'd been shocked to sense his desire for her a moment ago. She'd felt it palpably. As palpably as she'd ever felt anything in her life. And as tempting.

She shuddered at the memory of how tempting.

Yet hadn't she finally come to grips with the fact that God must not want her with this man? For years she had pined for him, dreamed of him, and held every other man at arm's length because of him. And then last summer he'd told her that he didn't feel enough for her for there to be more to their relationship. But just now…

Confusion, thy name is Cade Bennett!

Well, if the man had changed his mind he was going to have to prove it to her in a big way. Because she never again planned to wallow in the humility of making her feelings known, only to be rejected by him.

With Brandon trudging along behind him, Cade led their way to the Greens through the woods around the perimeter of the town. The concealing thicket of forest reached out clawed fingers to snatch at her skirts and tickle the back of her neck.

She couldn't help a check over her shoulder. But only darkness and eerie shifting shadows greeted her.

A shuffle and a grunt returned her focus to the front in time to see Brandon, who had apparently tripped on a root, sprawl flat directly in her path. With a soft gasp she stepped to one side to avoid treading on him. Something sticky and cloying coated her face and neck.

A spider web! She knew the moment the shriek escaped that Cade would not be happy about it. But at the thought of a spider crawling across her face, or maybe tangled in her hair, she jigged a circle, slapping and snatching and flinging and doing her best to keep the screeching to a low whimper.

His firm hand clapped over her mouth and his broad chest pressed up behind her. "Do you want to bring the whole town down on us?" he hissed in her ear.

She shook her head, heaving great draughts of air in through her nostrils. Her legs trembled to the point of uselessness and she sagged against him. And then just as suddenly, she realized she was doing it again, and stiffened.

She didn't need Cade Bennett. She didn't.

"Whoa! That was bully!" Brandon whispered from where he still lay prone on the forest floor.

Cade ignored the boy and spun her to face him, a goodly portion of irritation jutting his jaw to one side. He assessed her from head to toe, but didn't let go of her arms. After a moment his hands rubbed up and down from shoulder to elbow, soothing her trembling. "Can you stand on your own?"

Sharyah flicked remnants of web from her fingers and dusted at her shoulders, calling on every ounce of resolve not to step forward and beg him to wrap his arms around her. "It was a spider web."

His hands settled on his hips. "I gathered that from the number of times you screamed 'spider.'" A hint of humor ticked up one corner of his mouth. "Do you think you will be alright, now?"

"I wasn't screaming. I was actually quite calm." She couldn't suppress a shudder. "Do you think it's still on me?"

His soft chuckle escaped. "Somehow I think that spider is still running for its life."

A sheepish smile curved her mouth even as another shiver shook her. "Sorry. I'm not very good with spiders."

Brandon stood and dusted off the seat of his pants. "Is that why you never ate your lunch the day we put that spider in your pail?"

She pinned him with a narrow-eyed glare. "So that *was* you, was it?"

"Ah," his jaw dropped, "well... let's just say I know'd who done it."

"You *knew* who *did* it." Sharyah fell into line behind Cade once more. "And yes, that's why I didn't eat my lunch that day. And," she turned back to nail him with a glance, "when we get back to school, I better never find a spider in my pail again."

Brandon and Cade both chuckled. "Yes, ma'am."

Cade held out one hand for them to stop. "We're at the Greens' place. Just stay put for a minute."

Cade darted across a small clearing and knocked on the kitchen door. The door creaked open and Judge Green lifted a lantern sending a golden square of light to engulf Cade's shadow on the ground. Cade said a few words too low for her to hear from where she still stood inside the edge of the trees.

Beside her, Brandon shuffled his feet. "You in danger, Miss Jordan?"

Cade turned and motioned for them to hurry to him.

She took Brandon's hand and darted into the open space. "I'm going to be just fine, Bran—" Something burned across the inside of her arm and she froze and glanced down with a slow blink. Cade dove on her and pulled Brandon to the ground at the same instant she recognized the report of a gunshot echoing through her thoughts.

A rock bit into her ribs. She grunted and tasted dirt, and then Cade was yelling in her ear, "Go! Go! Go! Into the house! Move!" and she scrabbled forward.

Another shot splintered the wood of the doorframe as she clambered through it, and then Cade slammed the door and dropped the bar-lock into place.

The Judge and Missy both dove for cover across the room.

Cade's chest heaved and he took her shoulders and squatted

down pushing her below the level of the windows. Looking deep into her eyes, he asked, "Are you hit?"

She shook her head and quickly assessed Brandon. Had he been hit? Brandon sat in the middle of the floor, his arms wrapped around bent knees as he rocked back and forth, with his wide, frightened eyes fastened on her arm.

"Brandon?" Puzzled, she looked down.

Blood soaked her sleeve and dripped off the tip of one finger. "Oh." A wave of dizziness washed over her and sensible words failed to form. "I'm bleeding on their floor."

CHAPTER TEN

Cade murmured something low and menacing that Sharyah didn't quite catch. She looked at him, but he was already yanking his bandana from around his neck and reaching for her arm. "Judge," he glanced over his shoulder at the gray-haired man who cowered behind the butter churn, mouth slack, "I need to get us out of this kitchen. We're too exposed here. Is there another room we could move to that doesn't have so many windows?" As he spoke he tied the bandana tightly around her arm just above the wound.

The older man seemed to give himself a shake. "Right this way."

Sharyah started to stand to follow him, but Cade settled one hand on her forearm. "Stay low." He dipped his chin and held her gaze, not moving his hand until she nodded that she understood.

Judge Green led them to a small parlor that had only one round window set high in the peak of the gable.

"Thank you." Cade spoke to the Judge even as he motioned her into one of the chairs and reached for her arm once more.

Her whole body trembled now and she couldn't figure out why. "I'm sorry. I don't know why I'm shaking, so. I think it's just a scratch."

He paused and touched her cheek. "The trembling is normal. Just a reaction to the close call. You'll be fine in a few minutes. Let me look at your arm here." His jaw bunched and he swallowed hard, as he rolled up her sleeve and probed the area around the bullet wound on her forearm with gentle fingers. After a moment he let out a sigh. "Thank God, you're right. It's just a scratch."

Missy Green appeared, a roll of clean white bandages and a pair of scissors in her hands. But even as her friend set to wrapping her arm Sharyah couldn't take her eyes off of Cade who now paced the room like the caged bear she'd seen at a traveling circus one time. He kept glancing at her as he paced, and if his face turned any whiter, Sharyah was afraid he would faint dead away onto the floor.

A sudden thought struck her. "You weren't hit too, were you?"

He stilled. "Me. No. I'm fine. Just—" He glanced at Missy and apparently changed his mind about what he'd been ready to say. "I need you to quickly tell the Greens why we came, so we can get out of here before whoever took that shot at you can summon reinforcements."

"Okay." As Missy finished bandaging her arm and stepped away, Sharyah smoothed her skirts and looked toward the Judge leaning with one shoulder propped into the parlor doorway. "My suspicions have been confirmed now, I suppose. But I couldn't shake the impression that I needed to talk to you about a paper I saw earlier in the week when I was with the Rodale Gang."

Judge Green straightened. "Yes?"

"I didn't have enough time to read it. But they, well – maybe Katrina Perry? – had a letter addressed to you. From a De Beers mining company in South Africa."

Cade studied the man, a question clearly written on his face.

The judge shifted. "I have investments with them. I went to school with Cecil Rhodes. He is an explorer in Africa these days and started a diamond mine, over there. He needed investors, and I was happy to oblige. However, I've pulled out now. Most of my shares were wired to my bank, however I asked that a portion of them be sent in diamonds. They are supposed to arrive any day now. But I thought Cecil was going to wire me, not send a letter."

Cade turned back to her. "What did you mean when you said maybe Katrina?"

Sharyah shrugged. "I'm not sure if any of the men even knew the letter was there. I found it by accident when I started to pack up the chuck wagon, that day. And…" Her focus settled on Cade of its own volition.

Cade's brow furrowed. "Yes?"

"Well, when I was at the hotel, a note was shoved under the door. It said that I shouldn't say anything about the letter or you would be... killed."

In two swift strides he stood before her. The warmth of his palm settled against her cheek, and his eyes had never been more blue. She forgot to breathe. What would she do if she was the cause of his death?

"You let me worry about my safety, alright? You did the right thing, here."

She forced a nod, but the inhale of air didn't come until his fingers dropped away from her face. "The note was in Katrina's handwriting. I saw her writing something at the courthouse. And I think she must have known that I recognized her handwriting."

Cade paced the room, one hand working his jaw. "So you think Katrina might be the one behind this whole thing?"

Sharyah shrugged, not sure of anything.

Missy shuffled her feet. "Papa, I don't think Katrina would... she's made some mistakes, but I don't think she would go so far as to steal from us. And try to *kill* Miss Jordan?"

To Sharyah's way of thinking Judge Green didn't look so convinced. He tugged at his beard and studied Cade, who had finally stopped pacing but was staring at a spot on the wall with a far-away thoughtfulness furrowing his brow. The judge cleared his throat and Cade snapped out of his reverie with a light shake of his head.

He held his hand out to the older man. "Judge, best I get these two out of here right away. Sorry to bring this to your doorstep."

"Not at all. I appreciate the information. I'll wire Cecil first thing tomorrow to see what he knows. If you'll come this way...." He gestured toward the kitchen. "I've already sent my man, Jonas, to fetch your horses. He'll meet you in the trees by the old cedar stump. Just head straight back from the house and you can't miss it."

Cade released a long breath. "Thank you. Much obliged." He rested a hand at the small of Sharyah's back and lifted a brow. "Ready?"

She nodded.

Cade motioned for Brandon to join them, then spoke to her. "Just stick close to me and no screeching if you run into a spider web this time, alright?" One lid dropped in a quick wink, and a hint of humor lifted the corner of his mouth but there was a seriousness warming the blue of his gaze that sent a curl of fire through her belly and made her tremble in fear all at the same time.

She blushed even as she ignored his jibe and turned to give Missy a hug. "Thank you and I'm sorry to bring troubling news about your friend."

Missy gave her a squeeze and a kind smile before she waved away her concerns. "Kat will live or die by her own innocence, or lack thereof. Stay safe and come back to us – we need the best teacher we've ever had to return all in one piece." Missy blew out the kitchen lantern so their escape wouldn't be backlit, then opened the door and stepped aside, allowing them to pass out onto the porch. The door clicked shut.

The darkness of the night swallowed them, and despite all the upheaval she'd endured since Cade Bennett came to town, she couldn't suppress a wave of thankfulness to have him at her side.

Brandon started down the steps, but Cade snatched him back into the shadows of the porch. "Let your eyes adjust for a minute then we'll make a run for it."

After a few moments he tilted her a glance. "Ready?"

She nodded, swallowing the large lump of trepidation that had lodged in her throat.

"On three." Cade counted them off and then they ran pell-mell for the relative safety of the trees only a few feet away. Cade didn't let them stop but kept pushing until Sharyah felt her lungs might burst and knew her skirt had suffered several tears. Finally, he slowed to a walk.

"Did we miss the stump?" Sharyah gasped for breath.

"We didn't miss it." Cade slapped a branch out of their way and held it while she passed.

"How do you know?"

"He said to go straight and we couldn't miss it. I've been going straight."

She didn't know how he could be so sure of that when they'd been bolting through a thick forest in the dark darting this way and that to avoid trees, but she settled in beside him and held her silence.

Brandon strode a few paces ahead and Sharyah felt the brush of Cade's shoulder as he leaned close and spoke low in her ear. "Don't they have a rule about teachers having to be single?"

"What?" It took her a moment to equate his question with Missy's parting compliment. "Oh! Yes. So?"

He took her elbow and guided her over a rough patch of broken rocks. "Just that I don't think you'll be single for too much longer."

Her cheeks tingled and she was thankful he couldn't see her in the darkness. Maybe he was referring to Sam? "Sam has made no declarations of intent, yet."

He snorted. "I didn't me—"

"Found the horses!" Brandon called.

Cade took her elbow. "Come on. We can talk about this later. But let me assure you that Sam Perry was the farthest person from my mind, just now."

Sam jolted up in bed and glanced around his room, frowning and befuddled. Dim light at the window revealed it must be somewhere close to dawn. What had—? Another round of pounding commenced and as realization dawned he snagged his night robe and tied it about his waist. He rubbed his face, stumbled toward the stairs and was halfway down when someone called, "Sam! Sam Perry! Open up. There's been a fire in town."

"A fire?" Suddenly wide awake, he bounded down the last few steps and released the lock on the front door, jerking it open. "Where at?"

"The teacherage." Sheriff Collier blinked at him, his hat in his hands.

"Sharyah!" He bolted toward his room. "Let me get dressed and I'll be right there."

"Sam wait!"

There was something about the tone of Collier's voice that stopped Sam halfway to the landing. Dread blooming to life in the pit of his stomach, he turned and studied the man. "No."

Collier stepped inside and nodded. "I'm afraid so. Looks like the teacher didn't make it out alive."

All the strength gushed from Sam's legs, and he dropped like a stone right there in the middle of the stairwell.

"I'm right sorry. I know she meant something to yah."

Sam rubbed the back of his head and stared vacantly at the stair tread beneath his feet. "I— when? How?"

Collier shook his head. "I was to home. Then had to deal with the situation at the jail. So I never—"

"Situation at the jail?" Sam lifted his head, premonition raising his brows.

Twisting up his mouth and rubbing one hand over his cheek, Collier sighed. "The Rodale Gang done broke Mick and Red out tonight. Dynamited the wall. They was plumb gone by the time anyone got there. Most o' the citizens was off fighting the fire."

A cold chill tingled the skin all along the length of Sam's neck then cascaded into his fingertips. He glanced up the curve of the stairs to the door at the right of the landing. Katrina's door. Why hadn't she come out to see what all the ruckus was about?

"Sam you gonna be alright?"

Giving himself a shake, Sam returned his focus to Collier and nodded. "Give me a couple hours and I'll be in to town."

Collier dipped his chin, resettled his hat, and disappeared into the darkness outside closing the door behind him.

For a long time Sam sat with his hands hanging between his knees, simply staring at the floor of the entryway below. How could she have done such a thing? *You don't know that it was her.* Oh but he did. Deep inside in the places where he'd doubted his sister for a very long time, he knew beyond a shadow of uncertainty that his sister had gone too far tonight. Whatever her part in the night's events, he was finished with her.

He blinked hard. Then gripped the baluster and stood to his feet. He felt old and shaky and for a moment he stayed there, hanging onto the rail, swaying slightly as he stared at Katrina's door, working up the courage to do what needed to be done.

Slowly, he placed one foot on the next stair up and started the long climb to the top.

He knocked on her door quietly and she answered it only a moment later, pulling a robe around herself and doing her best to look sleepy, but her eyes were too bright to have just come to wakefulness.

He gritted his teeth. Her deception knew no bounds. "Get your things and get out, Katrina. You are no longer welcome in my home."

"Sam!"

He turned away, sorrow, frustration, and guilt weighing his shoulders down.

"You can't just kick me out, Sammy dear!" Her voice held incredulity. "And whatever brought this about? Who was that at the do—?"

"Don't!" Sam snapped. "You know good and well what this is about." He spun to face her, his hands coming to rest on his hips. "Be out in five minutes or so help me I won't be responsible for what I do."

"Sam really." She stepped toward him and rested one hand on his arm. "Let's be reasonable. Tell me what happened?"

"You killed her, that's what happened." Her wheedling would get her nowhere this time. He was done playing her little games.

Her eyebrows arched. "Killed who? I have no idea what you are talking about!"

"I don't believe you. I mean it. Be out in five minutes. I'll give you a twenty-four hour head start and then I'm coming after you with the law. I won't be part of this anymore, Katrina." With that he turned his back, stalked into his room and shut the door with a dismissive click. He would give her ten minutes and if she wasn't out by then, he would carry her out. No matter what, she would never spend another day under his roof.

Katrina blinked as the glossy mahogany grain of her brother's door closed in her face. This was most unusual. Usually Sammy capitulated to her desires so easily. Well... She turned for her room and collapsed on the edge of her bed. She would just have to think things through. Obviously, he didn't really mean for her to leave. He was just scared. Sam wasn't a man of action. *She* was always the one who took action. Action frightened him. Yes, that had to be it. He was terrified and overreacting.

So the teacher had died in the fire. Too bad, really. She'd halfway hoped the girl would escape, even as she'd jammed the plank under the handle to lock her into the cabin. It really was better this way. She'd known it then, when the thought of leaving Sharyah the door as a means of escape had begged for notice, and she knew it now.

Still... A cold chill settled into her stomach. What would it be like to burn to death?

Standing, she hurried to her closet and made haste to don her best day dress. She had some things she needed to take care of, then she would come back and see if Sammy was in a better mood, the ungrateful prig.

After all, she was doing all of this for *them*!

Fully dressed, Sam emerged from his room a few minutes later. Thankfully, Katrina seemed to have realized his seriousness, because she'd vacated the premises. He couldn't believe he'd let her take things this far. He'd never dreamed she would stoop to such levels. How could she want something so badly that she'd be willing to sacrifice another's life to get it?

Had she really set that fire?

He pulled his bowler from the peg by the door and stepped out onto the front porch with a sigh. They may never be able to prove it one way or another, but no matter what, he needed to alert the law. And he needed to find Cade. Had he heard about Sharyah yet? Sam blinked away the sheen of moisture blurring his vision. How could she be gone? And how would Missy feel when she learned? He knew the two women had grown close.

In the barn, Katrina's horse's stall stood empty. Quickly, he saddled his own mount and headed for town. Much as it pained him to do it, he rode straight for the sheriff's office.

Collier sat with his boots propped up on the corner of his desk, a mug of coffee in one hand, while he flipped through a stack of wanted posters with the other.

"Morning, Collier." Sam swallowed hard.

"Morning, Perry." Collier's boots thudded to the floor. "What can I do for you?"

Sam studied the gaping hole in the brick wall visible through the bars of the nearest jail-cell, then closed his eyes, willing away the guilt he felt for doing what he knew was the right thing. "Sheriff, I – I think Katrina may have been involved in the goings on, last night."

Collier was on his feet, in an instant. "Your sister?!"

Sam gave a barely perceptible nod. "I don't have any proof yet, though."

After a low whistle, Collier pursed his lips. "If that don't beat all. I'll ride out to your place and have a talk with her."

Sam's feet shuffled. "I asked her to leave. You won't find her there. I don't know where she is."

"I see."

"She's my sister." He felt his face heat as the defensive words slipped out.

"I understand. I'll put Cade to looking for her when he returns."

"Cade's gone?"

Collier nodded. "Said he'd be back in a couple days."

"Where did he go?"

"Don't rightly know." He shrugged. "He just said he had to be out of town."

"Does he know about Miss Jordan? He's a close friend of her family."

Again, Collier nodded. "I figured maybe he'd taken it on himself to ride home and let her family know in person. So I been holding off on sending a telegram to her folks, just yet."

"That's probably wise." Sam swallowed. A telegram seemed like such a cold way to find out a loved one had passed on. He hoped for their sakes that Cade had ridden to tell them in person. Still he ought to make certain too. "Since I'm the head of the school board, I should just make sure that's what happened, though. I'll telegram Miss Jordan's brother to see if he's heard from Cade."

"Alright. I'll just let you take care of that, then."

As Sam made his way down the walk toward the telegraph office he tried to decide the best way to word the telegram. He didn't want to say too much if Cade hadn't had time to make it home yet. But he needed to know if Cade had contacted them about Sharyah. He paused outside the telegraph office door, hands coming to rest on his hips as he stared out over the street. Had it really been only yesterday that he walked with her into the trial? Sat next to her? Heard her testimony?

He sighed and pushed through the doors into the office. "Hi, Earl. I need to send a message to the Jordans in Shiloh."

Earl picked up his pencil and licked the tip. "What'll it say?"

"Just say, 'Did Cade arrive? Will he be back soon?'"

"Alrighty. I'll git it sent on right away."

"Thanks, Earl." Sam dropped the payment on the counter and headed outside once more. He wanted to go look at the teacherage for himself.

The farther Katrina rode from the house, the more her anger mounted. She'd given years of her life to help Sam build a profitable spread. She'd even been instrumental in getting him the job at the bank to supplement their income during the early years when funds were low. Now when they were on the verge of something big, he had the nerve to kick her out.

Well, if he thought she was just going to give up without

a fight, he would know different soon enough. There wasn't a snowflake's chance in hell she was going to walk away from the opportunity to get her hands on a hundred thousand dollars.

She jerked the reins to one side to avoid a patch of scrub brush then reined the horse to a stop as a slow smile spread across her face. It was too early for calling, but she'd just wait here for a couple hours and then set her plan in motion. If Sam wouldn't get the information for her, she'd just have to get it herself. She swung down and pulled a book from her saddle bags, spread out a blanket, and settled against a tree. Nothing was ever gained by being impatient.

Time passed quickly, and three hours later, she decided she'd waited long enough.

When she reached the outskirts of town she made sure to keep back in the trees and skirted around to where she could tie her horse just south of the Greens' home. Darting down the alley between the bank and the feed store, she glanced both ways. All clear. Heart hammering in her breast, she stepped out into the open and set off with casual purpose. Had Sam made it into town, yet? She was only exposed to prying eyes for a few minutes as she hurried the one block down the boardwalk and stood on the Greens' front porch waiting for them to answer to her knock.

Mrs. Green opened the door only a moment later. "Katrina! How nice of you to stop by. Do come in." She stepped back and Katrina felt her shoulders ease as she brushed past the woman into the concealing welcome of the entryway. "Thank you, Mrs. Green."

Mrs. Green turned from shutting the door, folded her hands together and arched her brows, obviously waiting for Katrina to state her business.

Katrina swallowed. "Ah... I'm sorry to call unannounced, but I've been so remiss in coming to see Missy since... well, lately. Is she available for a visit this morning?"

"Certainly. How very thoughtful of you. I know she'll so appreciate the company." Caroline stretched out her hands. "Here, let me take your shawl."

Katrina resisted the urge to feel guilty as she undid the ties of her shawl, handed it off, and then followed Caroline to the parlor. She took the seat the woman indicated and waited while she went to fetch Missy. The silence wrapped around her, heavy and oppressive. She rolled her lower lip in and worked it with her teeth. She glanced around the parlor. The Greens had always been kind to Sammy and her. The parlor was spotless, as usual, the long gilt-framed mirror on the wall across from her reflected light from the window behind her, cutting off the head of her image with a blinding glimmer. She squinted and turned away, reminded of the time she and Missy had, as young girls, leaned over the back of the settee and made faces at themselves in that very mirror until they had fallen into giddy heaps on the floor.

She straightened her sleeves. Could she really do this?

Footsteps sounded in the entryway. She sat upright, pulled her bodice down with a firm jerk, and folded her hands into her lap as she pasted a smile on her face.

Yes. She could do this. Sam had left her no choice.

CHAPTER ELEVEN

Missy swallowed and hid her trembling hands in the folds of her skirt as she sank onto the chair across from Kat in the parlor, not knowing quite what to expect from her oldest friend. Her nerves were already raw from the shock of Sharyah Jordan's attempted murder right here in her own backyard. And she didn't really feel up to making small talk with Katrina, the woman suspected of being the mastermind behind the whole thing, in the parlor.

A lump of irritation lodged in her throat. She hadn't realized until this very moment how hurt she'd been by Kat's shunning after the attack. What kind of friend was she, to only just now be coming around for a visit? Maybe Papa was right about her.

Lifting her teacup Missy sipped quietly. If Kat thought Missy would be the one to break the silence, she was far, far from correct.

Kat squirmed a little on the sofa and Missy calmly took another sip, eyeing her over the gilded rim.

Twisting her teacup in circles on its saucer, Kat sighed. "I can see you are upset. And you have every right to be. I owe you a tremendous apology. I should have come sooner. I just...," she flipped her hand palm up and gave a little shrug, "...didn't know what to say."

A swell of forgiveness eased the lump in Missy's throat. Of course it wouldn't be easy to know what to say to a person after an incident like hers. Still, all she'd wanted was for just one friend to even come and simply sit with her – as Sharyah had done on several occasions.

She sighed. *I shouldn't be so selfish.* Kat was here now, after all. Forcing a smile, she stood. "Set your mind at ease, Kat. All is forgiven." She crossed the room to give her a hug, and she couldn't help but hold on a little longer than necessary when Kat returned the embrace. It felt so good to connect with her again.

Finally allowing her friend to resume her seat, she said, "What have you heard about the fire at the teacherage? And how is Sam handling Miss Jordan's… passing?" Papa had insisted that she tell no one that Sharyah had been here after the fire. Still someone out there knew! Someone who'd tried to shoot her!

Just the thought of losing Sharyah brought tears to the surface. She blinked hard to hold them back.

Kat peaked her brows, her mouth turning up at the corners. "You can't tell me you aren't at least a little happy to know that my brother's affections will no longer be directed elsewhere, now can you?"

Missy felt the blood drain from her face and lifted her teacup to hide her shock. Surely the woman couldn't think her so callous? To wish another woman dead just so she could have Sam to herself? She took too big of a gulp and the hot tea burned all the way down her throat.

Truth be told, she was the one who had pushed Sam away, in the first place.

The porcelain clinked as she plunked the cup down. "I could never wish ill on someone as nice as Sharyah – Miss Jordan. She is – was – the soul of kindness to me these past few weeks." She pierced Kat with a pointed look before she dashed at the moisture on her cheeks. Maybe Kat *was* behind the fire.

"Of course you couldn't, darling. Forgive me. I was trying to bring some levity to a very glum circumstance."

Missy fiddled with the lace at her wrists and studied Kat openly. "Mama says it was murder."

Kat flinched as though someone had just jabbed her with a quilting needle. "Murder? Posh! Why would she say that?" Her cup and saucer chattered as she set them on the side table.

"They are saying the door was wedged shut." She studied Kat's hands which were clasped so tightly in her lap that the color had drained from her knuckles. Then again, maybe she was taking this harder than she appeared to be.

"Wh-who would want to—" Kat leapt to her feet. "Oh, this is such a gloomy subject. I wanted our visit today to be cheery. Let's do talk of something else." She paced about the room as though searching for another topic, furling and unfurling her fan against one palm. "I know!" Rushing over, Kat sank down next to her on the divan. She squeezed Missy's hands, her eyes sparkling. "Tell me about the diamonds you have coming!"

Missy blinked, letting the surprise of the request sink in as she extracted her fingers from Kat's grasp. Sharyah *was* right. Katrina was interested in the diamonds. Cold terror crashed through her. How else could Kat know about the diamonds unless she'd had the letter Sharyah said she did?

Missy had told no one but Sam about them. Wait… Sam might have let something slip to his sister. She wouldn't be surprised by that. Kat could coax a secret from a rotting stump.

As the silence stretched so did Kat's lower lip. She leaned in and lowered her voice. "I know this can't be something you want told all over town. Sammy was just so excited! And you mustn't be upset with him," Katrina, tapped Missy's arm with her folded fan. "You know I've always been able to tell when Sammy had a secret. And I have to confess that I cajoled it out of him. But when he told me… Oh my, what a secret! I'm so thrilled for you!" She snapped open the fan and, with a few deft flips, set the tendrils of hair by her ears dancing. "Diamonds all the way from Africa! You'll be the talk of the town! Now do tell. I'm dying to know the details!"

Her wheedling smile brought a chuckle of relief to Missy's lips. "First off, they're father's diamonds. Not mine. He invested with a friend of his, Cecil Rhodes, and it appears to have paid off."

"I'll say! Sammy told me how much. A hundred thousand dollars in diamonds is quite a payoff!"

Missy felt another rumble of disquiet ease through her. "Yes, I suppose it is. We were all quite shocked when we learned how much Papa stood to make."

Kat's eyes sparkled. "So how soon until you'll be traveling to Boston or New York for a shopping trip?"

Missy pursed her lips and thought for only a moment before she said, "Oh, the diamonds don't get here until Friday's stage, but we won't be doing any extra shopping trips. At least not anytime soon. Papa did mention that he'd like to build a new church here in town." She shrugged. "After that, I'm not sure what we will do with it."

"Well, shopping trips or not, you will be the belle of the town!" Kat grinned and gave her a one armed hug, resting her head on her shoulder. "And speaking of shopping. I'm sorry I can't stay for long. Sammy has me running someplace for him today, so I really need to be going, but I simply couldn't stay away for another day. I'm so glad I stopped by."

Missy returned her hug, but a rock of dread settled into the pit of her stomach. "I am too. Thank you."

As she saw Kat to the door and watched her hurry down the walk, she frowned. Would her little deception work? The diamonds were due to arrive in two weeks, not on Friday. If Kat wasn't being honest, she and her compatriots would be jailed and awaiting trial before the diamonds were ever even in town.

She would need to talk to Papa however about what she may have just set in motion. People would need to be warned.

She sighed. Now only time would tell if Kat was friend or foe.

Collier, standing in the alleyway where Katrina Perry would soon pass by, fingered the badge on his vest and counted slowly to ten before he stepped out onto the boardwalk.

Katrina nearly crashed into him in her hurry to disappear down the alley to the safety of the woods where her horse stood tethered. She squawked in a most unladylike fashion and leapt back a step. "Why, Sheriff Collier, what a surprise!" She smiled coyly and flipped open her fan, flapping it so fast they might be in danger of a tornado if he didn't put a stop to it.

"Miz Katrina." He tipped his hat. "If you don't mind, I'd like a word with you." He stepped into the alley and willed his heart to beat sure and steady.

Trepidation immediately stiffened her stance. "Sheriff I don't know what my brother has told you but I can assure you—"

He held up a hand, silencing her. "Whatever beef is hanging between your brother and you is your business. I'm here to talk to you about the diamonds."

Her fan hesitated for half a beat before it resumed its tempo. "Diamonds? What diamonds, Sheriff?"

Collier folded his arms. "Coyness don't rightly suit you, Miz Perry. I help you get them, and you and I can split the proceeds fifty-fifty. But to do that you and I both know there'll be a sight o' people you'll need my help gettin' outta the way."

For the space of five strokes the motion of the fan slowed, and then she stopped flapping it, altogether. "Sheriff, I can't say that I have the foggiest notion what you mean. But it sounds like you want me to help you break the law. I simply can't be a party to that. Good day." She lifted her skirts and started to brush past him.

Not even bothering to turn and watch her leave, he leaned one shoulder into the building and spat, taking his time before he spoke quietly. "Your brother was by to see me today. He done tol' me he thinks you were party to murderin' the school teacher. If you was to walk any further, I'd have to pull out my gun to prevent your escape, and it'd be a shame for a purty little hide like yours to end up with holes in it."

The sound of her footsteps stopped so quickly one might have thought she ran into something. He suppressed a smile of satisfaction. He had her attention at the very least.

Slowly he turned to face her. "What do you say, Miz Perry? Partners?"

Jason Jordan hammered the last board down on the floor of the barn loft and stood, arching his back in satisfaction. He let loose with a loud whoop. He couldn't help himself. Their church had helped them erect the shell of this building but ever since he'd been working on the finishing touches and lots of little projects had kept him from getting it finished – tilling Nick's garden, putting up the deer fence around it, clearing the field to the south where he planned to build their house next spring, breaking in the new horses and a host of other things – it felt so good to have the last of it complete.

He moved to the loft edge and looked down onto the stalls, so thankful for this blessing from the Lord.

Ron poked his head out of the tack room. "I take it you got finished up there."

"Yep! Prettiest loft floor you've ever seen."

Ron chuckled. "Well best you get down here and get your pretty *gal* out of the garden. It's a might hot out there and I tried to talk her into going inside, but she told me she was expecting, not dead, and that I should leave her be."

Jason swung a leg over the edge and caught the first rung on the ladder. "You should have told me earlier! Where's Sawyer?"

"I just come in through the tack room door to get you. She's been in the garden for about ten minutes. I figured giving her a little leeway couldn't hurt. Sawyer is with Conner down to the south corral."

"All right, Ron. Thanks. Sorry to snap, I've just been a bit worried about her lately."

Ron nodded and stepped out of the door way. Swinging out one hand palm up, he gestured Jason by. "Go on, now. She just set to puttin' up a fuss in Spanish, so I figured I'd let you handle it, instead of trying to talk her into going back in again myself." There was a twinkle in his eyes and one lid dropped in a quick wink.

Jason hooked his hammer on the two nails pounded into the tack room wall for just that purpose and slung the nail bag onto the corner of the work table. "Spanish, huh?" He rubbed his palms down the legs of his pants.

"Yep."

He couldn't help the grimace as he strode out the door and headed left down the path toward the garden lot. Anytime Nick was talking Spanish it meant someone was about to receive the sharp side of her tongue. He came around the end of the barn and stepped into sight of the garden but he couldn't see Nicki anywhere. His pulse jolted. "Nick?"

"Aye!"

At the soft exclamation his heart started to pump in earnest. "Nicki?"

The bushy tassels at the top of a row of corn rustled violently. "Where have you been? I've been calling and calling for someone to come and you *men*.... Aye!" She launched into another string of unintelligible Spanish.

Jason jumped into a full out run. The only gate in the high wire deer fence lay at the far end of the garden. "I'm coming, Nick. Hang in there. Is it the baby?"

"*Si!*" She groaned.

Jason caught the post at the end of the fence with one hand and used his momentum to swing his body around the corner. "Ron! RON! Go for the doc!" He hoped the man had heard him through the barn's wall.

"I'm already on my way," Ron's calm voice came from the saddle of a horse a few paces away on the trail toward town.

Jason tossed a glance over his shoulder as he jerked open the gate. "You knew!?"

"I had a feeling when she started gasping and snapping those catchy little Spanish phrases."

Jason heard the slap of reins against haunch as the man called, "Gid'up, now," but he was already through the gate and leaping over tomato vines on the shortest route to the corn patch.

"I'm coming, Nick!" He burst through a row of corn and almost stomped on her. She was lying on the ground, her head resting right in the dirt by his feet. He squatted beside her and reached for her arm to pull her to her feet. "Come on. Let's get you to the house. Jed's gone for the doc."

She brushed him away. "I'm having this baby, right now!"

"Oh, no you're not! Doc isn't here yet. How long have you been in labor?" He scooped her up into his arms with a grunt.

She cried out in pain, but her arms wrapped around his neck

as she rested her cheek against his shoulder. He was thankful for that, because he didn't know if he could carry her dead-weight all the way to the house. Of course he didn't dare tell *her* that. He still wanted to marry her next month.

She cried out and one hand dropped to clutch her stomach.

"How long?" he demanded.

"About three hours."

"Three hours?! You stubborn—! Why didn't you say something sooner?"

"I'm soooorrry! Ooohhh!" She stiffened and squeezed his neck so hard he thought he might be suffering from blocked blood flow. "It was so much longer with Sawyer. I don't think I can do this."

It was the fact that she whispered those last words that sent his heart plummeting to his toes and then jolting back into place to pump like a locomotive. "Come on, Nick. You can do this, now. You've done this before remember. And look at what a blessing Sawyer has been to you." He hefted her over the last tomato plant and pushed open the gate with his shoulder.

"I don't want to remember. And I certainly don't *want* to do this again!" She smacked him with a balled up fist. He grunted. That was more like his Nick, but he'd be feeling that spot for a few days.

He rounded the corner of the barn and that's when he felt the warm wash of liquid spread down his arm and onto his chest. "Whoa! Nick you have to slow this down! Take deep breaths or something."

She was already huffing like a freight train and the glare she leveled at him could have set fire to a stack of green cord wood.

Her eyes widened and she pressed one hand to her stomach again. "Jason! You have to put me down. Now!"

"No,no,no,no! The house is just there. See?"

She groaned and huffed, huffed, huffed. The hand that still clung to his neck clenched tighter than a sprung bear trap and he wanted to groan right along with her.

Instead he ground out, "We're almost there, Hon. Come

on, just a few more steps." His breathing was coming hard too and the stretch of yard from the barn to the door of the soddy seemed miles long. He adjusted his grip on her and she cried out in pain once more. "Sorry… we're… almost… there…" Finally he reached the door of the house and pushed it open.

He rushed over to the bed and laid her down as gently as he could, prying her rigored fingers from the back of his neck. What in the world was he going to do if Doc didn't get here? He needed to get water on to boil. He remembered that much. But what he was supposed to do with it, was another matter altogether.

She clutched at his arm as he started to pull away, her eyes round and wild. "Don't. You. Dare. Leave. Me. Here!"

He leaned over her and adjusted the pillow behind her head then framed her sweat soaked face between his palms. "Nick, I'm not leaving you. Ever. I promise. I just need to get some water on to boil so that when Doc gets here it will all be ready."

She pulled a long breath in through her nose and pushed it out between pursed lips, shaking her head back and forth her fingers sinking like talons into his arms. "There isn't going to be time for Doc." She tugged him closer. "You are going to have to deliver this baby!"

His heart about pounded a hole in the wall of his chest. Surely Doc would get here on time. All he needed to do was reassure her. "Okay, Hon, okay. We're going to be fine. Just let me go get some water to put on."

She seemed to relax a bit after that. At least her claws retracted enough for him to get free.

He dashed out the door, snagging the water bucket on his way by.

At the pump, he ripped off his soaked shirt and tossed it on the ground then set to pumping the handle with a fury. The water shot out so fast that when it hit the side of the bucket it toppled over. With a grunt of frustration, he set it upright and pumped the water more slowly.

When it contained an adequate amount, he snatched it up and spun back toward the house. He almost barreled into Conner.

"Jason?" Conner gripped his shoulders and gave him a worried look. Sawyer, who was by Conner's side, looked up with wide eyes.

Jason forced a calming breath and crouched down before Nicki's son, setting the bucket down for a moment. "Hey buddy." He tousled the dark mop of curly hair. "Listen, Mama is going to have a surprise for you sometime tomorrow, but for tonight she needs you to go with Conner to the Snow's place, okay?"

The little tyke clapped his hands. "Tiwwy make good cookies!"

Jason grinned. "That she does, buddy. You eat one for me, okay?"

Sawyer stepped forward and wrapped pudgy arms around Jason's neck, pressing a soft little cheek to his face. "'Kay."

Jason raised a glance to Conner one eyebrow lifted in silent question as he gave the boy a squeeze. *Can you please take him over to the Snow's?*

Conner nodded his assurance. "Did Ron already head into town?"

Jason set Sawyer away from him, stood and lifted the bucket. "Yeah."

"Everything under control here?"

Jason started for the house. "I hope so. And thanks." His gesture encompassed the little boy by Conner's side.

Conner grinned. "Oh, it's such a chore to have to go over to the Snow's."

Jason chuckled. "Enjoy Tilly's cookies." And with that he lurched into a jog back to the soddy.

"Where have you *been*?" Nicki greeted as he opened the door.

Nicki still lay on the bed, but her knees were bent and both hands pressed flat against her belly.

Whoa! "I'm right here, Hon. Everything is going to be alright." Jason sloshed some water into a large pot and plunked it down on the stove top. "Just hang in there for a few more minutes and Doc should be here." He jerked open the stove and tossed two logs inside.

"This baby is coming NOW!" She lifted her head, chin tucked to her chest and grunted long and hard.

Oh, Lord! A little help here?! His eyes darted around the room searching for any answer other than the obvious.

CHAPTER TWELVE

Sharyah followed Cade into the yard of a little ranch with a new barn and an old soddy house just after noon. A bunkhouse stood on the edge of the yard and Cade pulled up before it.

Exhaustion coated her eyes with grit and when she swung down from her horse she hung onto it for a moment to ensure she had her balance. Her arm throbbed relentlessly but she was thankful that they'd made their escape from town without further incident.

Sliding down, Cade pulled Brandon into his arms. The boy lolled like a rag doll, sound asleep. He'd shared Cade's horse and stayed awake for most of the trip – only just an hour ago falling asleep.

Cade nodded to the bunkhouse and she hurried ahead of him and opened the door. The room was empty. All the hands were probably out working the cattle. Cade chose the nearest bunk and tucked Brandon under the blanket. The boy didn't even stir.

Cade looked as bad as she felt. His eyes were red rimmed and shot through with scarlet veins. His hat pushed back on his head had loosed a hank of tousled hair that splayed across his forehead making her want to brush it back.

She curled her fingers into her palms and held her hands to her sides.

His gaze dropped to the tear in her sleeve that revealed the bandage on her arm. "You doing alright?"

"I'm fine. Thank you."

They stepped back outside and looked around the yard. "Jason's done a lot with the place. You should have seen it six months ago." He nodded toward the soddy. "Nicki must still be living in the soddy, though." Striding across the yard he knocked on the door.

"Doc! That you?" a man called from inside the house and it was only a moment before the door jerked open. "Sharyah? Oh thank God!" The cry was nearly a screech as Jason pulled her into a quick embrace.

Pain squirmed up her arm and she caught her breath as she blinked and took a step back. She pressed away the pulsing reminder of her own close call. Her cousin was normally calm and… sane. What could be happening?

Jason's blond curly hair poked from his head in every direction and he was stripped bare to the waist, but he didn't seem to even notice. He stretched out one arm toward the interior of the home. "Sharyah, whatever you're doing here, God sent you! Come in! Please! It's Nicki, you have to help her." He grabbed her hand and dragged her into the dim little room.

A woman with dark damp curls groaned on the bed in the corner. Sharyah had never met the widow Jason had fallen in love with. But this was evidently her and she was quite obviously in labor. "Oh my!" Sharyah gulped. She was going to have to deliver this baby.

"Yeah." Jason rushed to the bed and knelt by the woman's head. "Nick, hon, this is my cousin Sharyah. She's going to help you."

The woman grunted out a string of unintelligible words.

Sharyah set to rolling up her sleeves and scrubbing her hands as Jason asked, "What was that, hon?"

The woman gritted her teeth. "Get your sorry self out of here this instant and take that man with you." She fluttered a hand in Cade's direction. He was standing in the doorway, eyebrows raised in surprise and looking like he'd rather be just about anywhere else on earth than right there.

Sharyah took over. She gave Cade a shooing motion and nodded her head toward Jason.

"What about your arm?"

"I'll be fine. Just get him out of here."

"Ah," He stepped forward a half step. "Jason, come on outside. Sharyah will have everything under control in no time."

Jason stood but it was plain that he didn't want to leave the woman's side. "Nicki, I'll be just outside, just send Sharyah out if you need me."

"Go!" Nicki gritted her teeth, all the tendons in her neck popping out like taut lasso lines.

Jason scurried out the door and Sharyah couldn't help but share a grin with Cade as he pulled the door shut behind them.

Nicki moaned and flopped her head to one side.

Sharyah swallowed. She'd never done a birthing on her own before, but she'd assisted at plenty and the woman needed her.

Hot water steamed on the stove, she noticed. At least the man had thought of that.

She strode across the room. "Alright, Nicki. You can do this. I'm just going to check you out and see how soon we might expect this little one to arrive, alright?"

Puffing short breaths, the woman seemed to relax slightly but her eyes were snapping fire. "Don't you dare look and then tell me it will still be hours yet."

Sharyah chuckled. But after a quick check she knew the woman didn't have much to worry about. This baby would be here any minute now. "Not hours. Do you feel like pushing?"

Nicki's head flopped back onto the bed. "*Si!*" She let loose with another groan and her face paled till it almost matched the color of the sheet. Sweat glistened in the lamplight, a sheen on her forehead.

"Okay, good. I'm ready. With the next pain, I want you to push."

A few minutes later when the baby slid into her hands, she thought her heart might stop from sheer amazement. "It's a girl! You have a little girl!"

The baby gasped its first breath and whimpered a mewling wail, one tiny fist waving in the air. Sharyah watched in awe as the little body turned from pale grey to a healthy pink, and grinned like a crazy woman. "Look at all that black hair!" She cupped the baby in the crook of one arm and wiped her face clean with a warm damp cloth. "Hello there, sweetness," she crooned.

Nicki collapsed back in utter exhaustion, her breaths still coming in great puffs, but a little easier now. A tired smile lit her face as Sharyah raised the baby so she could see her. *"Gracias, Jesus!"*

Yes. Thanks, Lord. Thank you for letting me be a part of this. Sharyah tied off and cut the cord, then nestled the baby into her mother's arms.

A knock sounded on the door then. "Sharyah? The doctor's here."

Relief surged through her. "Come in!"

Sharyah turned everything over to the doctor and stepped out the door. Tilting her face to the sky, she came to a standstill near the pump in the yard. Sheer thankfulness, pleasure, joy and love swirled through her in a heady mix and she realized she was trembling from head to toe. But it was a good feeling this time, so different from the night before. One that made her want to raise her hands to the sky in sheer adoration of her creator. New life had just come into the world and she'd been a part of it.

Cade stepped up beside her and began to work the pump handle.

Without thought, she stretched out her hands and washed. The soap lathered and drained away and still she said not a word.

"Sharyah?"

Jason watched her, worry and tension tightening the lines of his face.

"It's a girl." She gave him a tired smile. "Everything is fine."

Jason's knees buckled and when they hit the ground he turned his face to the sky his lips moving in silent prayer. For the first time Sharyah noticed the damp crumpled shirt next to the pump.

An older man emerged from the bunkhouse with a clean shirt hanging from one hand just as the doctor opened the door of the house.

The doctor smiled and tipped his head back toward the

house. "The baby looks healthy and Widow Trent appears to be doing just fine. You can go in and see them now."

Jason scrambled to his feet but the old ranch hand touched his shoulder and pressed the shirt against his chest. "You want her to be speaking English when you see her."

Jason grinned and slipped his arms into the sleeves and started on the buttons. "That I do."

"Tell her I stopped by her parents place on the way back from getting Doc. They should be here shortly."

"Thanks, Ron." Jason fastened the last button and swung a gesture to include Sharyah and Cade toward the house. "Come on in. I'm so glad you two are here."

Sharyah's heart felt too full. She and Cade sat at the table sipping coffee as Jason knelt beside the woman he loved and stared at the little baby like she might be the most amazing thing he'd ever seen in his life.

Doc had washed the baby girl and wrapped her tightly in a soft square of cloth. She now lay snuggled securely in the crook of Nicki's arm. Nicki set the rocker into motion with a little push of her foot.

Jason and Nicki's eyes met, a softness settling into their depths and Sharyah smiled gently. She was so glad Jason had found a woman that plainly made him so happy. She thought of Sam. Could she ever see herself that smitten with him? She twisted her cup and studied the rim, knowing the answer, but afraid to give it root. The only man she could ever feel that way about sat right next to her. And last night he had seemed to… her gaze flickered his way, but his attention lay fixed on Jason and Nicki.

Sharyah worried her lip. Last night…well, what if she had misunderstood something? The memory of the humiliation she'd felt last summer coursed through her on a tremor. No. She renewed her resolve again. If he really had changed his mind, he would have to prove it to her. She was certainly done throwing herself at the man. She forced the thoughts aside, turning her focus back on the couple.

Jason reached out and touched Nicki's face. "You are amazing."
Nicki blushed.

The corners of his eyes crinkled as he leaned forward ever so
carefully and brushed a light kiss across her lips. He whispered,
"If you ever wait so long to tell me you're in labor again...."

She reddened in earnest and tossed a glance toward where
they sat at the table. "You talk too much." He chuckled and she
reached up and brushed a damp curl off his forehead. "What
would I have done without you?"

He grinned. "Given birth in the corn patch."

Beside Sharyah, Cade shifted and she looked at him.

"Corn patch?" he mouthed with a wry grin.

She shrugged and returned her attention to the beautiful
sight of the new little family in the corner.

Nicki dropped her head against the rocker and closed her
eyes.

Jason turned his focus to the baby. "Beautiful." His voice was
soft and filled with wonder. He reached out one finger to touch a
round little cheek.

Nicki held the baby girl out to him. "Here."

Carefully, like a man picking up fragile china, he took the
little one and settled her into the crook of his arm. "Hi there," he
whispered, bouncing her gently when she let out a tiny bleat of
protest at the slight jostling. He bent forward and pressed a kiss
to her wrinkly forehead his blond curls a sharp contrast to the
baby's thick black hair.

Sharyah felt the prick of tears. Had she ever been witness to
something more beautiful?

"What are we going to call her?" Jason asked.

Nicki opened her eyes and tilted her head toward him. "I
want to call her, Haven Jaycee."

Jason blinked at Nicki, a look of total honor and awe on his
face.

Sharyah swiped the flats of her fingers under her eyes and
rested one cheek in her hand. This woman was perfect for Jason.

Nicki smiled softly her gaze never leaving Jason's face.

"Through you, the Lord has been such a haven for me. I want her name to always be a reminder of what God did for me by bringing you into my life."

He cleared his throat and blinked rapidly a couple times, then nodded and turned to look at the baby. "Hello little Haven. I'm so happy to finally see you." Jason's stubbled cheek pressed gently to the baby's head, his eyes closed, and his lips moved in quiet prayer.

Sharyah traced the grain of the table, the scene almost too reverent to watch anymore.

Cade reached across the corner of the table and tilted her face toward him. His eyes shimmering with quiet emotion, he studied her for a long moment. "You're beautiful when you are happy," he whispered.

Her stomach rolled. "I am happy." She reached out and brushed back the dark curls splayed across his forehead. Her heart dropped as she realized what she'd just done. Why was she constantly making herself vulnerable to this man? Hadn't she just promised herself that she was done doing that? She looked away, curling her fingers into her palm and shoving her hands into her lap.

Cade stood and tipped her face up toward him, fingers under her chin and his thumb tracing a hot caress across her cheek bone. He nodded toward the door. "Let's go outside. I need to talk to you."

Fear clenched a fist around her throat. All these years she'd longed for him to show an interest in her. And now… there was such warmth in the blue of his eyes. Had that time finally come? And what if he was misinterpreting his feelings? What if the fact that she'd nearly died twice the night before, not to mention his obvious exhaustion, was confusing him? She knew he cared for her in a brotherly way. But it had never gone beyond that and she'd be a fool to allow herself to believe that anything had changed.

Sharyah let him pull out her chair and hold the door open for her, but she wasn't about to stand still and listen to him try to explain his obvious confusion. He needed rest and a few days distance from her near death, then he'd realize what he was really feeling, and it would be better if she didn't let him muddle the situation up by promising her things he didn't truly feel.

Outside, he reached for her hand, but she stepped away. She would save him the awkwardness.

"Sharyah—"

"Cade, I'm exhausted." She scanned the buildings. "Do you think there's somewhere I could sleep for awhile?"

There was enough truth in the statement to assuage her guilt at avoiding him.

The door to the bunkhouse opened and the old ranch hand poked his head out. "You two look pretty tuckered. I've fixed up beds for you both inside." He tilted his chin in a gesture of welcome.

Sharyah hurried to accept the man's offer. "Thank you." She brushed past him.

The man nodded. "There's a second room there. You go on in. Cade can sleep out here next to the boy."

"That will be perfect." Sharyah bustled past him, shut the door to her little room, and pressed her forehead to the cool of the wood. How long could she get away with hiding in here? Maybe if she stayed long enough he'd be gone by the time she came out.

With a little groan, she flopped back onto the bed. Simply put, the man made her crazy.

Cade blinked slowly at the closed portal then glanced over at Ron.

The old man smiled sympathetically.

Rubbing a hand over his face, Cade tried to think. Exhaustion tugged at him, but he needed to ride into Farewell Bend and telegraph Shiloh. They would be getting a message from Beth Haven that Sharyah had been killed in the fire and he wanted to let them know she was alright and at Jason's. "Ron? Our horses need a rest. You have a mount I can use to get to town?"

Ron scratched the back of his head. "You don't mind my saying so, you don't look like you should be going anywhere but straight into the sack."

Cade smirked. "That bad, huh?"

Ron nodded.

"I got a couple hours sleep last night before the fire." And only two hours the night before that, but he didn't add that fact. "And I need to send a message to Sharyah's family that she's alright."

Ron took his elbow and pushed him down onto an empty bunk. "You leave that to me. I'll ride in and do it for you."

Relief from the responsibility sapped the rest of Cade's resolve to stay awake. "Much obliged." He pulled his boots from his feet and nearly groaned in pleasure as his head settled against the pillow and all went black.

Smith Bennett pulled his horse to a stop at the top of the hill overlooking the ranch where he'd spent twenty-five years with the woman he loved. Everything looked about the same. Cade was doing a good job then, keeping the place up. The way he himself had run off after Brenda's death though, wasn't right. The boy had deserved better than that. But grief had blinded him to what Cade would need.

God, forgive me.

How many times had he prayed that? God had forgiven him, he knew. Now it was time to ask his son to do that same.

"Gid'up." He heeled the horse forward, skirting a low hedge and angling down the hill.

He rode into the yard from behind the barn and could hear someone inside whistling a tuneless cadence. Reining up he swung down and dropped his horse's reins on the ground. He'd trained the animal himself and knew it wouldn't go anywhere.

Poking his head around one of the large sliding doors he called, "Cade?"

The whistling stopped and Rocky Jordan appeared out of the far back stall, a pitchfork in his hands. "Smith!" The young man strode his way holding out one hand, a genuine smile lighting his face. "It's so good to see you."

Smith shook his hand and nodded. Cade must have partnered up with Rocky. Smart move. Rocky was a hard worker and knew his way around a ranch. The kid had never really had his heart in the law. "How've you been, son? Good to see you."

Rocky set the pitchfork aside and settled his hands on his hips. "I'm doing real well. How about you?" True concern darkened the young man's eyes.

Smith blinked and rubbed one hand over the back of his neck. "I'm starting to breathe again, son. Starting to breathe again." The corners of his mouth pulled up slightly. "For awhile there I wondered if life was worth living, you know?"

Rocky nodded. "I think I'd feel the same if I lost Victoria."

Smith didn't comment on that. Give him another quarter of a century with the woman and then he might be close to being able to understand how he really felt. "How is she?"

"Doing real good. Come on." Rocky tipped his head toward the house. "She'll skin me alive if I don't bring you right in for refreshments."

Smith shuffled his feet and glanced around the barn. The last thing he wanted to see was another woman standing over Brenda's stove. "Actually there's something I need to take care of right away. Is Cade around?"

Rocky hesitated. "He's not, actually. A friend of his from Beth Haven came by and needed his help. He was having trouble with rustlers." Rocky's jaw bunched. "But some trouble must have gone down. We received a telegram from the head of the school board over there asking us if Cade had arrived here and if he'd be back soon. Then right after that we got a telegram from Cade. Something must have happened because he says he's got Sharyah safe in Farewell Bend at my cousin Jason's place and not to worry."

Smith sighed. He'd been hoping to get the burden of apology off his chest tonight. Looked like that would have to wait for a bit longer. He forced a smile. "Alright, then. Come on and let me see that young woman of yours. But I'll need to catch the first east-bound train there is."

Rocky nodded. "One leaves this morning at nine. I'll drive you to town in our buggy."

Smith felt a small weight lift from his shoulders. One step closer.

★

CHAPTER THIRTEEN

Sharyah slept the day away and awoke that evening to the lilting strains of a guitar. For a long moment she stared at the patch of stars outside her room's one small window, trying to place her whereabouts and where the music was coming from.

Then she remembered their all-night ride to Jason's spread, delivering the baby, and finally her escape from Cade.

She rolled to her side and sat up, eyeing the door. Would he be out there waiting for her? Or maybe he was still sleeping himself? The bunk springs groaned in protest as she stood and padded softly to the window.

Knowing Cade, he was wide awake and waiting to stubbornly insist that she let him talk to her.

Perhaps she should simply stay put until morning. But, as she pushed the window open to better hear the song, a tantalizing waft of smoky roast pork set her stomach rumbling with the reminder that she hadn't eaten since yesterday.

The music floated through the window, alluring in its beauty. Despite the begging of her stomach, she stood still to listen, her eyes falling closed. Each note wrapped around her, soothing frayed nerves and calming the fear that had lain just beneath the surface since her near escape from the fire the night before. Who would be playing so beautifully? Was it Jason? Or maybe one of his ranch hands? Finally, aided by the mouth-watering enticement of the delicious scent, the melody lured her to her door.

She eased it open and peered into the other room. Only when she saw that Cade didn't occupy one of the room's four bunks did she relax and step through.

Brandon, still sprawled on the bed they'd laid him in, head tousled and mouth gaping open, slept as the dead.

She smiled softly. Poor boy. This was probably the best night's sleep he'd had in a long time. She soothed the hair off his forehead and adjusted the covers, pausing for a moment by his side. *Lord, help us to know how best to help him.*

Straightening, she glanced at the outer door. She could hear voices and laughter now, along with the clatter of utensils on plates. Curious to see what all the commotion could be this late at night, she poked her head outside.

A roaring fire blazed in the middle of the yard, several stools, logs and rocks pulled up around it, and she blinked at the number of people gathered there. Where had they all come from and who were they all? A man with a long drooping black mustache and wearing a large sombrero slowly turned the spit of smoldering meat above the fire and tapped his toe in time to the guitar which had picked up the beat, now. Off to one side a long table with a lantern at each end held a wide array of food, just the sight of which had Sharyah's stomach rumbling so loudly she feared it could be heard across the yard.

"You must be, Sharyah?" A young woman about her own age, eyes dark as almonds and high cheek bones framed by a cascade of straight black hair, stepped up next to her with a soft smile on her browned face. "I am Rosa Vasquez. Nicki, she is my sister. She tell us that you help her during her time."

Sharyah dropped a quick curtsy. "It was my pleasure and I'm pleased to meet you."

"We are here to celebrate." Rosa held one hand toward the food table where a portly matron busied herself straightening and refilling and smacking the hands of hungry boys she apparently deemed had enough food on their plates. "You are hungry?"

"Famished!"

Rosa giggled. "Well then, come." She led the way through several darting children and offered Sharyah a plate. Then leaning forward she said quietly, "You will get not only a feast for your belly, but one for your eyes as well, when you see the one who makes the guitar sing."

"Rosa! For shame, talking so!" The hearty woman who'd been

standing behind the table launched into a string of Spanish that set Rosa's cheeks aflame and then her hands to wringing.

Sharyah scooped several different foods onto her plate, her curiosity piqued even though she couldn't understand a word being said. When the plump woman hurried off to scold a couple of small boys that had fallen into a tussle, Sharyah grinned at Rosa. Rosa's levity instantly returned and she rolled her eyes. "My mama, she… how you say? She howls bigger than her teeth."

A laugh bubbled forth. She couldn't help it. "Her bark is worse than her bite?" She popped a small bit of flatbread into her mouth.

Rosa snapped her fingers. "That is it. Now come," her dark eyes sparkled, "we will go on the pretense of getting some meat from Papa, and then you will see I speak truth about *el músico*."

Taking another bite of her tortilla, Sharyah glanced around. She should really just make her escape back to her room before Cade decided to pop out of hiding. But Rosa was already halfway across the yard, and she didn't want to disappear on her without an explanation. Besides, the smell of the meat would torment her all night if she didn't get at least a small slice of it. Balancing her plate on one hand, she lifted her skirt with the other and followed Rosa's calico skirt.

"*Papa, esto es Sharyah. Desearía un trozo de carne.*" Rosa spoke to her father.

"*Si, si.*" The man with the sombrero nodded his head and set to carving off a thick slice of the roast pork.

Rosa touched Sharyah's shoulder and nodded to the man. "This is my Papa, Carlos Vasquez."

Sharyah smiled. "It's a pleasure to meet you, Mr. Vasquez."

He nodded, his eyes glinting with good humor as he used his huge carving knife and fork to set the steaming pork onto her plate. "*Si, si. Es una Hermosa noche para celebrar el nacimiento de mi nieta. Ella es tan bonita! Gracias.*"

"Papa says it is a good night to celebrate the birth of his beautiful granddaughter and thank you for your help to Nicki, today."

Sharyah dipped her head. "I'm glad I was here to help."

Rosa lowered her voice. "Now come," she gestured toward two logs upended near each other, "let us sit and *feast*." With a little giggle, she pumped her eyebrows twice in quick succession then trotted away before Sharyah could state her intention to head back to her room.

Rosa sat, fluffed her skirts, and then clasped her hands around one knee and leaned back, looking for all the world like she was settling in for a long concert.

Several men standing in a group and wearing big hats and ponchos blocked her view of the guitarist Rosa stared at with gleaming gaze.

Sharyah grinned. She'd only known the girl for five minutes and already she could tell they would be lifelong friends. Cade Bennett be hanged. Suddenly she wanted to stay right here and get to know this new friend better. She settled herself onto the log next to Rosa. "Alright where is this *el músico* you were talk—" Her sentence ended on a squeak as her eyes settled on the man with the guitar across the fire.

Rosa chuckled and leaned over to bump her with her shoulder. "See? It is as I said, no?"

Sharyah's mouth gaped open, the bite of meat she'd just taken forgotten. Cade Bennett was the *el músico!* How had she not known he could play a guitar, much less so beautifully?

His black Stetson pushed back, and a red bandana crumpled around his neck, he had his head tilted to one side and his eyes closed as he plucked a harmonic melody from the strings.

Realizing her mouth could be mistaken for an unsprung bear-trap, Sharyah snapped it shut and remembered just in the nick of time to chew a few times before she swallowed. She tossed Rosa a sheepish look that was met with a giggle.

"Just remember, I saw him first, yes?" Rosa teased.

Oh no you didn't.

Just then, as though he had sensed her there, Cade's focus zeroed in on her without so much as a flicker right or left. His chin lifted in a quick gesture of greeting, but his fingers never missed a beat. Nor did his gaze waver.

She lifted a finger in acknowledgment, but then pretended great interest in the food on her plate. All she could bring herself to do, however, was push the beans into little piles and twirl her fork through the mound of fried potatoes and then she lifted her eyes, only to find him still studying her, one corner of his mouth quirked in a crooked little smile.

Her heart stalled, then rushed as though to make up for the lost beat even as heat surged into her cheeks. And immediately following, a swell of anger washed over her. How many times would she have to take herself in hand before she finally extracted this man from her heart? He didn't want her. How could she still be so attracted to him? Why couldn't she get it through her head that he would never see her as more than a little sister needing protection?

"Rosa, if you will excuse me. I think I will head off to my room for the night. It was very nice to meet you." She stood and offered her new friend a smile.

Rosa glanced back and forth between the two of them, a glimmer of confusion in her eyes. "Of course, you are... Forgive me. I did not know that you and he... that you were—"

"Rosa, please." Sharyah kept her voice low. "We are not. You have done nothing wrong. Will you be here in the morning?"

The music stopped and out of the corner of her eye she saw him stand and pass the guitar to another man. Cade straightened his hat and started her way.

Sharyah pressed down her instinct to run as she waited for Rosa to respond. She needed to make her escape quickly, or he would catch up to her.

Rosa nodded. "Our family will sleep in the barn and spend a few days here to help Jason and Nicki so they can take extra time with the little ones."

Sharyah started backing away, balancing her plate in one hand. "Good. Maybe we can go riding, tomorrow?"

Rosa's shoulders eased perceptibly. "*Si.* I would like that."

"Me too. See you then." She turned quickly, lifted her skirts with one hand, and started toward the bunk house. Only a few yards to go. Once in the safety of her room she could plead fatigue and wouldn't have to face the man until morning.

"Miss Jordan!" a woman called.

Sharyah's heart sank even as she tossed a glance over her shoulder. Rosa's mama waved to her and hustled her way, one hand gripping several plates. Maybe she could just pretend she hadn't heard the woman. She kept going.

"Miss Jordan!"

Her eyes slid shut and her feet unwillingly shuffled to a stop. She turned to face the woman well aware that Cade was only a few paces away. "Yes, ma'am?"

A grin to rival the Deschutes canyon split Mrs. Vasquez's face. "I bring you peach pie. You like?"

"Oh, I'm fine. I'm not really hungry right now, thank you." Sharyah's stomach rumbled a revelation of her lie just as Cade sauntered up to them. He cocked one eyebrow and took in the plate she'd heaped high with food and barely touched before he turned to Mrs. Vasquez.

"Evening, Mrs. Vasquez." He fingered the brim of his hat.

The woman gave him a chiding look. "Juanita, *por favor*! Juanita!" She thrust a plate, laden with the largest slice of pie Sharyah had seen in a long time, into her free hand and another into Cade's. A young girl by her side held out a tray filled with steaming mugs of coffee, and only when Cade had taken one and Mrs. Vasquez had noted Sharyah's lack of a free hand, did the woman seem satisfied. "Take! Eat! Be happy!" And with that she threw her hands into the air and rushed off hollering a string of Spanish at a little boy walking the top post of the corral like a balance beam.

Cade watched the woman for a moment, then turned back to Sharyah with a grin. "I do believe you were running from me, Miss Jordan."

Sharyah swallowed. To admit the truth would only inflate his ego more. But to deny it would be an outright lie. "I do believe you were chasing me, Mr. Bennett." She cocked one brow at him.

A light of amusement dancing in his eyes, he cupped his

chin and looked down at her. "It's about time I started, don't you think?"

Her cheeks tingled with warmth and she studied the darkness around her feet. She worked her teeth over one lip and held her silence.

He gestured to a make-shift table of lumber balanced on a barrel where Jason and Nicki were already seated. "Will you join me?"

"Actually, I'm very—"

Jason and Nicki noticed them and waved them over.

Sharyah sighed and angled him a look. She couldn't very well escape now without being very rude.

He studied her. "I promise to be on my best behavior."

Humor quirked her lips. "That's not saying much."

His head tipped back on a laugh before he led the way to the table and held out one of the chairs so she could be seated next to Nicki. He took the seat across the way, next to Jason.

Nicki looked tired, but oh so happy. Her hands curled around a steaming mug of tea, rested on the table as she smiled a greeting at them and spoke to Sharyah. "I'm so glad you woke up in time to get some food."

"Everything has been simply delicious. Thank you. How are you feeling?"

A chuckle escaped as Nicki twisted the mug in circles. "When I had Sawyer, I did everything myself. This time, Mama won't let me lift a finger. I'm doing just fine."

"She's going to go inside to sleep in just a moment." Jason gave Nick a pointed look.

Nicki opened her mouth, her shoulders tensing in obvious protest, but Sharyah cut her off before she could speak. "Where is the baby?"

Apparently deciding to let the matter with Jason drop, Nicki gestured to a woman about Sharyah's age the next table down. The baby lay along her forearms, her tiny head cupped in gentle hands. Next to the woman sat a young man with sandy blond hair and a quiet sincerity. "Tilly is our neighbor. She also works for us."

Tilly studied the baby, but the young man's eyes never left Tilly's face. Sharyah smiled softly, her focus flickering to Cade. His gaze captured hers and refused to release it, even when he took a slow sip of his coffee.

Sharyah bit the inside of her lip as her heart launched into a crazy erratic flip. She turned to concentrate on her plate but after only a moment glanced back up. He was still watching her, a serious, thoughtful tilt to his head, his pie seemingly forgotten as his gaze roamed her face.

He must be trying to decide how to word an apology. If she just let him say it she could be done with this tension between them. He would move on, and all could return to normal.

Brandon's sleepy voice broke the spell as he touched her hand. "Miss Jordan?"

Relieved to have something to distract her from those alluring blue eyes, she smiled at the boy. "Brandon! Hi. Are you hungry?" She brushed the hair back off his forehead.

"I sure am!"

She chuckled. "Well, let's go get you a plate and some food then."

"I'll help him." Jason stood. "You finish." He gestured to her still almost-full plate.

"Really, I can—"

He waved her off. "Nonsense. It's fine. Come on young man." He settled a hand at the boy's neck, but stopped by Nicki's side. "Nick, please…"

Nicki sighed and stood also. "I am being sent to bed like a little child, it seems." She lowered her brow in mock anger, but the fatigue in her stance betrayed her.

Jason touched her cheek and dropped a quick wink. "Now I know where Sawyer gets that stubborn look."

She batted his shoulder. "Oh, I do need to find Sawyer. I'll be back in a moment."

"Oh, no you don't." Jason took her elbow and halted her. "I will have Tilly bring Sawyer in just as soon as I get this young man a plate. And Haven too." He turned her gently toward the door. "Go."

"Aye! So bossy." Nicki tossed another pretend glower over her shoulder even as she complied. Jason shook his head, glancing at Sharyah with a chuckle, then took Brandon to the food table.

Sharyah couldn't hide her amusement at the exchange.

Cade didn't waste a moment as Jason walked away. "Sharyah, I need to say something to you."

She sighed. "Cade, you don't have to say anything. I know already and it's alright."

His brow furrowed. "You know what?"

Her mouth dropped open. He was going to make her say it? Fine. "Cade I know that you will never—"

Cade's face paled as his attention snagged somewhere behind her.

"What is it?" She turned to see who he was looking at, then froze.

A rider emerged from the shadow of the barn, and trotted to the corral, then swung down and looped his reins around the top pole.

Her mouth dropped open and joy welled in her heart. "It's your father." No one had seen Smith since he rode out of town the very hour of his wife's funeral.

"I can see that."

Smith Bennett stood, hands on hips, next to his mount, scanning the festivities. By the way his gaze moved methodically from one group of people to another, Sharyah could tell he was searching for a familiar face in all the hubbub.

Sharyah rose from her seat and started toward him, then paused when Cade didn't join her. "Aren't you coming?"

Cade rubbed one hand over his jaw, then finally stood and trailed after her toward his father.

Smith noticed them when they were almost to him and his eyes lit up with pleasure. "Sharyah!" He pulled her into an embrace. "How are you, girl?"

She grinned and squeezed him hard then set him at arm's

length. "I'm fine. How are you?" She arched her brows and knew by the slight tick in his jaw that he knew she meant more than just his physical well-being.

He swallowed. "I'm gonna make it." He nodded. "Gonna make it." Then his gaze transferred to his son, and Sharyah had to blink away tears as the two men stood and stared, each the spitting image of the other. Hats pushed back at a familiar angle. Hands resting on narrow hips. Even the cock of their shoulders tilted the same direction.

Smith's throat worked. And Cade's eyes held a sheen of moisture that matched his father's own, but neither man spoke. Finally Cade held out one hand. "Pa. Good to see you."

Smith took his hand and pulled him into a fierce embrace. "I'm sorry, son. I'm so sorry."

Cade swallowed hard and clapped him on the back. "You're here. All's well."

Smith, shook his head. "I shouldn't have—"

Stepping back, Cade ran one hand down his face. "You'd just had a terrible blow."

"That doesn't excuse me running off on you like that. Leaving the ranch for you to deal with all on your own."

Cade nodded his forgiveness and gripped his father's shoulders. "What are you doing here? How did you find me?"

"Looking for you. Rocky told me you were here. Said he got a telegram from you saying not to worry and that you and Sharyah were here with Jason. But there must have been some sort of trouble he hadn't heard about yet. Was there?"

"He didn't get a telegram from Sheriff Collier saying Shar had been killed?"

Smith took a step back, astonishment sending his eyebrows into his hair. "No."

Cade glanced at Sharyah, and the depth of emotion in his eyes nearly took her breath away. "Someone tried to kill her, so I got her out of town, hoping that whoever tried would think they succeeded. We just got here today about noon." He turned back to his father. "That's interesting that no one telegraphed them."

Smith nodded and rubbed his jaw. "Yes. It is."

Sharyah frowned. "Why is that so strange?"

Cade shrugged. "I'm not sure why Collier wouldn't have immediately telegraphed your family. It just seems odd." He rubbed his jaw and then hooked his hands on his hips. "I did tell him that I was leaving town, so maybe he thought I was headed to Shiloh to let them know Sharyah had passed on."

A cold shiver traversed Sharyah's spine.

Smith nodded. "Could be."

Cade looked at her the worry still lingering in his gaze. "Judge Green could also have told Collier that you were alright."

Sharyah sighed in relief. "Of course. That's probably what happened."

An awkward silence stretched for a moment. Both men shuffled their feet as though unable to think of anything to say.

Sharyah's heart went out to them. These men who had lost so much, yet neither who seemed to know how to comfort the other. "Uh, we were just eating, Smith, you must be famished. Would you care to join us?" She stretched her hand back towards the table they had just vacated.

Smith scratched the stubble on his cheek, eyeing Cade thoughtfully. He reached to adjust his hat and gave her a soft smile. "Well now, can't say I'd mind if I do."

Cade piled up a little mound of dust with one boot. "You two go on ahead. I'll take care of your horse for you Pa." Stepping past his father he gathered the reins in one hand and led the horse towards the barn.

Smith's shoulders sagged perceptibly, as though the weight of the world had just landed there.

Sharyah gave him what she hoped was an understanding smile.

"Can't say as I'm surprised, but I'd hoped things would be a little easier between the two of us."

Sharyah fiddled with the lace at her wrists. The man had ridden off within an hour after his wife's funeral and now he wanted his son to welcome him as though nothing had changed?

"I'm sure he just needs a little time. There's Jason." She pointed to her cousin just emerging from the low door of the soddy. "Why don't you go and talk to him and I'll go in and see about Cade?"

Smith sighed. For moment he eyed the door of the barn where Cade had disappeared, then with a slow nod he headed towards Jason.

Sharyah watched until her cousin exclaimed in surprise and pulled Smith into a manly hug, then with a sigh of her own she headed into the barn.

★

CHAPTER FOURTEEN

Cade jerked the cinch loose and yanked the saddle towards his chest. Marching across the room he flung the saddle onto a saddle rack against the wall, then leaned his fists into the planks and dropped his head between his arms. Fury coursed through him in trembling waves and he gritted his teeth. Six months he'd been gone. *Six months*! And now he waltzed back into his life with an apology and the hope that everything would be the same?

With a guttural cry, he sent his fist into the wall. He flinched and examined the split skin of his knuckles. No matter. The pain eased some of his frustration. He turned back towards the horse, snatching up the curry comb on his way, and began to wipe down the animal with sure swift strokes. The horse's withers flinched and he eased up the pressure.

"Sorry boy." He patted the horse on its flank. "Shouldn't be taking my frustration with him out on you."

Behind him a floorboard creaked.

He glanced over his shoulder. Sharyah stood in the soft golden glow from the lamp hanging overhead. Her eyes were large and luminous with concern. She didn't speak. Merely stood there waiting.

He returned his attention to the horse giving it a few more strokes. Finally he dropped the curry comb back on its shelf, led the horse to a stall, and forked in a pile of hay. The latch clicking shut was loud in the silence. He faced her, leaning against the gate arms folded across his chest. He didn't know what to say. He had no words. With a soft huff of breath he rubbed his chin against one shoulder and looked away.

Her skirts rustled as she stepped closer. "Cade?"

He met her gaze. "He's been gone six months, Shar." He bit his lip, hating the sound of vulnerability in his tone.

She tilted her head, her eyes softening even more. "I know." She took another step closer. "It was very hard for you when he left so suddenly, wasn't it?"

His jaw pulsed and he chided himself for even allowing that much exposure. He should be able to handle this without getting all emotional. Still... "I don't know if I can–"

Another step and she stood right by his side. Her skirts brushed against his legs, and the floral scent of her wafted up to him. He shouldn't be noticing such things at a time like this. He rubbed the back of his neck and looked down at her.

She laid one small hand on his forearm. "You can do this. Your mother would want you to forgive him."

He nodded. "I know." Her eyes were still big and full of concern as she studied his face. He allowed a small smile and tapped the end of her nose. "Don't worry about me. I'm going to be fine. His arrival just gave me a bit of a surprise, is all."

Her head tilted. "You sure?"

"Yeah." He nodded.

"Alright then. I'm just going to—" She gestured in the direction of the bunkhouse— "Head back to my room. I'll see you in the morning."

He swallowed, not wanting to lose the soothing comfort of her presence. Besides, their earlier conversation had been interrupted by the arrival of his father. She turned to go, but he grasped her hand, stilling her. "We never finished our conversation." Purposely, he laced his fingers through hers.

Her gaze darted to their hands before she asked, "O-our conversation?"

He tipped his head towards the doors enjoying the feel of her small, smooth fingers intertwined with his own. "Out at the table."

"Oh." She fidgeted, then sighed. "Cade I know that you feel – that you have—" her face paled and she tried to pull away but he tightened his grip just enough to let her know he wanted her to stay.

She gave a little huff and angled him a look.

He swallowed, allowing his thumb to caress the soft skin along the back of her hand. Her eyes, dark and full of soft emotion, drew him a step nearer. His heart knocked on the walls of his chest. She didn't know the first thing about what he was feeling.

Sharyah cringed inwardly, somehow unable to form the words that would let Cade know she understood he didn't want to hurt her. She tried again, "I know that you—"

"—You know that I've finally realized I'm in love with you?"

Her mind stuttered to a standstill and her gaze flew to his. "Excuse me?"

He tugged her closer and wrapped a tendril of her hair around his first finger. "That I must be an idiot for taking so long to recognize it, and that I don't want to live another moment without making sure you know?"

"Ah…" From somewhere far away a breathy, high-pitched squeak of disbelief rang out. Other than that, no reply made itself available. Her mind seemed to have been scrubbed clean of all thought. All thought except one. She needed space and she needed it now.

She scrambled away from him, pulling her hand free. Lifting her skirts, she made her escape toward the bunkhouse.

Jason stood, excused himself from the table, and strode over to meet the young woman who had just returned from taking the toddler and the baby into the soddy.

Smith grinned. He'd always had a niggling worry about that young man but it appeared the good Lord had changed his heart. Jason had grown into a man to ride the river with.

Smith glanced back to the barn. Sharyah had disappeared in there almost ten minutes ago and he wondered if she would have any success in talking Cade into forgiving him. He sighed. Grief was a wearisome thing. For several weeks before Bren had passed on, he'd known down deep in his heart that things didn't look good, but he hadn't been able to bring himself to discuss it with anyone, much less his son whom he could see was barely hanging onto his own sanity. Then that morning when the doc had come out, and he'd seen the look of sorrow and dread in his eyes, something inside him had simply broken open. It had taken him six months eating dust behind a herd of cattle. Six months of hardscrabble living with cowboys who resented him because he refused to drink with them, afraid that if he started, he'd never stop. Six months of running from the only place he'd ever known true happiness and still his grief rode just beneath the surface, ready at any moment, any little drop of a hat, to bubble over. But his son was all he had left. It was time. Time to face life without his beloved Bren and move on. A task he was sure to fail. But one he must attempt. He couldn't shirk it any longer.

He dropped his head toward the table and massaged the weary muscles along the back of his neck.

A plump woman, her hair streaked with the evidence of her age, stopped beside him and set a thick slice of apple pie drizzled with cream in front of him.

"I bring you coffee, Señior?"

He smiled his appreciation and nodded. "That'd be right fine, ma'am."

He watched her for a moment as she made her way toward the fire, where he could see the coffee pot keeping warm on a rock to one side, and wracked his brain trying to remember the last thing Bren had done for him. That morning she'd died, there had been a bowl of pie ingredients half mixed together still sitting on the side board in the kitchen. Neither he nor Cade had been able to bring themselves to throw it out. Now he wondered how long the bowl had sat there before someone had dealt with its contents. A soft touch to his shoulder and a steaming mug of coffee appeared next to his plate.

He nodded. "Much obliged, ma'am."

She smiled acknowledgment and turned, leaving him to his thoughts.

Movement snagged his attention. He glanced up. A young

boy, his hair a mop of dark curls, and big dark eyes full of wonder, studied him.

For a long moment he met frank appraisal with frank appraisal, and then finally the boy spoke softly. "You look like someone I know."

"That right?" Smith stuffed a bite of pie into his mouth and gestured with his fork to the bench across the table from him.

The boy obliged him and slid along the seat until he sat directly across from him. "Yes, Sir."

Smith cut the generous slice of pie in half and handed a section to the boy.

In half a second flat, the boy accepted the slice and had a quarter of it stuffed into his mouth.

"Well now, I been told a time or two I look a lot like my son, or should I say my son looks a lot like me. You wouldn't be speaking of Cade Bennett, would you?"

The boy's eyes widened. "You know Cade?" He swiped at his chin, the words barely understandable around the bite in his mouth.

Smith slurped his coffee and tried not to think how much this young man reminded him of Cade at his age. He cleared his throat. "Cade's my son. How did you come to know him?"

The boy shifted slightly, glanced both ways, and then leaned forward conspiratorially. "Well don't tell no one, but I think he's a mite sweet on my teacher."

Smith chuckled. "Is that so?" *'Bout time he wised up.* "So you're a student in Miss Jordan's class, are you?"

The boy's eyes lit with surprise. "Why, yes Sir. You sure is smart for a newcomer."

Smith winked at the boy. "A wise man learns to keep his mouth shut and his eyes open. You'd be surprised the things you can pick up when you keep quiet and just watch what's going on around you. But the truth is I've known Miss Jordan since she was a tyke younger than you are."

The boy screwed his lips over to one side and mumbled, "Bet she weren't much fun to play with when she was little."

Smith chuckled. "I think you'd be surprised." He mashed the last crumbs of the apple pie into the tines of his fork. "I recall a day when my son came home with the remains of a jelly sandwich mashed into his hair. His mother had to make him take a bath midweek."

Brandon shuddered.

Smith suppressed a grin and continued, "The story he told was he'd been helping Miss Jordan do her math when all of a sudden she up and lost her temper, slapped her sandwich on top of his head, and stormed off."

"Miss Jordan did that?"

Smith winked. "Well that was Cade's story anyway. As I recall, at the time there seemed to be some discrepancies between their accounts of the incident. But mind you, I don't think Miss Jordan would take kindly to me having told you."

The boy made a key turning motion in front of his lips, an impish gleam glittering in his eyes. "I won't say nothin'."

Smith reached over to shake the boy's hand like a man as he gave him a nod of thanks. "You wouldn't know where a man could get some shut-eye around here would you?"

With a nod back over one shoulder toward the bunkhouse, the boy stood. "We been sleepin' in the bunkhouse. There's an extra bed in there."

"Well alright then. Sounds good. Just let me get this plate and cup to the nice lady that brought them to me and I'll join you. Then you can show me where I can catch a few winks."

The boy nodded and scampered off through the last few people still milling about the yard.

Smith shook his head as he watched the lad disappear into the bunkhouse. If the last few minutes didn't take him back in time, he didn't know what would. *Ah Bren, I need you here.*

Sharyah burst out of the barn, but Cade was hot on her heels and he caught her before she'd gone five steps. His hand wrapped gently around her arm. "Shar, please, just let me have my say. Then if you want to walk away, I won't stop you."

Spinning around, she pierced him with a look. "Cascade Bennett I—" She broke off as she realized that her raised voice was drawing some attention since they were now in full view of the gathering.

He took her by the elbow and led her around the corner of the building. The sound of voice and song receded. Somewhere in the bushes a cricket chirped lustily and overhead the stars were sprinkled so thick a swath of light seemed to be spackled against the sky. Cade remained silent as she quietly studied the expanse, willing her heart back into her chest and coaxing it into a proper rhythm. But his gaze, warm and full of desire, heated her face and made all the willing and coaxing in the world a near impossible feat.

After a long moment he stepped in front of her, blocking her view of Orion's canted belt.

"You were saying?"

She shook her head. "It's not important."

The backs of his fingers grazed the curve of her cheek. His words were barely audible when he said, "Tell me."

Pulling in a shuddering breath, she closed her eyes, thrusting away the curl of fire in her belly that urged her to lean forward and lift her lips to this man, the only man she'd ever wanted. She would not make a fool of herself again. Her resolve hardened and she clenched her teeth, stepping back.

He stepped after her.

"Cade, I'm sorry, I can't—" She wet her lips. The air around them seemed thin and elusive as she took another retreating step. The wall of the barn met her, firm and unyielding.

He leaned close, arms resting on either side of her against the barn wall planks. His gaze roamed her face. "You can't what?"

Her heart pounded so hard she could hear the beat of it in her ears. Yes indeed... she couldn't what? Believe that after all the years of longing for him to notice her, he was finally standing before her with that look in his eyes? Couldn't allow her hopes to be raised only to be dashed again later when he moved on to someone else? Couldn't, *wouldn't*, be naïve enough to make herself vulnerable to him, yet again?

"I'm sorry, Cade, I just can't." Her mind scrabbled for any excuse. "I-I've got to think of Sam."

He shifted and adjusted his hat. "Sam, huh?"

"Yes." She took advantage of his movement to step around him.

But the warmth of his fingers settled around her arm and he stepped close, once again. His hand slid up over her shoulder and came to rest against the side of her neck, his thumb tracing a hot trail along her jaw line. "Listen, I can understand that this has come as a surprise. It's certainly taken me long enough to open my eyes, but Shar, I've felt this way for some time and was just too... afraid, maybe... to admit it. But last night," his voice broke and he lifted his face to study the sky for a moment before looking back at her, "last night, when I woke up and saw those flames... I knew, I *knew*, I didn't want to live the rest of my life without you."

Be strong. She forced a chuckle and patted the pocket of his shirt. Big mistake. Her hand disobeyed the order to drop back to her side. "Of course you didn't. What man would want to live without his little sister for the rest of his life?"

"Little sis—?" He caught her hand in his free one and pressed it against the beat of his heart. "Is that what you think I'm feeling for you? That couldn't be further from the truth." The hand resting at her neck slipped behind her head and, slowly but steadily, he bent toward her, his gaze never leaving hers.

She should step back. Pull away. Run for her life. "Cade, please..." The plea was ragged and thready, but she did manage to exert a little pressure against his chest.

He stilled, his face only inches from hers. "Maybe when we were kids, I did see you as a little sister. But ever since that day in the schoolhouse— You remember the day I came to apologize for whatever I'd done to make you slap me?"

Her chin dipped ever so slightly in acknowledgement. How could she ever forget that day?

"Ever since that day, I haven't been thinking of you as anything but a woman – a very beautiful one."

Her face warmed at the declaration. Still… She swallowed. "But later… at the picnic…"

He leaned down to rest his forehead against hers and for the longest time he remained silent. Finally, in a voice choked with emotion, he whispered, "I knew Ma was dying. I couldn't deal with more on that day. Then after… Pa took off, and by the time my head cleared you were gone."

She pressed her lips together. Of course she'd left town. She hadn't been able to deal with the sympathetic glances from everyone who knew her heart had always been set for Cade Bennett.

Cade's hands came up to cup each side of her face. "Shar…" His breath brushed warmth against her lips and her hand betrayed her wishes and gripped a fistful of his shirt.

Of their own volition, the fingers of her other hand slid into the curls at the base of his neck.

Footsteps crunched through the gravel in front of the barn. "Uh, Cade?" It was Jason's voice.

Sharyah jumped back, smoothing her hands over her skirt, but the sound stilled and her cousin remained just out of sight.

Cade sighed, slanting her a look that indicated the last thing he wanted to do right now was answer. Then, as though he intended to follow through on that idea, he held one finger to his lips with a quick wink, and reached out for her again.

But just that split second of time and fraction of distance had been enough to clear her head. She needed to think over the implications of his declaration before she allowed herself to fully enter into this fantasy. And she had better hang onto this reprieve – and her sanity – while she had it.

As his fingers grazed her forearms, she leapt sideways out of his reach, cocked one brow, and nodded her head toward the still unseen Jason with as stern a school-marm look as she could muster.

Smiling sheepishly, he rested his hands on trim hips and

gave her a lingering look that almost weakened her resolve, once more. "He's waiting," she mouthed.

His eyebrows winged their way upward and humor lit his blue eyes as he adjusted his Stetson. "So am I."

She couldn't stop a grin. "Answer him! We can…" She searched for a word, feeling her face heat as she thought of and discarded several. "…*talk*… more later."

Gravel crunched as Jason apparently shifted.

Cade's mouth quirked and he wrapped a strand of her hair around one finger.

Hands clenched in the smooth, soft material of her skirt, she held her breath.

After a long moment, he gave her curl a gentle tug and whispered, "I'm going to hold you to that… *talking*."

The tension left her on a little breath. She would have her time to think over his declaration.

His gaze never leaving hers, he directed a louder call toward the front of the barn. "Yes?"

"There's a man here. Claims Judge Green sent him. Says he needs to talk to you right away. Uh… Sorry to interrupt."

"Him and me both," Cade muttered for Sharyah's ears alone. "Be right back."

Sharyah waited just a moment and then followed around to the front of the barn intent on making her escape.

Cade stood across the yard with Jason and the man who'd been holding the horses for them in the forest the night before. The glimmering light from the fire highlighted the frown of concern on Cade's face. Looked like he was going to need more than just a few moments with Judge Green's man.

A sigh of relief escaped even as disappointment curled through her. She couldn't help but laugh at herself. He'd only been back in her life for a few days and already he was making her insane. She lifted her skirts and headed toward the bunkhouse. Tomorrow was another day and right now exhaustion coated her eyes with grit. A good night's sleep was what she needed before she made any decisions about Cade Bennett's proclamations.

★

CHAPTER FIFTEEN

Katrina Perry tucked her hands inside a fur muff to disguise their trembling, but she knew, by the short quirk of his lips, that Sheriff Collier had noticed. No matter. The day she'd been planning for since moving here was upon her and she wasn't going to let him have an ounce of control, no matter how condescending he came off.

Judd and his men had arrived at the clearing a little while ago and had set about building a fire and hobbling the horses. But she had insisted she and Collier stay hidden in the shadows. It was better that way. Judd didn't need to realize they'd been here waiting for several hours. Finally, when she was sure she could comport herself with calm assurance, she spoke quietly, "Wait here." Stepping slowly from the hiding place, she sauntered towards the men.

Judd saw her first. "There you are," he called. Two swift strides and he jerked her roughly against him, his breath hot and fetid as he glowered into her face. "I was about to think you'd done gone and left us in the cold."

Stay calm. "Now would I go and do something like that, Judd?" She leaned closer, pretending the vile stench of his breath had no effect on her. "You've lived too long with men you can't trust, Judd honey. Of course I wouldn't leave you out in the cold. We're in this together. And," she rested her hands on either side of his face, "I have good news."

"You better." He let her go abruptly and stalked over to the fire Billy Montell had just finished coaxing to life.

Behind her the brush rustled. She tugged one hand free of the muff and gestured impatiently for Collier to wait, then followed Judd toward the fire.

They were all there. Billy tucked his flint into the front pocket of his shirt then pulled out the makings for a smoke and set to rolling it. Red and Mick had already dragged a log over near the fire, now they both sank down onto it. Seth hadn't bothered to find something to sit on. He'd already sprawled out in the grass.

"I have the information we've been waiting on." Katrina allowed herself a moment to study each man.

Everyone glanced at her, stilling in anticipation.

She smiled softly. Talk about being the center of attention. "The diamonds will be on tomorrow's stage from Farewell Bend."

Mick and Red clasped each other's fists and bumped their chests together in a show of celebration.

"Finally!" Seth tossed his hat high in the air with a yelp of excitement.

Billy finished rolling his smoke and lit up, remaining stoic. But there was a hint of a smile about his eyes when he met her gaze a moment later.

"Alright then." Judd stepped forward to take control as she'd known he would. "We've got some plans to make. First—"

"—There's just one more thing, boys." Katrina stepped up by Judd's side. "There is someone I'd like you all to meet. And I think you'll all agree that with him on our side this job should go smooth as butter." With a flip of her wrist she indicated the general direction of the brush from which she had just emerged.

Sheriff Collier stepped into the light. "Howdy, gentlemen." He adjusted his hat.

The crackling of the fire was the only sound that followed his greeting. Katrina suppressed a smile of satisfaction. If Judd and his boys, and Collier for that matter, only knew what she had planned for them.

Cade took a step back and assessed Jonas, Judge Green's messenger. "Tomorrow's stage?"

Jonas nodded and spat a stream of tobacco into the dirt. "We can make it and still get a few hours rest if we leave right now." The man seemed more than a little irritated about missing his sleep.

"And he knows for sure that there will be an attack?"

"No." He shook his head. "It all depends on whether Miz Katrina is on the up and up, or not."

Cade rubbed the back of his neck, wanting to make sure he had his mind wrapped around the plan the judge had laid out. "So let me make sure I have this straight. Missy Green told Katrina the diamonds would be on tomorrow's stage – but they really aren't?"

Jonas nodded. "That's right. His friend, Mr. Rhodes, says he gonna wire him when the diamonds be coming, but no wire's come through. They's not supposed to come for another couple weeks, yet."

Cade smiled, beginning to like this plan more and more. "Give me ten minutes and I'll be ready to ride."

"Yes, Suh. I'll be waiting."

Cade turned and headed for the bunkhouse. He'd seen Sharyah go that way. Excitement built up inside him. Just a few more days, hours even, and this job would be done. Then they could move on and hopefully... Well, he wouldn't count his chickens before they were hatched.

Stepping into the bunkhouse, he lit the lamp.

She was in her room but he needed to let her know that he would be gone come morning. He knocked softly. "Shar?"

Brandon, who had apparently stuffed himself full of good food and then gotten sleepy again, shifted restlessly on his bunk. And he noticed that Pa had sprawled out on the top one across the room.

Cade tapped on her door again but kept his voice low. "Shar?"

Soft rustling came from inside the room. And then she appeared at the door. She rubbed her face. "Sorry. I was waiting to hear from you, but I must have fallen asleep."

He resisted a grin at the site of her disheveled curls. "Don't worry about it. Listen," he shoved his hands into his pockets, "Judge Green needs my help with something. I'll be gone for a couple days."

Was that disappointment he saw?

"Does this have something to do with catching the men who want the diamonds?"

He nodded.

She studied him. Soft concern darkened her eyes and highlighted the sleepy flush of her cheeks. "Be careful."

His thoughts turned serious. "Listen. No one knows you're here. So you should be fine. Just lay low and don't go anywhere until I get back, alright?"

Dainty fingers tucked a curl behind her ear. "You just make sure you come back." Desire warmed her dark gaze, ripping through him like flames through a dried corn silo.

He took a deep breath and stepped back, willing down his calf-kicking pulse. There was no time for this now. It would have to wait until he returned. But... He allowed a lazy grin. "Oh, you can believe I'll be coming back. I'm looking forward to finishing our *talk*."

Even in the dim light from the lamp he could see the flush that pinked her cheeks. She tried to glower, but it was mirth that lit her face just before she disappeared and her door clicked shut.

He started toward the exit, elation energizing his steps. But as he neared the bunk closest to the door, he paused, glancing back toward his father. Pa had come all this way and, at the least, deserved an explanation of why he couldn't be around for a couple days.

Cade lifted his hat and ran one hand through his hair. Indecision kept him rooted to the spot. The man had deserted him at a time when he'd needed him most. Yet... he thought of how he'd felt when he'd seen the flames engulfing Sharyah's front porch. If Pa had been feeling something akin to that, well, it was no wonder he hadn't been thinking straight.

Two quiet strides and he stood by the man who meant more to him than any other man in the world. His hair had grown a little thinner, a little lighter, and the bags under his eyes a little more pronounced. A new scar angled across his whiskered chin and Cade pitied whatever poor sap, beast or man, had put it there. A grin bloomed at that thought, even as moisture blurred his vision. Chagrin curled through him and he dashed at his eyes with the sleeve of his jacket.

Pa was alive. The months of not knowing.... He cleared the emotion out of his throat.

Pa sat up with a jolt. His Colt appeared from thin air and the cold muzzle slammed into the middle of Cade's forehead. The ratcheting of the hammer reverberated through the room.

Cade's heart lodged somewhere in the vicinity of his brain and his hands shot up on pure reflex. "Pa! It's me!"

One slow blink and then recognition dawned. Pa jerked the Colt up and away and then relaxed with an exhale of air. "What are you doing sneaking up on me like that? I might have blown your head clean off."

"Yes. I'm abundantly clear on that point." Cade rubbed at the pain throbbing from between his brows and hoped his heart would return to his chest sometime soon.

"You alright?" Pa shoved the pistol under his pillow and jumped to the ground.

"I'm fine." Cade forced his hand away from the pain and glanced at his fingers. His eyebrows shot up and the wave of pain that spiraled through his head made him wish they hadn't. "Am I bleeding?"

Pa lifted his chin and surveyed Cade's forehead. "Yep. I must have thumped you a good one. Here let me see."

Cade waved him away and stepped back. "I'll be fine. It'll quit bleeding in a minute. Ah...," he tried to remember what he'd been doing by Pa's bunk, in the first place, "I wanted to let you know that I need to be gone for a couple days. Judge Green from Beth Haven needs my help and sent a man to get me." He swiped at his forehead and examined his fingers again, then met Pa's gaze. "I didn't want to go without letting you know."

A nod tipped Pa's head to one side. "I appreciate that." A question still remained in his expression.

Cade swallowed. "I'm glad you're here, Pa."

Pa nodded again, a soft gleam easing the tense lines around his eyes. "Me too, Son. Me too."

"So…" Cade stepped toward the door, "I'll see you in a few days, then?"

"Want I should ride with you? Or would you rather I stayed here…," a mischievous humor quirked up one corner of his mouth, "…to keep an eye on a certain pretty school teacher I hear you've gone all soft on."

Cade blinked. "Wha—who?"

Pa indicated the bunk where Brandon still sprawled in sound sleep. "There's not much that young man misses, if I have him pegged correctly."

A chuckle escaped. "I'd say you have him pegged fairly well." His glance took in Sharyah's closed door and he hesitated, thinking out loud. "No one knows she's here. She should be fine. And Jason will be here with her. Why don't you come along? I might need an extra gun for this run."

Pa cleared his throat and reached casually for his hat, but Cade didn't miss the sheen of moisture he quickly blinked out of his eyes. So maybe the man had missed him a little too. He stepped out and headed toward Jason. They would both need fresh horses. It would be good to ride with Pa at his side, once more.

Her room was still dark when Sharyah bolted upright and glanced around in sleepy confusion. A knock sounded at her door and she realized that must be what had woken her.

"Just a moment," she called. She quickly scrambled into her clothes, reminded once more that the sleeve of her dress was still torn and bloody.

Wondering who could be knocking on her door at this hour, she eased it open and peered into the other room. The older ranch hand, Ron, indicated she should follow him. He crossed the room and sat on one side of Brandon whose legs draped over the front of his bunk. The other ranch hand, the younger one who was smitten with the neighbor girl, still lay on his bed. His head was propped on one hand, but weariness clouded his countenance. Jason, who was also sprawled out with his head on one hand, didn't look like he was quite awake yet, either. Smith, and of course Cade, were nowhere to be seen. Smith must have ridden with Cade, then.

Brandon hiccupped and swiped at his face, and in the dim light of the lantern she suddenly noticed the glistening rivulets of tears trailing down his cheeks.

"Brandon what's the matter?" She kept her voice low, but hurried over to the young boy and squatted down before him.

"I want my mother."

"Your mother?!" She gaped at him. "You mean to tell me— but, at the diner that morning you told Cade and I..."

"I know!" Brandon sniffed long and hard and rubbed one forearm under his nose.

His mother must be frantic with worry!

She glanced at Ron.

He arched one brow as if to say, *You're the one that brought him here, don't look at me.*

"We didn't know. He told us..." She waved that thought away and stood. "It doesn't matter. We need to get him home as soon as possible. Oh honey!" She pulled Brandon into a fierce embrace. "I'm sure your mother is just sick with worry and wondering where you are."

She paced the room massaging circles at her temples. What kind of the teacher was she? She'd taken one of her students hours across the country without his mother even knowing she had him. She spun and pierced the boy with her best brook-no-nonsense look. "Where do you live?"

One leg swung out and back as he scuffed his toe across the floor. He glanced up at her through his bangs. "Just outside of Beth Haven, a spell."

"Brandon!" Sharyah tried to keep the exasperation out of her tone but some of it filtered through anyhow. "What were you doing in town that morning eating out of Mrs. Shane's rubbish bin?"

His toe slid across the ground again. "I ran away." New tears welled up and spilled down his face, and to her surprise the boy glanced over at the bunk Smith had been on earlier. "My Pa... died..." Emotion clogged the boy's throat and he paused, swallowing hard. "I told that man earlier that he reminded me of someone. He thought I meant Mr. Cade, but it weren't. He reminded me of my Pa. And when I woke up and he was gone, I...."

Ron settled one hand at the base of the boy's neck. "Mr. Bennett went to help his son with an errand. He ain't hurt."

The boy nodded his understanding, then looked up at Sharyah, shame filling his face. "I was mad at Ma. We didn't have no gunny sacks and Ma wouldn't let me bring a pillow slip to school that day of the leaf collecting." He shrugged as if to indicate he knew it was silly now. "She hasn't been herself lately. What with needing to watch after my little sister and keep up the farm all by herself, I think she must be real tired. But I was mad..." His face crumpled again and he collapsed against Ron's chest.

"There now." Ron soothed one hand over the boy's back. "All's going to be fine. We're gonna get you home."

Sharyah thought of Cade. He'd skin her alive if she showed up back in Beth Haven, letting everyone know she was alive. But he'd only needed her to play dead until he caught the Rodale gang and whoever else might be involved. And he'd said it would all be over today. By the time she got back to town, everything should be fine.

She looked at Ron. "Would you mind saddling my horse so I can take Brandon back to Beth Haven?"

Ron glanced across the room and an unspoken message seemed to pass between him and Jason. He scratched at the white stubble beneath his chin. "Well now, that horse you rode in on the other night had come a far piece. She's got a leg that still needs restin'. I'm sure Jason and Nicki wouldn't mind lendin' you one but..." He shrugged. "There's a stage leaves Farewell Bend at nine o'clock. It makes a stop at Beth Haven 'fore goin' on to Prineville."

"Well then..." Sharyah reached out and squeezed Brandon's knee. "It looks like it's the stage for you and me at nine o'clock."

Jason flopped onto his back and scrubbed his hands over his face. "And me. But I don't have to be up to do chores for another three hours yet, so in the mean time, let's all try to get some more sleep, huh?"

CHAPTER SIXTEEN

"Cade, wake up." Pa was shaking his shoulder.

They had reached the Greens' in the wee morning hours and been shown to the guest room. Pa had taken the bed. He had collapsed in exhaustion on the room's settee. He blinked the grit out of his eyes and was embarrassed to note that sunlight lit the room in full radiance. Quickly, he swung his feet to the floor.

"Sorry to wake you. I know you've ridden hard the last few days." Pa held out a steaming mug of coffee.

Cade accepted it, gratitude coursing through him. He waved away the concern as he drew a deep drought of the black brew. "Is Green ready to go talk to Collier?"

"He and his man Jonas are just waiting for us."

Cade stood and swung his gun-belt around his hips. "I was thinking last night, there's only one place that makes sense to hold up that stage. That corner with the really deep ruts out near Powell Butte? The stage would have to slow almost to a stop to negotiate that. I think that's where it will be hit."

On the ride here the night before he'd taken time to carefully fill his father in on all the pertinent details he would need to know for today's showdown.

As they came down the stairs into the parlor where Green and Jonas waited, Cade glanced over at the judge. "First off, have you told anyone that Miss Jordan is still alive?"

The judge shook his head. "I saw no reason to. I figured the fewer who know, the safer she'd be."

A sigh of relief escaped and he realized he'd been more nervous than he'd thought, leaving her at Jason's place. "Good. Let's keep it that way." Someone still knew – whoever had taken that shot at her the other night after the fire. But he hoped they would be too busy trying to rob today's stage to be off tracking her down. Still then, why hadn't Collier wired her family to let them know of her passing? "Why didn't anyone contact her family to tell them?"

Green shrugged. "Sam told me Collier had figured you were riding there to tell them personally."

Relief eased the tension in his chest. That explained it then.

"Alright… did you inform the stage drivers of what might be happening today?"

"No." Green shrugged. "I couldn't trust the information to the wires and I didn't have another man I trusted enough to keep quiet and ride straight to the station house and let them know."

Unease at that information tensed Cade's shoulders. He prayed no one would get hurt today.

"Anyhow, Collier's waiting for you down at his office. We decided it would be best to keep knowledge of this to as few people as possible, so it will be just you, your father, me, my man Jonas here, and Collier out there today."

Cade ran his tongue along the inside of his cheek and pondered that. Judd had at least five men besides himself, and maybe a couple more, but if he, pa, and the others placed themselves strategically they shouldn't have any trouble taking them down. He'd prefer to have better odds on their side. But there was good cover out there and he could almost guess where at least two of Judd's men would be positioned. With a little luck they might find a couple more before the incident started. Still, he couldn't help wishing that Sky, Rocky, or Jason were here to help him. He'd thought about asking Jason to come the night before, but with Nicki having just had her baby girl, he'd decided against it.

Downing the last of his coffee, he handed the cup to Missy who stood to one side of the room. "Much obliged," he nodded his thanks then turned to face Green. "We're ready when you are." He lifted his hat and settled it on his head.

Green led the way to the Sheriff's office where they found

Collier whistling as he leaned over a map of the stage route between Beth Haven and Farewell Bend.

Cade introduced Pa to Collier then stepped up beside him and pointed out the rutted turn near Powell Butte. "If they are going to attack, I think that's where they will hit them."

Collier grinned. "Oh, she's definitely planning to. And you're right. That's where she's going to execute her heist alright."

Cade met Pa's slight frown of puzzlement with one of his own as he responded, "You sound like you know for sure."

If possible Collier's grin widened. "That's because I do. Gentlemen," he stretched his arms wide and spun in a circle, "I'd like to introduce you to the newest member of the Rodale gang."

Jonas smirked. "You, suh?"

"Sure as shootin'." He strode to the stove and poured himself a cup of coffee. "And get this, Katrina, that little conniver, plans to let the Rodale gang help her pull off this heist, and then wants me to arrest them all so that she and I can split the diamonds between the two of us."

Cade's eyebrows shot up into his hairline. "So Judd and his gang have no idea she's planning on backstabbing them?"

"Well," Collier tipped his head to one side and scratched his neck in thought, "Judd might be a tad suspicious, but I'd say he mostly believes her."

Cade sighed. *Poor Sam. Ever since I've known him he's been trying to reform Katrina.* Speaking of which… "Where's Sam?"

Judge Green folded his arms. "Sam asked if he could stay at our place with Missy and my wife during all this." His wave encompassed the map on the table. "Missy is going to be crushed. I haven't had the heart to tell her that Katrina betrayed her trust, yet. She really hoped Katrina would do nothing with the information she gave her. Sam figured he might be able to break the news to her easy-like. He's some broke up too, what with thinking—ah, what with the death of the teacher and all."

Over by the stove, Collier stiffened. If Cade hadn't happened to be looking right at him, he might have missed the slight tenseness that passed over the man for a split second before he glanced down at his coffee and took a lingering sip as though he hadn't a care in the world, and then moved a stack of papers from the top of his desk into the a drawer.

Cade mulled that over. Collier wasn't the brightest star in the sky, but he wasn't a dummy either. Had he tensed because he'd just figured out Shar was still alive? Or because there was something in that stack of papers he didn't want the rest of them to see?

He rubbed his jaw. He'd have to ponder on that.

And what would Sharyah think if she knew Sam's interest in Missy had reignited the moment she'd "passed on"? Would she be hurt? *Or was her stated interest in Sam merely to keep me at arm's length?* He shook off the thoughts. Now was not the time to worry over such things.

"Alright," Cade leaned over the map, "so how are we going to run this?"

Collier took a loud slurp of coffee and then plunked his cup down on one corner of the map. "So long as they all stick to their plan, Mick and Billy will be here." He tapped the map. "There are a few aspen there that will offer some cover for them. Seth should be somewhere here 'long the top of that cliff on the north side of the road. Judd is going to be here to the south of the road and Red is going to be here, on the north side."

Judge Green rubbed his jaw. "Where's Katrina going to be?"

Collier's lip tipped up. "Katrina is going to play the damsel in distress. It's her job to get the stage stopped."

The judge sighed. "If at all possible, let's try to make sure that Katrina doesn't get hurt."

Every man in the room nodded.

Cade glanced at the clock on the wall. "Stage will get to that spot around eleven?"

Collier agreed. "That's about what I figured."

"Alright then, we better get going. We go in quiet and each try to take our man silently."

Every man nodded, knowing that at the first sound of alarm, the whole gang would be on the alert.

Cade met Jonas' gaze. "You think you can manage Mick and Billy? Mick will be the one to take down. He'll be the one with blond sandy hair and the cowhide vest. Billy's a follower. You take out Mick and Billy'll belly up and cave right in."

Jonas dipped his chin, calm assurance shining from his dark eyes.

He's a man to have in your corner. Cade moved on. "Pa how about you take Seth?

Pa nodded and Cade knew he wouldn't have any trouble getting the drop on the youngest of the outlaws.

"Judge you take Red. Sheriff you take Katrina and I'll take Judd?"

Collier checked the loads in his Winchester. "Sounds good to me."

Cade was glad to hear Judd would at least somewhat be on his own out there. The man was pure venom and he had a feeling he would have his hands more than full trying to take him down quietly. Judd would be gunning for him with extra motivation because of the way he'd hauled in Mick and Red.

"Alright," Collier scanned each face, "let's move out."

Cade followed, once again praying that no one would be hurt today. But something niggled at the back of his mind. Something that didn't feel right. Something he couldn't quite put a saddle on.

Sharyah stood on the platform at the stage stop trying to ignore the woman sweeping the boardwalk in front of the mercantile who kept eyeing her torn and bloody sleeve with something akin to horror etching her face. She shifted and rested her hand over the tear, hoping the move looked unintentional. The woman obviously had never had all her possessions burned up and her only remaining dress shot through with a hole, all in the same night. *Not to mention my arm.* That thought nearly brought a chuckle and she caught herself just in time. The woman would be summoning the nearest asylum attendant, if she wasn't careful.

Beside her Brandon shifted uneasily.

"Just a few more hours, Brandon."

He squirmed again, glancing up at her through the mop of his bangs. "Ma's gonna be some sore at me."

Some? "Yes. I imagine she will be. But first she is going to be beside herself with joy to know you are well and safe."

His lips tugged over to one side of his face. "I shouldn't o' run off."

"No. You shouldn't. But she will forgive you. Mother's always do."

Jason stepped up beside her holding three tickets and for the third time that morning she said, "You really don't have to come with us. We'll be fine."

"Won't take me more than a day to make sure you get home safe, and I wouldn't want to have to face Cade if I let you go off without an escort. Besides," he grinned at her, "what are cousins for?"

"What do you mean you wouldn't want to face—" Her cheeks heated up like a cast-iron griddle and she decided she'd rather not pursue that conversation, after all. "—oh, never mind."

Jason grinned full-out and crossed his arms. But he was gentleman enough not to embarrass her with further comment.

Brandon, however, held no such compunctions. "I do think Mr. Cade's some sweet on you, Miss Jordan."

"Do you, now? Oh look, here comes the stage." She snatched up her skirts and stepped to the edge of the platform, leaving the two annoyingly male individuals grinning at each other like goats in a kitchen garden.

The arriving passengers disembarked and Jason had his hand on her elbow, ready to help her to the first step, when a horse galloped around the corner of the farthest building down the street.

Jason's hand tightened and they paused to see what the commotion was about.

The lathered horse, flecks of foam spurting from its sides with each stride, slid to a stop only feet away, sides heaving. The rider relaxed visibly when he noticed the stage driver seemed more interested in learning his business than getting the stage off on time. He pulled a bandana from his shirt pocket and mopped his face, then swung down.

"Boy," he gestured Brandon over to him, "you walk this horse for me. Just for a few minutes, until I complete my business with the stage driver here. He's a good horse and I don't want him ruined because he cooled down too quick after such a long hard run."

Brandon glanced at Sharyah for permission and she nodded. "Just take him down to the end of the street and back."

"Walk him at a good clip, son." Jason clapped the boy on the shoulder.

The rider handed the reins to Brandon with a tired smile. "Thanks, lad. I'll make it worth your time." Then, as Brandon led the horse back the way it had just come, the rider turned to the stage driver. "Can I have a moment of your time before you make the next run?"

The driver shrugged. "Don't suppose a few more minutes will make much difference one way or another."

The rider scrubbed the bandana over his face and neck once more. "You have any room on there for one more passenger?"

The driver cast him a skeptical look.

"Oh, don't worry. I'm a paying customer." The man smiled. "I have to get to Beth Haven and I've had nothing but trouble trying to get there."

At the mention of money, the stage driver perked right up. "If you're paying, we got room."

"Good then. Can you give me thirty minutes to cool down my horse, stable it, and send a telegram?"

The driver turned to glance at them. "You have any problems with that?"

Sharyah looked at Jason. They really should get Brandon home as quickly as possible.

Jason hooked his thumbs into his belt buckle. "He's already been gone for several days. I don't presume a few more minutes will hurt anything."

She fiddled with the strap of her reticule. "You're right, I suppose."

Jason nodded their consent.

Returning his focus to the rider, the driver said, "You got thirty minutes."

"Much obliged." The man tipped his hat and strode off toward Brandon to gather his horse.

Jason escorted Sharyah and Brandon into the local boarding house where she fidgeted through a second cup of coffee and Brandon had a warm doughnut. Sharyah kept thinking of Brandon's poor mother. Every minute they remained away, was another minute she would be worrying over her missing son. But, true to his word, thirty minutes later the rider was back and everyone climbed aboard the stage.

The driver cracked his whip with a shouted, "Gid'up!" and the coach lurched into motion.

Sharyah and Brandon, occupied one seat, while Jason and the rider occupied the facing one.

After a moment the rider held his hand out to Jason. "Name's Baylor. James Baylor."

"Jordan." Jason clasped his hand. "Jason Jordan." He gestured across the coach. "This is my cousin, Miss Sharyah Jordan, and her charge Brandon McBride."

"How do?" The man shook Brandon's hand as if he were an equal gentleman, then touched one finger to his hat brim and nodded at her. "Ma'am."

Sharyah smiled her reply, liking him immediately.

They made small talk for over an hour and they had almost reached the beautiful vista of Powell Butte when Jason finally asked the man, "What brings you out this way?"

Baylor shrugged. "I'm a courier on a delivery errand. "I work for a man who has a friend that lives in Beth Haven. My boss has me delivering a… well, a package to him."

Sharyah stiffened and took a calming breath.

Collier walked out of the jail office with the group, his rifle held in one hand. Too bad he'd made that little slip up – tensing when he'd noticed the telegrams plainly visible on his desk. Cade had been looking right at him. Hopefully, Cade thought his surprise had something to do with the judge's slip about Miss Jordan's well-being. Cade, after all, didn't know that he was the one who'd narrowly missed cutting the lovely Miss Jordan out of the picture for good. Well, in the end her escape into the judge's house hadn't mattered. Apparently the girl hadn't seen enough of the letter to do any damage. And Cade taking her out of town had really been an advantage.

He sniffed and scanned the street. At least he didn't have her death on his conscience.

One worry niggled at the back of his mind. Why hadn't Bennett and Green confided in him of the girl's safety? Were they doubting his loyalty?

He shoved the thought aside. No. They were probably just playing their cards close to their chests.

The judge didn't even know his diamonds would be on that stage today. Providence had made sure of that when he'd intercepted a telegram that had come through for Judge Green.

It had been quite by accident, really. He'd been strolling by the telegraph office, when Earl had gimped out with a message to deliver to Judge Green. Collier had been headed to meet the judge anyhow, and had said he'd be happy to deliver the telegram. He hadn't planned on reading it. But curiosity had gotten the better of him and he'd never been more happy that he decided to give into that curiosity, than now.

The telegram had stated that the judge's diamonds would arrive earlier than he expected on one of this week's stages from Farewell Bend and further details would be forthcoming. It had been the easiest thing in the world to simply slip that message into his pocket and neglect to give it to the judge. The next step had been to butter ol' Earl up some and commiserate about his bum leg, torn and irreparably damaged during the War Between the States. He'd said there was no need for Earl to walk the messages all the way to the Greens' place. Just to bring them on by the sheriff's office and he would take care of delivering them for him. Earl's leg gave him a sight of pain and he'd been more than happy to agree to that arrangement.

And it was a good thing they'd made the agreement when they had, because the very next day the telegram had come in saying that the courier was on his way and that he would send a wire from Farewell Bend on the day he was to arrive.

Only moments before Green and Bennett stepped into his office, Earl had delivered a telegram stating that the man was on his way and should be here by early afternoon.

Yes. He held in a whoop of triumph. All was falling into place.

Katrina didn't know that he was bringing half the best guns in town to her little party. And the judge didn't know that his diamonds really were in danger of being stolen. And no one suspected that he of all people planned to make off with the whole shooting match.

They would get the drop on Katrina and her gang, give them the sad news that the diamonds weren't even on the stage, and haul them off to their respective hangings.

Only he and the courier would know the diamonds really were there, and the courier wouldn't live long enough to spill that information. In all the chaos, and with Cade and his men sure to be caught off guard by his false information, it wouldn't be suspect at all for the man to end up shot. Then he would pocket the diamonds, but only after arresting Katrina and all her compatriots, leaving Green, Bennett, and the rest thinking he was still on the up and up. Then he planned to get out of town while the getting was good.

He was careful to keep any expression off his face, but on the inside he was smiling. Oh he was smiling to beat the band. He had no doubt Cade and his men would eventually gain the upper hand. They'd all make the arrests then he could light a shuck out of town with no one the wiser.

All his planning was finally coming to fruition. Yes sirree. He would soon be a very rich man with a future stretching out before him full of infinite possibilities.

They mounted up and trotted their horses out of town but they'd only gone a couple miles when Bennett's father pulled to a stop and gestured for all of them to do the same.

"I've been pondering on the best way to keep everyone safe today," he said. "Coordinating each attack without some central signal will be too difficult and would likely result in one party or another of the outlaw gang, being alerted that their plans aren't going as scheduled. Seems to me that as soon as the stage gets near enough that we're sure all their attention is fixed on it, that would be the time to make our move. The stage should still be far enough away that none of the passengers, or the driver for that matter, should come to injury from a bullet, but still be close enough to offer a little distraction. And like we've already said, we need to strike unanimously, so it seems the best way would be for Collier here to be the signal for the rest of us. When he steps out to take down Katrina, that's when we strike all at once. She will need to be in the road before the stage comes into view to keep the driver from getting suspicious, not to mention barreling right on by her. When Collier confronts her, all of the outlaws will have their attention fixed on her at that moment, for just a split second, all of them will be surprised and it will give us the best shot at safety, both for us and for the stage passengers."

Collier cursed silently. He *needed* the stage to be within shooting range for his plan to work. But to express descent would draw suspicion. He couldn't have that – at least not too soon. First they had to take out Katrina and the Rodales for him.

There was only one way to handle this, then. He'd hoped to keep up the ruse of honesty all the way until he lit out of town, but… Well, he'd just have to travel a little farther and be a little more careful in the long run.

He leaned over and spat on the ground then forced himself to grin at the men gathered around him. "Ya'll just be sure you don't leave me out there, exposed and vulnerable, for too long, ya hear?"

As they all rode out once more, under his breath he cussed them all soundly for the do-gooders they were.

Chapter Seventeen

Sam Perry crushed the brim of his bowler in one hand as he waited on the Greens' front porch for someone to answer the door.

When Missy herself opened the door, he thought his heart might stop on the spot.

"Sam?" She glanced past him, as though expecting he would be with someone else.

"It's just me. May I…" He cleared his throat. "May I come in?"

"Of course. Papa isn't here right now." She didn't move out of the way.

"Yes. I know. He asked me to come, actually."

"Oh."

Was that disappointment he heard in her tone? His heart thudded out renewed hope.

"I wanted to come, though. I mean I had a choice to be somewhere else or to be here and I chose… well, here." He gestured inside with his hat. "May I…?"

Blushing, she stepped back. "Of course. Yes. Do. The parlor is…" Her hands fluttered toward the settee he could just see through the door. "But then you already know that. Ahh," she hoisted her skirts and fled the room calling over her shoulder, "I'll just get us some tea."

Sam hooked his hat on the tree and only stood for one moment of indecision. Then he followed her toward the kitchen. Forget this dancing-around-the-subject business. He'd let her put him off for far too long. And heaven knew that he'd tried to forget her. It simply wasn't going to happen. They needed to have this out and have it now.

He pushed open the kitchen door and stepped inside.

She squeaked in surprise and dropped a teacup. It shattered at her feet.

Ignoring the mess, he stepped over it and took her hand, brushing the softness of her cheek with the tips of his fingers.

Her jaw dropped slightly, but she seemed paralyzed and didn't try to pull away as he'd feared she would.

"Missy..." Sam closed his eyes and inhaled long and slow, savoring the familiar scent of her lavender toilet water. Leaning forward he pressed his forehead to hers.

"S-sam, we can't..." She swallowed hard.

He eased back a fraction and cupped her cheek. "Why can't we?"

"I'm ru-ruined. It can never work." She didn't meet his gaze.

Anger surged through him toward the man who had robbed so much from them. "You are *not* ruined." He gentled his tone and thumbed the tears from her cheeks, lowering his head until she finally looked at him. "Hasn't enough been stolen from you? From us? Don't let him steal anything more."

Tears welled up and spilled down her cheeks. "You deserve so much better."

He shook his head. "That's not true. If anything I don't deserve even the half of you. I'm so sorry, I never should have...left. Not when you needed me the most."

Missy stiffened and jerked away from him. "Wait! Are you here because you think Sharyah is dead?" Sam started to shake his head, but Missy forged on. "Because she's not, you know. Someone tried to kill her but Mr. Bennett helped her escape."

Sam's eyebrows shot up. "She's not dead? That's great news!"

Resignation filled Missy's face. "I knew—"

Sam's fingers against her lips cut off her words. "I don't want her. All the time with her only made me long all the more for you."

"Really?"

"Yes."

"Sam, I don't know." Her face crumpled and she folded her arms tight against herself.

"Shhhhh." He pulled her head down against his chest. "We'll just take one day at a time. Alright?"

She made no response for the longest time, then finally her arms slipped around him.

Gratification released his pent up tension on a breath. "That's my girl." He kissed the top of her head as she sobbed against his shirt. But he knew these were healing tears. Tears that had needed to fall for a long time. He closed his eyes and rested his cheek atop her curls, thanking God for giving him the courage to do what he'd been longing to do since the day of her attack.

As he stood there, he realized he still needed to tell her about Kat. It would be another blow. But, together, they would make it through this.

He lifted a glance toward the ceiling. *Thank you, Lord.*

Cade belly-crawled along the ground, rifle in one hand, careful to keep from crushing any twigs that might snap under his weight, or brushing up against any of the sage brush that grew freely across the hillside. He didn't want to alert Rodale that he was only yards from him.

He'd left his horse ground hitched a ways back, knowing the well-trained steed would come trotting the moment he whistled for it.

The scent of Judd's cigarette came to him now, so he was closer than he'd thought. He stretched out behind a length of bunch grass and stilled, breathing shallowly. From here, on the knoll just south of the road, he could see one of Judd's boots, and had a fairly good view of the path the stage would come on from Farewell Bend.

He should have no problem seeing Collier's signal for attack when he confronted Katrina after she stepped out into the open.

Judging from the angle of the sun, the stage should be rolling through any moment now. All he had to do was hunker down, keep quiet, and wait.

When fifteen minutes went by and the stage wasn't even a

speck of dust on the horizon yet, he hoped Green, Collier and Jonas would hold their positions and not do anything stupid before the right time. He wasn't worried about Pa. That man had more patience than an old maid had wrinkles.

The minutes crawled by. The high desert in September was still warm in the middle of the day and the sun glowered unmercifully. Sweat trickled down his temples and he would have loved nothing more than to remove his hat and swipe it away, but any movement this close to his quarry might alert him to his presence. His one consolation was that Judd had to be just as hot as he was.

He worked his tongue over his lips, tried to swallow, and realized his mouth was bone dry. Moving as little as possible he picked up a small pebble, polished the dust off with his thumb, and then put it into his mouth. His tongue immediately moistened up. He'd almost forgotten about the old trick he'd learned from Uncle Sean when they'd been tracking a horse thief down in the Deschutes canyon one day.

Thirst somewhat abated, he occupied his mind with more pleasant thoughts. And there was one pleasant topic his mind couldn't seem to keep away from lately – Miss Sharyah Dawn Jordan.

He remembered the disbelief in her eyes when she'd recognized him as one of her captors in the schoolhouse, the shaking of her small hands when he'd unwound the cord he'd inadvertently wrapped too tight. The way she'd trembled when he'd stepped between her and Mick Rodale in the field.

His hand fisted. He should have done better by her. Even later...

Her blond curls, wet and cascading all around her, eyes wild with fright, the night of the fire. Then there was the close call with the bullet.

If ever there was a moment he'd nearly gone off his senses, that had been it. He'd been a fool to leave her alone for even those few seconds when such danger dogged her. The sound of her gasping for breath, alive and well with only a scratch, afterwards, had been the only thing that kept his sanity intact.

A quiver of unease traversed his spine. He'd gone off and left her, once again. Was she truly safe? He forced away the worry. Tucked safely miles away, there was no chance of her getting hurt today. Anyone who wanted to harm her would be right here.

He'd never known a woman could make his knees weak, until last night. The feel of her pulse dancing beneath his thumb, when he'd almost kissed her…. The way her blush magnified her dark eyes, when he teased her about the *talk* they needed to finish….

He smirked. *You've got it bad, Bennett.*

He suddenly realized he'd been watching a cloud of dust grow bigger as it came toward them on the horizon. The stage was late, but it jounced toward them at a steady pace.

Alert and ready for action, he flexed his hand on the grip of his rifle, tension coiling every muscle in his body.

Movement in the road just below caught his attention. Katrina. Leading a horse from the brush with a bloody bandage wrapped around its leg. But the animal wasn't limping, so the bandage was most likely just part of the ruse.

Collier should be taking out Katrina any moment now. Just like they'd all agreed.

He scanned the brush, but Collier was doing a good job keeping out of sight from those on the hills above him.

Cade could see the stage driver now. And the scabbard by his side held a rifle. At least he had that.

How many passengers would be on board? He hoped they would have sense enough to keep their heads down when all the ruckus started. If they came much closer it would be too late to ensure their safety.

Cade spat out the pebble and licked his lips. Where was the man? He had to start the whole thing. He should have taken Katrina several minutes earlier. *Come on, Collier!* He scanned the brush again.

Still nothing. Something wasn't right.

The curtain at one of the coach windows pulled to one side and a blond woman stuck her head out to peer ahead.

He blinked and looked again. *Sharyah!* He would recognize those blond curls topped by that little green hat anywhere.

His heart forgot to beat for a full three seconds, and then he leapt to his feet even though Collier hadn't initiated the attack yet.

What was she doing here!?

He snugged his rifle into his shoulder and sighted in on Judd. "Rodale, put your hands up where I can see them!"

"Judd! Look out!"

Mick? Cade started to turn. Heard three pounding footsteps and then a body slammed into him and pain burst to life in his skull. He grunted and slumped forward, losing his grip on the rifle. It clattered into the brush at his feet.

Mick's momentum carried him off balance and he stumbled two steps sideways. Cade thrust the heel of one boot into a high kick that connected with Mick's chin. The outlaw's head snapped back, his eyes rolled up into his head, and he slumped to the ground.

Hadn't Collier said Mick would be across the ravine with Billy?

Cade shook his head to dispel the encroaching blackness. *Judd...*He needed to move. Now!

Leaving his rifle where it lay, he shucked his Smith and Wesson Safety Revolver, and headed in a full out sprint toward Judd. This was going to be a job that required close quarters.

"Whoa!" The stage driver's call to the horses as he neared the sharp, rutted corner sounded as clear through the desert air as if the man had been standing only a few feet away.

Judd had already leapt to his feet. Now his hand descended toward his Colt, his eyes alert but still wide with surprise.

Cade let loose with a bird call he hoped Pa would recognize as a distress signal, and then kicked one foot toward Judd's gunhand. He could just shoot, but he wanted to take him alive.

The man was fast for a person so large and he managed to twist to one side at the last second.

Seeing that his boot was going to miss its target, Cade landed on the balls of his feet and spun in a roundhouse to plunge his fist with all his might into the soft spot at the base of the man's sternum.

With a whuff of air rushing from his lungs, Judd brought his Colt to bear.

Lord! It was the only prayer Cade could come up with as he slapped the gun sideways.

It discharged.

A white hot shard of flame grazed along his ribs. A grunt of agony burst forth. But at least he'd managed to knock the gun loose.

It flew into the brush beside them.

Another blast echoed from across the canyon.

In the moments where Cade's concentration honed in on the pain, Judd kicked out, and connected with his wrist. Numbing tingles paralyzed his grip and one more kick from Judd sent his revolver end over end down the hill.

It didn't appear Judd had another weapon. So they would settle this man to man now.

Behind them, Mick moaned and brush rustled.

One at a time. And Judd was the one to take out first.

Cade smashed his fist into Rodale's face, but Judd's hands wrapped around Cade's throat, and the punch jounced harmlessly off his cheek.

Cade tried to pull in a lungful of air, to no avail. He thrust his arms up between Judd's and gave a swift jerk to the sides, breaking Judd's hold. He gasped for breath, knowing he only had moments before Judd came at him again. He touched his side. His hand came away sticky and red with blood. Wincing, he swung out one boot and heard a satisfying crunch when heel connected with knee cap.

Judd screamed, but didn't go down. If anything, he grew angrier. "I'm gonna kill you, Schilling!" He limped a step forward and swung a sledge-hammer fist with all his might.

Cade dodged inside. Let loose with two quick jabs to Judd's brisket. Danced back. "The name's Bennett." If it came down to a sheer slug-fest, he could take Judd on speed alone – so long as he didn't lose too much blood.

What was going on with the others? He'd only heard one shot. Other than the one Judd had almost bought him a ticket to eternity with.

Judd swung again, and again Cade dodged inside.

Snatching him close, Judd caught him to his chest in a mighty bear hug and Cade realized his mistake.

Set on squeezing the life from him, Judd trembled with the crushing force he exerted around Cade's ribcage.

Face buried in Judd's chest, arms pinned to his sides, and unable to breathe, panic nearly set in. But then he remembered Judd's knee. He pulled his leg back as far as he could and smashed his own knee into Judd's.

Judd hissed and his grip loosened just enough for Cade to gasp for a lungful of air. He snapped his head back, then smashed it forward into Judd's nose.

Blood spurted and the man instinctively let loose to grab at his face. Still heaving for breath, Cade stepped back, planted one boot in the middle of Judd's chest, and kicked him away.

Judd tripped over a low growing sage shrub and sprawled flat on his back. Then his hand came up with his Colt.

Sharyah's heart beat from the region of her throat. Somehow she had a sinking suspicion, based on Mr. Baylor's reluctance to reveal details about the package he was delivering, that it must be very valuable – diamonds were very valuable. James Baylor was delivering his package to Judge Green!

But she needed to be sure. "Are you delivering diamonds to Judge Green?"

The man blinked, taken aback. He glanced from Sharyah to Jason, his hand settling on the stock of his pistol. "How do you know that?"

Jason showed the man his palms. "We don't mean you any harm. Just take it easy." Facing her, he questioned, "What is it?"

Sharyah ignored the question, as she wracked her brain. Cade had ridden off the night before saying he was going to deal with a situation for Judge Green that had something to do with the diamonds. Katrina Perry had tried to have her killed simply over the fact that she'd seen a letter about these diamonds.

Where the diamonds were, Katrina and the Rodale Gang were sure to be close by.

She leaned over to peer out the coach's south-facing window. Powell Butte had been visible off in the distance for the past half hour or so. She leaned further out the window to get a better look at what lay ahead. Another low knoll rose just to the south of where the road turned sharply east. They were about to head into a narrow canyon of sorts between the butte and the knoll.

The perfect place for an ambush!

As soon as that thought registered the stage driver hollered, "Whoa!" and they slowed to take a sharp, rutted, bone-jarring turn.

She jerked her head back through the window and swallowed hard. Bracing her feet, she gripped the seat to keep from sliding forward. Her pulse raced so fast she could hear the thrum of it in her ears, even over the jangle of the trace chains, the jouncing carriage's groans of protest, and the crunching dirt. "Jason, I think we are in for some trouble."

It was then that the distinct echoing report of a gunshot blasted through the air!

Smith took another cautious step toward Seth Rodale, who was on his belly under a clump of brush, his rifle aimed down to where the stage would momentarily arrive.

The Sheriff was sure taking his sweet time calling out the woman.

From up on the hillside where Cade would be, Smith heard the warbling bird-call he and Cade had practiced so much when Cade was a lad.

That boy! Never did have the patience God gave a squirrel.

Well, he'd better take Seth out, before the man realized what was going on.

Apparently Cade's warning hadn't alerted him. Seth, his back to him, remained focused on Katrina in the ravine below.

Smith shucked his gun and said quietly, "Don't move. I've got you in my sights and one twitch of a muscle will be your last."

Seth tensed up but did the smart thing and didn't move.

From up on the hillside a gun-shot sounded, and Smith jolted a glance that way. He thought his heart might stop. The blast had been too loud for Cade's Smith and Wesson. *Lord, please…*

Forcing himself not to panic, he snapped his attention back to the man before him. Keeping his gun trained on Seth, he stepped up behind him. "Just toss your weapon over the edge."

The man hesitated, slow to follow orders.

"You just keep on thinking, young Mr. Rodale. You think mighty hard about what the fires of hell might feel like. My guess is, if you keep on the way you are, you'll be finding out here pretty quick."

Rodale grunted and tossed his gun over the edge.

"Good thinking. Now with two fingers you reach into your boot and pull out your back-up piece."

He complied.

"Toss it."

He did.

"Much obliged. Now…" Smith pulled a length of rawhide from his vest pocket. "Let's truss you up good and tight, like a calf at a branding." Another gunshot rent the air. This time from across the canyon where Jonas should be.

A few moments later, the man bound hand and foot, Smith squatted next to him. "Which of you was up the hillside there?"

Seth only glowered at him.

Smith slipped the tip of his knife against the young man's chin and raised his eyebrows.

Fear widened the boy's eyes. "Judd and Mick."

"Only them? I thought Montell was supposed to be over there too?"

"Plans changed at the last minute. How did you know that, anyway?"

Smith narrowed his eyes in thought.

"I ain't lyin'!" Seth cursed him.

"Where's Montell?"

"I already said more than I ought."

Smith allowed the point of the knife to bite a little more deeply.

And it only took that little urging for the boy to indicate the near side of the canyon to the southwest with nod of his head.

Unease clenched Smith's fists. That was the direction Judge Green had taken. And he wouldn't be expecting a second man.

Smith shoved the knife back into its sheath and tied his bandana around Seth's mouth to keep him quiet. After securing him to a tree where he would be well-shaded until he could return for him, Smith turned to the right and crept forward.

It took fifteen minutes to find Judge Green, but when he did there was no doubt that the man would be some laid up for quite a bit of time.

Green lay face-down in the blazing sun, a gash the length of a man's little finger splitting the hair along the back of his head and oozing blood into a caked matt. The only thing to indicate he still lived was an occasional moan.

Much as he wanted to, Smith didn't approach the man right away. Instead he circled him, needing to make sure he hadn't been left there as bait for a trap. Only when he found two sets of fresh footprints leading away into the canyon did he feel safe to approach the judge.

Smith stripped off his shirt and laid it out so that when he turned the man over dirt wouldn't get into the cut. "Judge," he grabbed the man by the shoulder, "I'm going to turn you over now."

The judge cringed but was alert enough to help, and Smith dribbled a trickle from his canteen into the man's mouth.

Green moaned. "Thanks." The word rasped out in a whisper. "He got the drop on me."

"Were there two of them?"

Green wet his lips and Smith gave him a little more to drink. "I think so. I was talking to Red, and something hit me from behind."

"Alright, listen. I think Cade's in trouble. I'm going to have to leave you here for a bit. First, let's get you to that shade over there. Think you can make it?" He tipped his head toward a juniper a few paces away and started to help the man up.

That's when he felt the press of cold metal against his neck.

"I think we ought to leave the judge lay right there where we left him. Let's you and me take a trip down to see your boy. What do you say?"

Disgusted with himself for giving his full attention to the injured man instead of his surroundings, Smith lifted his hands wide.

How had he not heard footsteps?

The man behind him chuckled. "I might be a big fellow, but I've learned a thing or two about walking quietly."

"Appears that way." Smith left his canteen lying in the dirt next to Green. At the moment it was all the help he could give the man.

"Come on, Billy, let's you, me and this hombre here go on down and join the party." His assailant leaned forward to peer at Green. "I don't imagine the judge there will be much of a problem to us."

A second man a little further away guffawed. "Nope, I gave him a good whack."

Red spat to one side. "Let's move."

Discouragement weighed heavy on Smith's shoulders as he led the way, hands held up, down the steep trail into the canyon below.

What were they all going to do now?

Chapter Eighteen

Hands lifted and his heart kicking like a bucking bronc in his chest, Cade fully expected to be passing through the gates of eternity at any moment.

A snarl lifted Judd's lip. "Not so tough now that you have a gun in your face, are you?"

Cade held his silence, not wanting to offer any fuel to the man's temper. He pulled in a slow, steady breath.

Judd clambered to his feet, never turning his cold calculating gaze away.

Cade swallowed. Wondered how long he had left on this earth. Strained to hear if anything was happening with the stage coach in the ravine below.

Where was Sharyah? And why on earth had she been on that stage?

Judd spat and swiped at the blood coating his upper lip. "Got to say I'm actually a sight glad to run into you. We Rodales got a bit of a beef to settle with you. But I think I'll let Mick have the pleasure." He gestured with the gun to where Mick was still sprawled out on the ground, his mouth thinning into a grim line. "He better be alright."

Gun and eyes still trained on Cade, Judd squatted by Mick and jostled him. "Mick. Shake it off. Wake up."

Mick moaned, his head rolling from side to side.

Cade analyzed his chances of taking Judd while he was preoccupied. But decided against it. The man still hadn't looked away, and Cade didn't want to buck the odds that he'd be able to dodge another bullet.

After a few moments, Judd was finally able to get Mick onto his feet.

A narrow path led down the hill into the canyon. Judd pointed to it with the barrel of his pistol. "You first."

Air eased through Cade's lips. So he had at least a few minutes to come up with another plan. He started down the trail, with Judd, supporting Mick with one arm, only a pace behind him. The descent was steep. Pebbles rolled over under his feet.

Behind him, Mick's boots scrabbled over the ground as he slipped. Judd caught him and held him up. He swore. "Slow down, Schilling!"

Cade didn't bother to correct him a second time.

They reached a hair-pin turn on a point jutting out into the canyon. Below them, Katrina still stood in the middle of the road.

Why hadn't Collier taken her our yet? Where was he?

Katrina bent over her horse's leg examining it.

The lead team from the stage trotted into view, going considerably slower since they were just coming out of the turn into the canyon. It was only a moment before the driver saw her.

"Whoa!" The driver pulled back hard on the reins and the coach jolted to a stop. "Lady are you crazy?!"

Katrina stood and spun to face him, sunlight glinting off the barrel of a pistol in her hand.

Judd prodded Cade's spine. "Keep moving."

The last thing he saw before the path turned was the driver shoving his hands toward the sky.

Cade licked his lips, his mind scrambling to make sense of the circumstances.

Collier hadn't done his part. That meant he'd probably been taken out by one of Judd's men. Maybe that other shot he'd heard. Unless… What if Collier was working *with* Katrina and Judd? That would make sense with the fact that he'd given them faulty information about where all the outlaws would be positioned.

The thought so stunned him that he stopped in his tracks.

Judd crashed into him from behind and nearly lost his grip on Mick. He cursed and gave him a shove. "I said, keep moving!"

Cade stumbled forward. It couldn't be could it?

The path leveled out as they stepped onto the canyon floor

and skirted around the last boulder that blocked their view of the stage and Katrina.

"Put your gun down!"

That was Collier's voice. So he wasn't dead.

Relief eased through him. Maybe all was not lost.

"Whoa!" The stage driver called and the stage jolted to a halt. "Lady are you crazy?!"

Lady? It had to be Katrina! Dread shimmied down Sharyah's spine. She peered out the window but her side of the stage was angled away from whoever the driver had spoken to.

She gripped Brandon's arm. "You keep your head down and do as you're told. Everything is going to be fine."

Oh how she wished she could believe those words.

Both Mr. Baylor and Jason had their pistols out now.

Sharyah snatched up her reticule and shoved her hand inside to pull out her own derringer. Then she heard a ratcheting hammer, and froze. The coach door jerked open.

Heart stuttering somewhere between beating too fast and not beating at all, she glanced up. *Collier!* A puff of relief rushed from her lungs and she relaxed against the seat.

He had had his gun leveled at Mr. Baylor's chest but both Jason and Mr. Baylor tilted their guns toward the roof as soon as they saw Collier's badge.

"Sheriff, thank—"

"Put your gun down!" Collier yelled.

Confusion swirled through her. What threat did Collier see? Neither Mr. Baylor nor Jason had their guns pointed at him.

Something hardened in Collier's gaze and a muscle twitched at the corner of his eye.

A prickle of premonition raised bumps on her arms.

"I said, guns down."

The men dropped their guns onto the floor of the carriage, in compliance.

She leaned forward. Something wasn't right. The Sheriff must be confused. "Sheriff this is Mr. Baylor and my cousin Mr. Jordan. I don't think we have anything to fear from them."

"Miz Jordan…" Sheriff Collier grinned, but it didn't reach his eyes. "I'm just not the man you think I am."

A cold chill gripped her. He wasn't here to help them!

He glanced toward the road. "Miz Katrina, you want them down there with you? Or just leave 'em inside?"

So Katrina *was* here.

Jason spoke, low and reassuring. "Everything is going to be fine, Shar."

But Sharyah noted the grim glint of anxiety in his gaze.

"Collier!" Katrina cursed him soundly. "It's about time you showed your face! I could have been shot!" She paused for only a second before adding, "Out here in the road where we can keep them all in sight."

"Alright you heard her." The sheriff jerked his head toward Katrina's voice. "Everybody out of the stage, now! Driver, you come down nice and easy. And if your hand even goes anywhere near that rifle you'll be eating lead." He backed away a step, his tongue flicking out to moisten his lips even as his gaze darted back and forth between each group. "Move! I said everybody out!"

Baylor jumped down first, followed by Jason who turned to help them down. Sharyah let Brandon go first, then took Jason's hand, clutching her reticule and praying Collier wouldn't demand she leave it behind. Her Derringer only had two bullets, but they might come in handy in the next few moments.

Footsteps crunched over gravel in the roadway. Judd Rodale stepped into sight.

Where he is, Mick won't be far away. Her stomach rolled.

Judd was holding onto the arm of someone she couldn't quite see yet. "Collier, you didn't happen to know anything about Schilling, here, skulking around, did you?"

Schilling? Sharyah froze. Held her breath. Fear threatened to paralyze all thought.

Judd pulled his prisoner into sight.

Cade! She gasped.

He stood in the road, hat pushed back on his head, and hands lifted at shoulder height, somehow looking relaxed and confident. He gave her a quick wink and a little nod, as if to assure her everything was going to be just fine. Judd shoved him further into the road ahead of the lead horses.

Blood soaked one side of Cade's shirt, and still glistened wet in the sunlight. *He's been shot!*

Sharyah gritted her teeth, refusing the tears that begged for release, and folded her arms against the trembling that shook her. And he still had a gun to his back!

Katrina strolled down the line of captives, giving them each a once over and now her parasol blocked Cade from sight. She jolted to a stop in front of Sharyah with a gasp. "You! But—I thought—"

Sharyah pressed her mouth into a grim line. "Surprised to see me alive, I take it?" Come to think of it, Sheriff Collier hadn't batted an eye when he saw her alive. Why not?

Judd leaned over to peer around the edge of the parasol and whistled. "Well, I'll be!"

"Shut up, Judd." Katrina's chin lifted and fire glittered in her gaze. She jerked a gesture toward Mr. Baylor, and snapped at Collier. "This one has to be the courier. Line the others up in the road next to him." Her hand flapped toward Cade.

Collier and Mick pulled Mr. Baylor from the line, and then Collier pushed Sharyah down onto her knees next to Cade in the roadway with Brandon to her right and Jason and the driver after that. Collier stepped in front of them all, keeping his rifle trained in their direction.

Judd immediately set into asking Mr. Baylor if he was transporting diamonds, to which the man responded negatively.

Sharyah suppressed a moan. None of this could end well. Hadn't God promised that goodness and mercy would follow those who tried to live for Him?

Cade bumped her with his shoulder. "What are you doing here?"

"Brandon…" her eyes flitted to Collier's gun, and she clutched her reticule close. "Brandon confessed that he ran away. He has a mother. We were taking him home."

For just a split second Cade's eyes slid shut and defeat seemed to cloak his shoulders. Then he lifted his chin and something softened in his expression. "We're going to get through this."

Despite her determination, tears welled. "You're hurt."

"This?" He gave a little shake of his head. "Just a scratch. I'll be fine."

Collier stepped up before them. "No more talkin'!"

Off to the right, Katrina paced a short path from one direction to the other scanning the hills around them. "Judd, just hurry up and let's get out of here. And where are Red, Billy, and Seth?"

"Patience woman! You think he's gonna hand over that much in diamonds without so much as a protest? Stop worrying like a wet cat. They'll be along shortly. And I'll have your diamonds in no time." His voice dropped low as he continued talking to Mr. Baylor.

Cade shifted slightly. "What Collier hasn't told you two is that he brought me and several others here with him to take you all out. He wants the diamonds for himself, don't you Collier?"

"Shut up!" Collier stepped toward him.

"Your three compadres have probably already been—"

"Shut yer yap, I said!" Collier rammed the butt of his rifle into Cade's forehead. "He's lyin'! I didn't know anythin' about him bein' out there, I swear." He hoisted the gun again, as if to prove his point.

"Stop!" Sharyah lunged forward and stretched out a hand to prevent another strike. "He'll be quiet." Her whole body trembled. "I'll keep him quiet."

"What's he talking about, Collier?" Judd ceased his interrogations and stepped over to glower into the man's face, although he kept his pistol directed toward Mr. Baylor.

Maybe Cade's comment would work? Did he really have other men out there who might help them? Smith maybe? Blood oozed down his cheek from the fresh gash over his eye. She plucked the hanky from where it was tucked into her cuff and pressed it to the cut. He couldn't afford to lose any more blood.

"Nothin'!" Collier swore. "He's just tryin' to get into yer head! Now let's get on with it."

Judd stood still for a long time, and like two bulls neither of whom wanted to back off, the men stared each other down, chins lifted.

Finally Judd must have been satisfied that Collier was telling the truth, because he stepped away and spat to one side. "Alright, let's find the diamonds. Mick," he gestured his brother over to a seat on a boulder across the road and pressed a pistol into his hand, "watch them and shoot the first one that tries anything."

Judd, Collier, and Katrina took Mr. Baylor with them toward the stage.

Mick lounged lazily, the pistol resting on one thigh. But his eyes, anything but lazy, raked her from the ground up and back again.

Sharyah shivered and looked away to dab at Cade's cut. The man had that same feral look he'd had when he'd accosted her in the meadow. A rock bit into her knee and she shifted to a less painful spot.

Cade's fingers brushed hers and a muscle pulsed in his jaw. His gaze dropped to her reticule, darted to Mick, and then met her own. "You still carry my tintype in your bag?"

She swallowed, knowing good and well it wasn't his picture he was really asking about. "You asked me never to go anywhere without it."

"Did you listen?" He kept his voice low and darted another look toward Mick who was still ogling her.

Sharyah pressed away a roll of nausea and tried to lighten the mood. "I always listen."

He arched his brows. "Uh huh. Like you listened when I asked you to wait at the Hanging T until I came back for you?"

Yes, there was that, wasn't there? But she had a good reason! "There is a mother in Beth Haven who has no idea her son is alive and well. What was I supposed to do?" Brandon shifted and she patted his shoulder. "This is not your fault."

Across the way Mick stood from his perch on the boulder. He swayed slightly, and for the first time Sharyah noticed that his jaw was quite swollen and purpling with a bruise. His predatory eyes never left her but he hesitated as though trying to make a decision.

Cade snatched the hanky down and leaned closer. He lowered his voice. "Do you trust me?"

She darted a look toward Mick as he took a slow step forward, then nodded. "Yes."

"I need you to distract him. Just for a minute. Drop your bag."

"Cade…" She shivered at the thought of spending even one second talking to Mick Rodale, but even as she uttered the small protest she let the drawstring slip from her wrist and her reticule slid to the ground between them.

"I won't let him hurt you. I just need a couple seconds."

That was what made every muscle in her body weak with fear. She knew he'd fight for her, but in doing that he might be hurt – hurt worse than he already was.

Yet what other options did they have?

She lifted her chin, ready to face Mick head on, but at that moment Smith stumbled out from behind the stage, hands lifted high in the air. Billy and Red shoved and prodded him from behind with their guns.

Mick, still several strides away, paused, his attention on the newcomers.

"There you are!" Katrina stepped into view, Collier right on her heels with a strange emotion in his eyes.

Was it happiness to see Smith? Or worry? Sharyah couldn't quite tell.

"Where's Seth?" Katrina snapped.

Red and Billy looked at each other, then Billy stuck his lower lip out with a shrug. "Don't know. Figured he was down here with ya'll."

Katrina raked Smith with an assessing gaze. "And who's this?"

Red gave Smith a shove. "Found him up on the hill, trying to help Judge Green who'd just tried to waylay me a few minutes before that. We figured we'd better bring him along to the party."

Katrina cast a sharp glance toward Collier. "Where's the judge?" Even though she was glowering at Collier, her question wasn't directed to him.

Red guffawed and the sound sent a swirl of horrible apprehension through Sharyah.

"He won't be bothering us anytime soon."

They killed him?

As if sensing her worry, Smith said, "I left him my canteen."

"Hush up, old man!" Billy cuffed Smith from behind.

So the judge had at least been alive when they left him. And Smith *had* been out there supposedly coming to their rescue just like Cade had claimed. Along with the judge. Was there anyone else?

Smith sent Cade an apologetic glance.

Cade shook his head, giving his father a little shrug, as if to say, "Don't worry about it," but Sharyah could read the defeat in his eyes.

"Well, we're lucky nothing came of it." Katrina turned to fully face Collier now, and leveled her pistol at his chest. "But you lied. There were other men out there. And I think Cade was telling the truth."

Alarm filled Collier's face and he lifted his hands. "No wait—!"

Katrina shot him. Right through the heart. He fell, staring sightlessly at the brazen blue sky overhead.

Sharyah couldn't stop the little yelp of shock that burst forth. And in that moment she knew Katrina had no intention of leaving any of them alive. She thought of Brandon, so young and full of youthful vigor, his life cut short in such a manner. Jason and Nicki, who had just celebrated the birth of their little girl. Cade… she closed her eyes unable to finish that thought.

Breathe.

Katrina dismissed Collier's body with a flip of her wrist and reloaded her spent chamber as she spoke to Red and Billy. "Roll him into the ditch." She gestured from Mick to Smith to where they all knelt in the roadway. "Get him over there next to them, and then come help me search the inside of the coach. Those diamonds can't be that hard to find. Billy, you keep an eye on everyone."

Red and Billy rolled Collier over the embankment, leaving a dark splotch of blood in the roadway. Red followed Katrina as Billy came toward them.

Sharyah couldn't seem to pull her gaze away from the dark stain that stood in stark contrast to the dirt around it. Evidence of a soul who'd had a choice, a chance at *Life*, only moments ago, but now no longer had any options.

How much more blood would be shed here today?

Mick shoved Smith onto his knees in front of Brandon. "Don't go anywhere now, old man." He patted Smith on the head giving a dry chuckle as he reached out to trail one finger over Sharyah's cheek.

She jerked her face away.

And beside her, Cade stiffened. "Keep your hands off her."

Mick only chuckled again, his gaze never leaving hers. "I guess we'll just have to delay the pleasure of getting reacquainted for a few minutes." He sauntered toward the coach.

Sharyah's shoulders slumped in relief. *The snake!*

Billy, left as their only guard, winked, took a seat on the boulder across the road, and watched them all intently.

Over by the stage Judd bellowed a curse, something crashed, and Baylor grunted.

Still jittery, Sharyah wrenched around to see what was happening. Apparently Katrina, Mick and Red were all inside the coach, because it jostled from side to side as though people were moving in there and the only people in view were Judd and Mr. Baylor.

Judd, his beefy hand wrapped in a firm grip around Mr. Baylor's neck, screamed into the man's face. "I'm done playing games! You have exactly ten seconds to give over the diamonds, or someone dies!" Judd's voice warbled, shredded ragged by rage and insanity. He shoved Mr. Baylor up against the side of the coach and rammed the barrel of his pistol into the man's cheek. "Where! Are! The! Diamonds!?"

Sharyah spun around to face the front, she had no desire to see another man killed as she watched.

Cade squeezed her hand, his palm warm against hers as he gritted, "The diamonds aren't even here."

She met Jason's gaze over top Brandon's head, then looked back at Cade and nodded. She whispered, "That man has them. He galloped into town at the last minute and delayed our departure, but he told us he has them."

Cade's eyes slid shut. "Don't worry. We'll think of something."

Judd bellowed another curse and Mr. Baylor grunted.

Brandon cowered and Sharyah wrapped one arm around him. She glanced down to murmur a word of encouragement but stilled. Brandon had slunk down, but what she had perceived as cowering was really him gathering up small pebbles.

His slingshot! How could she have forgotten that the boy always had that thing shoved into the waistband of his pants?

To their left, Judd cursed again, ramming one fist into the door and kicking the hub of one wheel.

The horses shifted nervously and the coach rolled forward and then back before they settled and held their ground.

Kneeling to Jason's right, the stage driver huffed and mumbled, "Stupid idiot's gonna spook them hosses and they's gonna gallop right on outta here, if he don't settle down."

Sharyah exchanged glances with Cade. *The horses!* That was it!

The lead, nigh horse was only a few feet in front of them and to the left.

She closed her eyes and pressed one hand to her forehead. They needed to act now. It would be too late in a few minutes. Too late for all of them. She let go of Cade's hand and squeezed his arm, hoping he would catch her signal, and then spoke loud enough so she was sure Billy would hear her. "Cade, the sight of that blood is making me dizzy."

"Shar, what are you doing?" he whispered. "Please be careful."

Swaying in a manner she hoped was convincing, she pulled her hat from her head, secured the hatpin in her hand, and fanned herself with the green felt brim. "Oh, I think I'm going to be sick!"

At least that much was the truth.

She lurched to her feet. Bending double, she clutched her stomach and staggered forward.

She heard Cade scramble to his feet. "You'll have to excuse her, she does have a very weak stomach."

Sharyah stumbled another few steps closer to the horses.

Billy swung his gun toward her. "Wait a min—!" Then, in her peripheral vision she saw him jolt and slap at his head. "Ow! Hey! What the—"

"I got 'im!" Brandon cried exultantly.

Billy pointed the gun at her again, but she only had two more steps now and the horse blocked her from his view. She leapt forward and jabbed the haunch of the lead horse with her hatpin. "Ha!" she yelled.

With a screech of terror the horse reared in the harness.

"What in—!"

Judd started to turn toward her, but she couldn't worry about him. She was at the rear team now, and put the hatpin to good use again.

The feet of the first horse landed back on the ground. "Ha! Ha! Ha!" Sharyah flapped her hat and Cade gave a sharp whistle. The same one he'd always used to call his horse.

Dirt spraying in every direction from sixteen hooves, the coach lurched forward.

The far horse's shoulder must have rammed into Billy, because she saw his gun hand fly up and then he toppled over backwards.

Sharyah leapt to one side just in time to keep from being knocked down and run over by the coach wheel, as the horses lurched ahead.

"Judd!" Katrina screeched from inside. Her small hand grasped at the edge of the window, but to no avail. Red's body,

234 ★ Lynnette Bonner

also falling, collided with hers. "Red!" She tumbled backward and as the coach shot by Sharyah saw her head smash into the back seat and Red scrabbling to keep from falling on her. But to no avail. With a squawk of cursed protest from Katrina, and a loud thud, both disappeared below the ledge of the window. Then the coach was gone, leaving nothing but a swirling cloud of dust in its wake.

Sharyah coughed and waved a hand in front of her face.

Mr. Baylor took advantage of Judd's distraction. He shoved him away and landed a solid kick to his groin. Judd bent double and Mr. Baylor kicked the gun from his hand.

Sharyah pulled in a relieved breath. Her curls had come loose from their pins and cascaded over her face. She swiped them out of her eyes, looked up, and froze.

From the other side of the road, Mick grinned at her over the top of the pistol he held steadily on her chest.

Shoulders slumping, her eyes blinked slowly in defeat. She raised her hands. He'd been examining the other side of the coach, not inside it.

"Well, well, well… Nothing but a trouble maker, are you?"

"Rodale!" Cade yelled.

Mick's eyes darkened. His finger tightened on the trigger, and Sharyah knew her end had come.

CHAPTER NINETEEN

A gunshot ripped through the air. Something tugged at her shirtwaist. A second blast ricocheted around her.

I've been shot. She took a step backward. Looked down to see where she'd been hit.

"Shar!"

Pounding footsteps. Crunching gravel.

Knees so weak… She sank to the ground.

"No. No. No!" Cade slid to a stop before her and forked the fingers of both hands into her curls, pushing them out of her eyes. "Are you hit? Where are you hit?" He pushed her to arm's length, his terror-filled gaze darting down the length of her and back again. "Shar? Talk to me. Are you hurt?"

She wanted nothing more than to give in to the blackness tugging at the edges of her vision, but Papa's old admonitions kicked in and she took a deep breath.

No vapors!

Another breath. "Where's Mick?" A tremor raced through her.

"I shot him."

The blackness receded.

Inhale. "Judd?"

"Baylor got the jump on him. Jason and Baylor are tying him up right now." His hands tightened around her face. "Are you hurt?"

She assessed herself. She didn't feel any pain.

"Shar, talk to me." Cade gave her a little shake.

Pain sliced along her side then and she hissed involuntarily.

He jolted back. "What? What is it?"

Brandon was suddenly by her side. His eyes wide with fear darted from her face to her side and back. "Are you alright, Miss Jordan?"

"I don't—" She glanced down. Blood soaked the waist of her dress around a jagged tear in the material. "I guess it's good I hadn't had time to change into another dress, yet. That would have been two dresses ruined." She tried to smile, but was afraid it came out more like a grimace.

"What am I going to do with you? Let me see that." Cade carefully lifted her arm and examined the wound with gentle fingers. "This one will be worse than the one on your arm, but it looks like the bullet went clean through. That's good." Even though she could tell he was trying to sound optimistic, his whole body shook perceptibly.

Jason stepped up behind Cade and laid a hand against his shoulder. "Here." He pressed a sheathed knife into Cade's palm. "Your Pa and I are going to go after the stage. See if we can't catch that woman and the other man."

Cade nodded, even as he slipped the blade of the knife through the material just above the hem of her skirt.

Despite the pain now pulsing through her ribcage in waves, and the dizziness sweeping over her, Sharyah had the presence of mind to exclaim, "That's my dress you are slicing up!"

Cade ignored her and spoke over his shoulder to Jason. "Give me a minute and I'll come with you."

"You don't mind my saying so, you aren't in any condition to be riding along." Jason turned and looked at Brandon. "Brandon, bring me the canteen off that horse that just trotted in."

Cade used a section of her hem to wipe away as much of the blood as possible, and then wrapped the rest of the material he'd just torn from her skirt around her waist to staunch the bleeding. "I'll be fine. Just a couple more seconds."

"Uh huh." Jason pressed the canteen against Cade's chest and pushed him back down when he started to stand.

Cade sucked in a quick breath, his face scrunching in pain.

The corner of Jason's mouth ticked up. "Like I said. Your Pa and I will go. Take a good long drink, wait a minute, then drink some more. Both of you. You've lost a lot of blood."

Jason started away, then paused. "By the way, the guy you

shot is dead. I didn't know you packed a derringer. How'd they miss it?"

Cade took a long drink from the canteen, and sank down to sit next to her, apparently giving up on the idea of pursuing Katrina and Red. He swiped his mouth with the knuckles of one hand, and passed her the canteen. "The gun was in Shar's little bag."

Jason's lips quirked. "Count on a Jordan to come through with a gun when you need one."

Cade chuckled but exhaustion had suddenly gripped Sharyah so thoroughly, she couldn't bring herself to comment.

"Well it was a good thing you shot when you did, looks like your bullet knocked his aim off just enough." Jason indicated the fresh bandage around her ribs. "The big guy is tied up. The other one, the one who was guarding us there at the last, he got knocked a good one when the horses took off. Bashed his head into that rock he was sitting on. He didn't make it. And I sent Baylor up the hill to where they said they left that Judge."

"Thanks, Jace. I'm glad you're here. You and Pa."

Jason touched his hat and strode away.

Sharyah glanced around. So much death and destruction. All over a few little stones.

"Did they ever find the diamonds?" She clenched her jaw against a wave of pain.

Cade shook his head. "I don't think so. You sure they were on there?"

She nodded. "Mr. Baylor said he was delivering them to Judge Green."

Cade sighed. "Of all the days Missy could have picked to test Katrina's loyalty, she somehow picked the one that the diamonds actually were being delivered on." He glanced over at the row of bodies. "Discontentment sure causes a lot of trouble."

There was enough truth in that statement to keep her thinking for a long time to come. All this because people weren't content with their place in life. And wanted all the benefits of money without the hard work it took to get it.

Jason and Smith had laid the bodies all in a row. A light breeze rippled over them, fluttering material and hair. She swallowed and studied the ground by her side.

It was her fault Billy was dead. If she hadn't spooked the horses... She took another swallow of water and passed the canteen once more to Cade. Then picked up the knife and set to slicing off several more inches of her hem. Cade's side needed tending too. She faced him and gestured for him to remove his bloody shirt. "Let me see it."

He grinned, but pain radiated from his eyes as he shrugged out of the sleeves. "A real matched pair you and I make, don't you think?"

Despite all that had happened, her stomach curled at the thought, and her hands began to tremble as she used the canteen to saturate the portion of his shirt that was sticking to his wound. She'd come this close to losing him forever.

"Hey." He captured her hands and touched her chin, tilting her face up until she met his gaze. "I'm going to be alright. You're going to be alright. You did real good today."

"If I hadn't..." She couldn't help but glance again toward the row of bodies. Judd, trussed hand and foot, lay on the ground not too far from them.

"Shar." Cade pulled her attention back to him. "They all made their choices. You couldn't know that horse would knock him into the rock. As for Mick and Collier, no one forced them to be here. This all would have been over in less than five minutes if Collier hadn't betrayed us. Sometimes in order to prevent evil, tough choices have to be made. I never like to have to kill someone, but...," he shrugged, "if we don't stand up when evil men attack the innocent, what are we left with?" He pointed to Brandon, who sat with arms wrapped around his knees. "Your actions saved that boy's life today. And don't you forget that. Not to mention the rest of us."

She bit her lip and nodded. "You're right. But it doesn't make me feel any better about how it all turned out." Another wave of wooziness made her shake her head.

Cade caressed her cheek and leaned forward to drop a kiss on the top of her curls. "That's what makes you different from them."

"Yes. I suppose." She forced her attention to cleaning and wrapping the gash on his side and tried to ignore the tingling fire emanating from the spot he'd kissed. Cade's wound blurred and she blinked hard to bring it back into focus.

It was only a few moments later that Jason returned leading one team of horses from the stage.

Cade glanced at him questioningly. "Where's Pa?"

Jason swung down. "The stage tipped over at a corner just down the road a ways. The big man with long red hair, had broken his neck. And we found a black man shot in the head."

Cade's hands fisted. "Jonas. That must have been the first shot I heard. It had to have been Collier that shot him."

Jason handed the horses off to Cade. "The woman wasn't anywhere around. She'd cut loose one of the horses and we had to put the other down. Smith is scouting a circle to see if he can't pick up her trail but he said the judge was hurt pretty bad and wanted me to get him and you two to the doc in town as soon as possible."

"Is the stage drivable?"

Jason shook his head. I'm afraid we're going to have to ride."

At that moment Mr. Baylor came into view, leading a horse with Judge Green slumped over in the saddle. He rubbed his jaw. "He's some injured, but seems like he's got grit. I think he'll make it to town. This must be his horse, I found it tied back a ways in the brush from where he was laying up there. There's another man up there. Cussin' and fussin' like a boy yet in short pants."

"Seth!" Cade wore a chagrinned look. "I nearly forgot about him. He's his younger brother." He nodded toward Judd.

Jason grabbed the rope that tied Judd's hands together and hauled him to his feet. "I'll get him. You all go on and ride into town. I'll meet you there after I get this one and his brother locked up."

Cade helped her to her feet and but she couldn't seem to find firm footing. And everything around her swirled unsteadily. "Cade…" she reached for his arm, but met only air. Then all went black.

Two hours later, Cade leaned back into the slats of the chair in the corner of the hotel room, eyes heavy with fatigue. He was too tired and distraught to remain standing but couldn't allow himself the comfort of the bed.

In the room next door, Shar fought for her life.

The Doctor had been by to examine her, and had said only time would tell, but it didn't look good.

His jaw clenched and he rubbed at the grit behind his lids. *God*! He could think of nothing else to add to the prayer.

Judd and Seth were in jail. But Smith had ridden back into town a few minutes earlier, frustrated after losing Katrina's trail. He had quickly volunteered to take Brandon out to his mother.

The doctor had left to examine Judge Green, but since her father was in much better shape than Sharyah, Missy volunteered to sit with her through the night.

Jason had sent a wire to his aunt and uncle, letting them know about Shar.

And now all Cade could do was wait. Interminable hours stretched.

The fever came on Sharyah sometime during the night. Missy knocked on his door to let him know the prognosis looked worse and that Sharyah couldn't seem to find a comfortable sleep, either she kicked off the covers, too hot, or couldn't seem to shake wracking chills.

Sleep remained elusive for the rest of the night although he did doze off and on in the chair.

The boy squirmed from his seat on the horse behind Smith, as they took a trail off the main road.

"You think you might stick around for a minute or two, until Ma regains her head, like?"

Smith didn't respond right away. Cade had never run off when he was a lad, although he'd played plenty of pranks and caused his share of ruckus.

What would he have done if a complete stranger had returned Cade to him, several days after the boy disappeared? He bit back a smirk, he knew good and well what he'd have done.

Brandon leaned off to one side and peered up at him. "Just for a minute?" As the silence stretched, the boy resumed his seat behind him and murmured almost to himself. "Or a day? Or a *week*?"

It was nearly more than Smith could do to withhold a guffaw at the plaintive pleading in the boy's tone but he wasn't about to relieve his discomfort with an answer. The boy's mother must be fit to be tied.

A little cabin came into view ahead. The yard was swept clean and there were flower boxes at each of the two windows, although they stood empty now. The porch railing needed a few nails, and one of the steps had rotted through. One window pane had broken, and a hide of some sort covered the hole from the inside. The place looked run down, but it didn't have a feel of neglect, simply the feel of lack.

Smith pulled up at the rail, and helped Brandon slide down. He was just swinging down himself when the cabin door opened and a woman with a toddler on her hip stepped out. He swiped his hat from his head.

Her red-rimmed eyes honed in on Brandon. Then widened. "Oh!" She plunked the little one onto the porch and rushed headlong down the steps, snatching the young man into a fierce embrace. "Lord of Mercy and Grace. Thank you! Thank you. Thank you!" Just that fast she thrust him away to arm's length again, and gave him a shake. "Young man, I ought to tan you till you can't stand for a week of Sundays! Where have you been? Do you know how worried I was?" Tears came then and she clutched him close, once more. "I thought I'd lost you."

Smith tapped his hat against one leg, feeling a little awkward standing by, but he couldn't just ride off without so much as a word to the woman.

After a long moment in her arms, Brandon squirmed. "Ma!"

"Don't you 'Ma' me!" She set him back and cuffed his head, but gentled it with a ruffle. "And don't you think this discussion is over." She nodded her head toward the baby that hadn't moved, but had contented itself with slurping on several fingers, wide eyes on its mother and brother. "Go on now, and get Lissa and take her into the house while I talk to this gentleman."

The baby's face broke into a huge grin as Brandon trudged up the stairs, and without hesitation she raised her arms to her big brother. "B'andon!"

The woman wore a pendant around her neck and when she turned to face him, she was sliding it back and forth on its chain. "I don't know how to thank you." She blinked hard. "I looked everywhere. No one in town seemed to know what happened to him. I thought—" Her voice choked off and she looked away to stare across the small clearing of pasture.

"He's been with my son and his teacher. Safe this whole time. We're very sorry. We didn't know he had a family. He told us he was an orphan and had been living on his own."

Her eyes dropped closed, but not in time to shutter the pain he saw there.

"Ever since his father… passed, he hasn't been himself. It's been nearly a year now, but I haven't known how to help him. I've been so busy trying—" she gestured around the place, taking in the barn, pasture, and cabin— "…just to keep us alive…."

Smith glanced toward the barn. If he could talk her into letting him stay for a few days he could help her with a lot of the little repairs that needed done around the place. He stretched out his hand. "Name's Bennett. Smith Bennett."

Her hand was small and cold, but her grip firm when she shook. "Reagan McBride."

He smoothed his palm over the brim of his hat. "That barn have any extra stalls?"

She frowned. "Why?"

He shrugged. "Figured I could stay around for a couple days and help with some repairs and such. I can sleep in there if there's any extra room."

She raised one palm. "We might be hard up, but we are not a charity case. I thank you from the bottom of my heart for bringing my boy home. But I can't afford to pay you, and I won't take any handouts." She turned her back in dismissal as if all was a done deal.

Smith folded his arms and rubbed one hand over his jaw. "Well now, I don't know. The boy did take some caring for. And I currently find myself without a place to stay. I think it would only be fair payment to let me sleep in your barn for a few days."

She spun back toward him. Her chin lifted and her blue eyes snapped. She didn't like it, but oh, the stubborn in her was just a little too bullheaded to deny him his request. "Fine." She bit the word out, then lifted her skirts and stomped up the steps onto the porch. "I suppose that is only fair. I can give you a week." And with that she stepped through the door and shut it without so much as another glance.

Smith grinned and settled his hat back on his head. He glanced around. Might as well start by fixing the hinge on that barn door. He whistled as he lead his mount across the yard. Maybe the Good Lord had instigated Brandon to run off, after all?

Sometimes stubborn needed a good ol' whack with a fence post. He chuckled. Yes sir. He knew all about that.

CHAPTER TWENTY

S am Perry pulled his riding gloves from his fingers as he stepped into the entry way at his ranch. He glanced around. Maybe he would sell. He and Missy could move east. Give her a new start in a new place. She might like that. He would talk to her about it.

A sound from upstairs drew his attention. He glanced up to the landing.

A muffled grunt and the sound of drawers opening and shutting in Kat's room.

She didn't! His pulse thrummed in his ears as he slapped his gloves down on the side table and took the stairs two at a time. Her door was slightly open and he pushed it wide.

Clothes were flung everywhere. A suitcase lay open on the bed with various articles spilling from it like mangled spokes from a broken wagon wheel. Katrina lay on the floor reaching for something under the bed.

He folded his arms and took two deliberate breaths before he allowed himself to speak. "How dare you come back here."

She jumped, cracking her head against the thick wooden frame of the bed. "Sammy." She leapt to her feet, whatever item she'd been trying to reach apparently forgotten. "I need your help. They're coming for me!"

He inhaled, long and slow. This was partly his fault. He'd always been too easy on her. Let her weasel her way into his good graces time and time again. But this time she'd gone too far.

"Word is you killed the sheriff, Kat." Pain sliced deep, at the thought. "Is it true?"

She brushed her hands together. "He wasn't a good man, Sammy. He was out there trying to steal the diamonds from me! I did this town a favor."

His eyes dropped closed. There came a time when the most merciful thing to do for someone was to turn them over to justice. That time was now.

He opened his arms. "Come here, Kat."

"Oh Sammy, I knew you'd understand." She came to him, wrapping her arms around him.

He savored the feel of her there, for just a few seconds and then, before he could change his mind, he set her at arm's length and looked down at her. "I'm doing this for your own good. I love you, Kat."

"I know you do. Thank you."

She started to turn for her suitcase and he grabbed her wrist and twisted it behind her.

"Sam!"

He pushed her forward onto the bed and pulled her other wrist behind her too.

She called him every foul name under the sun.

Blinking hard against the tears that wanted to fall, he snatched a corset from the suitcase, and pulled the string loose with his teeth. It was only moments before he had her bound, trussed, and gagged for good measure. He couldn't stand to listen to even one more of her lies.

He would have called someone to take her into town for him, but this was something he had to do for himself. He had Millicent's boy ready two horses, tied her in the saddle, lead her into town and locked her into a cell himself.

Judd and Seth shared the room's only other undamaged cell across the room from her.

Without a word he turned his back. He'd given her everything. Ever since Pa died. He'd tried to make up for their past. Yes. He'd given her everything. And now, even this. One last mercy. One last chance to see the error of her ways and make a change.

God, let it be enough.

He strode from the jail without so much as a backward glance, not envying her the chilly night she would pass, since the gaping hole in the wall of the middle two cells had yet to be fixed.

The next weeks stretched on eternally and seemed to fade into a blur.

Sharyah's parents, Rachel and Sean Jordan, arrived and Rachel tended her daughter around the clock, but still the infection from the bullet wound raged. October's limpid sun gave way to November snow flurries and Sharyah's breathing grew shallow and raspy.

Cade stood at Sharyah's hotel window, hands clasped behind him as he studied the street below. Across the room, Rachel sat beside Sharyah's bed, periodically dabbing the moisture from her face and coaxing water between her lips.

The trials for Judd, Seth and Katrina had taken place each in succession. Judd, his past deeds taken into consideration with his present, was sentenced to hang and had been summarily executed. Seth and Katrina were sentenced to jail – Seth to ten years in the Oregon State Penitentiary in Salem, and Katrina to life.

James Baylor had given Judge Green his diamonds – turned out the man had been wearing them all along, sewn into the thick leather belt he wore – and now Missy proudly sported one on her finger as a pledge between Sam Perry and her.

It had taken some grit for Sam to turn his own sister over like that, and Cade couldn't be happier for him that he and Missy had been able to patch things up. Especially since that meant Sharyah would have no more excuses to avoid him if she got better.

When! When she got better.

He sighed. Truth was, Sharyah had slowly been getting worse for the past several days. He clenched his eyes tight and gritted his teeth. He had to remain strong.

His stomach rumbled and he turned from the window. Rachel would be hungry too.

"How did her wound look today?"

Doctor Rike had missed a small scrap of cloth that had gotten stuck in the wound when the bullet passed through her dress.

Rachel had only discovered it a few days earlier while changing the dressing. He'd hoped removing that, and the new medicines they were trying would have shown more of an improvement by now.

She looked down. "I want to say better, but I'm afraid it's wishful thinking. But…maybe a little better. Missy brought by some carbolic acid and I've been cleaning it with that for several days now. It's her lungs I'm worried about."

Cade nodded. "I'll sit with her. Why don't you get Sean and go on down to the diner? Take a little break?"

Rachel stood reluctantly, her hands fidgeting to smooth and straighten Sharyah's blankets. The knowledge of imminent loss weighed heavy in her expression. "I'll not be long." The barely audible words held the fear of missing her daughter's last breath.

He knew because he'd been living with the same fear every time he'd left the room for the past three days.

Cade swallowed hard and collapsed into the chair by the bedside, as Rachel left the room. He propped his ankle across one knee and steepled his fingers, studying Sharyah over them.

Her face, pale and almost gray against the sheets, shone with droplets of moisture. Lips cracked with fever lay slightly parted as each breath labored to grate in and out.

He leaned forward and lifted her hand from the blanket into his own, and though her body burned with fever her fingers were cool. With a cloth he carefully dabbed the moisture from her face, then took up the teaspoon and held water to her lips. Once. Twice. Three times.

"God," he looked toward the ceiling, pressing the back of her hand against his lips, "please…" He blinked hard. He wasn't versed in being blatant with his feelings. Feelings were better hidden behind humor and laughter.

Would God ask him to let go of another? Hadn't letting go of his mother been hard enough?

Didn't the Psalmist promise that God had good things in store for those who belonged to the Shepherd? That goodness and mercy would follow them all the days of their lives?

248 ★ Lynnette Bonner

God, this doesn't feel like goodness or mercy. Not for me. Not for her. Not for Rachel and Sean.

And yet, who was he to tell God what those looked like?

His own hands trembling with suppressed tears, he laid her hand back against the blanket and covered it. He'd prayed for weeks now. Done nothing but pray as he moved through the haze of each day. Maybe the time had come to let go.

Is this what You are going to require of me? Again?

He leaned forward and pressed a kiss to her brow.

He stilled. Did she feel cooler? He laid the back of his hand to her forehead. Maybe... or was it only wishful thinking as Rachel had said?

She stirred, moaning softly.

His heart lurched on the wings of renewed hope. "Shar?" He snatched up the cloth and dabbed her face. "Shar. Can you wake up?"

Her mouth worked and her face turned toward him slightly. She didn't open her eyes, but she rasped something he couldn't quite understand.

He leaned down. "What? Tell me again."

"So... thirsty..."

The words were more air than voice, but he wanted to whoop for joy at the sound. "That's my girl. Thirst I can deal with. Here, I'm going to help you sit up a bit." He slid one arm behind her and held the cup of water to her lips.

She clutched at it and sucked greedily at the rim.

He tilted the cup back to slow her intake. "Easy, Shar. There's plenty. Easy now."

She's not a horse. He grinned at the thought. Good thing she was only half lucid or she might send him packing for speaking to her like one of his mares-in-training.

She drank more than half the cup, and then sank back with a satisfied sigh. She was asleep again before he even had time to pull his arm out from behind her.

Cade clasped his fingers behind his head and simply stood there looking down at her. He hadn't been this happy in a long time. She still had a long ways to go, but she was getting better. Goodness and mercy. Maybe God wasn't asking him to give up this dream, after all. *Thank you.*

He was still standing there a few minutes later when Rachel came back into the room. She gasped. "What is it?"

"She's fine." He stretched a hand out and rushed to sooth her alarm. "She woke up. Drank half a cup of water. Then fell right back to sleep." He grinned. "I think she's on the mend."

"Oh Lord of mercy!" Rachel covered her face with both hands and wept.

"You may now kiss your bride."

Sharyah smiled from her seat at the back of the small group who'd gathered at the Hanging T to witness Jason and Nicki's vows.

The day couldn't be more perfect. March sunshine, softened by a gentle breeze, warming her shoulders. Small fluffy clouds floating on the horizon. Family gathered all around. All made even better because she was finally well enough to be here.

The past months, her recovery had proven torturously slow. Between Mama and Cade hovering over her at nearly every waking moment, and her body's refusal to regain energy as quickly as she would have liked, there were days when she'd been ready to bellow her frustration like a calf in search of sustenance. Only for the past week had she even been leaving the hotel.

Jason kissed his new wife with obvious relish, amid much whooping and heckling.

A sigh of contentment eased from her as she glanced around.

Grandma Eltha was there, seated next to Jeff and Marquis, Jason's sister. Sky held Sierra captive on one knee, his other arm wrapped around Brooke's shoulders. Neither of them were focused on Jason and Nicki, but instead on each other. Sharyah's insides melted. *Thank you Lord, for bringing Sky into Brooke's life just when she needed him most.*

The minister dismissed them all and Rocky, Victoria, and

their three adopted children stood and made their way through the benches toward the tables laden with food where Mrs. Vasquez already bustled back and forth.

"Jimmy, no going back for seconds until everyone has eaten," Rocky called. Then he reached over and tweaked one of Victoria's red curls, bending forward to say something into her ear. Victoria swatted his shoulder and gave a retort that made Rocky stop in his tracks and settle his hands on his hips, a huge grin splitting his face.

Smith, who had been walking behind them and had his attention fixed on something behind Victoria, bumped into him.

"Sorry," Rocky said over his shoulder and then hurried to catch up to his family.

Smith murmured a reply, but his gaze was still fixed beyond her.

Sharyah turned to see what had captivated his attention so thoroughly. A dark haired woman with a baby on her hip stood talking quietly with the minister and his wife. And next to her stood Brandon. *Interesting.* Sharyah felt a smile tug on her lips. She'd heard that Smith had been helping to keep things running for Brandon's mother. What she hadn't heard was that the woman was so beautiful. Brandon caught her looking and gave her a hearty wave.

She smiled and returned the gesture. Looked like his mother let him live, after all.

Turning back around Sharyah tipped her face up to catch the full effect of the sun. She should probably mosey on over to get herself a plate.

As if she'd read her mind, Mama leaned over and patted her arm. "Why don't you just sit right here, Sharyah? Soak up some sunshine and warmth and let me get you a plate. I don't want you to overdo today."

Sharyah started to rise. "Mama, I'm fi—"

"I'll sit with her, Mrs. Jordan." Cade touched her elbow, and urged her back onto the bench, easing down beside her.

Sharyah's pulse kicked around like a spring filly. Where had he come from?

"Thank you, Cade." Hefting her skirts, Mama bustled off leaving the two of them practically alone.

Sharyah swallowed. Although she'd seen him nearly every day since she'd started to mend, they hadn't had much time alone. So much had changed in such a short amount of time.

Cade planted his elbows into his knees. He pushed his Stetson back on his head then looked at her over his shoulder, his blue gaze warm and steady.

She smoothed at her skirt, picking at invisible flecks. If anything would make her overdo, it would be her racing heart.

"How are you feeling?"

"I said, I'm fi—"

"Shar."

She huffed. "A little tired maybe, but better than I've felt in a long time."

"Good." He studied the place where only moments ago Jason and Nicki had said their vows. Glanced down at the ground. Looked back at her. Rubbed his jaw, then leapt to his feet and paced two steps before spinning and straddling the bench, facing her. His intense eyes took in every detail of her face. "Sharyah, there's something I've been wanting – no *needing* – to say for months, now. I'd planned to – but then you were shot and I thought I'd lost you *again*. But now here you are and here I am and your whole family is here. And there's no point in having everyone make another trip somewhere when, well, what I'm trying to say is…" As the words trailed to a stop, Cade's focus wandered to those milling around them and a slight frown furrowed his brow.

She replayed every word he'd just said, but confusion refused to give up their meaning. "What?" If she'd thought her heart was beating fast before, it had held nothing on this.

He looked chagrinned. "I'm making a mess of this." He glanced out over the fields past the soddy. "Take a walk with me?"

Walk? She could barely breathe. "Sure." She started to rise.

He jumped up. "Actually that's a bad idea." He motioned her back into her seat. "I'm supposed to be keeping you from overexerting." Without another word, he dashed away.

Sharyah's mouth opened and shut, then opened again and hung there for a moment as she twisted to see him disappearing around the side of the barn.

Mama appeared by her side and handed her a plate piled high with delicious smelling beef and potatoes. "What's the matter?" She glanced around. "Where's Cade?"

"He's…" Sharyah glanced toward the barn once more. "He'll be back in a few minutes."

I think. Had he been trying to ask what she *thought* he was trying to ask? Maybe her fevers were back? She waited till Mama wasn't looking and then discretely felt of her forehead. She didn't feel warm. She closed her eyes. After so many years of longing… would the Lord finally grant her wish?

Her fork clattered against her plate and Mama cast her a worried look. "You sure you're feeling alright, dear?"

Oh, no. She was definitely not feeling alright. "I'm fine, Mama. Really." *Where did he go?*

She caught movement out of the corner of her eye. His blue shirt, black hat, familiar stride. He paused before Papa and said something. Papa stopped with a fork half way to his mouth and gave him a long level look, then a slow smile split his face and he held out one hand. They both glanced her way.

She fumbled to set her plate down on the bench before she dropped it. Her heart beat a tympani against her ribs. *Breathe.*

His gaze never leaving hers, Cade made his way through the benches and dashing children. He paused a stride away and settled his thumbs into his belt. His gaze darted to Mama, and when he returned his focus to her, humor danced in his expression. "Shar, I was wondering if you might be interested in taking a ride with me in the Hackney? I have it ready. There's something I'd like to… *talk* to you about."

Heat bloomed in Sharyah's cheeks and she worked her lower lip, unable to even formulate a response. The silence stretched.

Beside her, Mama squirmed and simpered, "That's a delightful idea, dear. Do go. A ride in the fresh air will do you some good."

Cade arched a brow and held out his arm. "Shall we, then?"

Could this really be happening to her? This was what she'd wanted ever since she could remember. Giving herself a little shake, she stood. "Y-yes. That sounds lovely. Thank you." She suppressed a grimace. She sounded like a nervous school girl giving her first oral lesson.

Cade helped her up into the Hackney and then climbed up beside her and set the team down the road at a smart trot.

He didn't go far before he pulled the team off the road and directed them out across a flowing meadow. Here and there purple crocuses poked their heads above the soil and yellow daffodils bobbed and swayed in the breeze. The sun arched high in the sky, the warmth of its rays chasing off the last vestiges of winter's chill and she turned her face to its welcome rays. Somewhere a squirrel chattered fiercely, apparently not appreciating their intrusion into its domain. Birds sang lustily and even a small herd of deer cropped grass at the far end of the meadow.

Cade pulled to a stop in the dappled shade of a cherry tree with blooms just beginning to open. He wrapped the reins around the brake handle then turned to look at her, his palms rubbing against his knees. He scooted closer.

She closed her eyes and held out one hand. "Cade please be sure you mean your words before you say them." Her heart couldn't take another breaking.

Warmth enveloped her hand as he clasped it and pressed it against the solid warmth of his chest.

She chanced a peek.

Moisture glinted on his lower lids and he reached out and traced a caress from above her eyebrow to her cheek bone. "I thought I'd lost you…" He slid his fingers into her hair. "First when I told you there could be nothing between you and me, then again when I woke to find your cabin engulfed in flames, and a third time when you were shot. Each time I told myself what a fool I was not to have made it more clear exactly how I feel about you." His thumb skimmed over her lower lip, his focus dropping to her mouth as he leaned closer. "I don't aim to let that happen again."

A tremor raced through her. "Cade, I just want you to be sure y—"

The silken caress of his lips sealed off her words. All her years of pent up longing escaped on a low moan, and she leaned into him as a curl of sheer desire rolled through her. Her fingers skimmed over the rough stubble of his cheek to the smooth skin just behind his ear, then entwined in his hair.

He scooted closer and deepened the kiss for just a moment before he eased back a fraction and rested his forehead against hers. He pulled in a rapid breath and cupped her face with both his hands, his thumbs resting against her mouth. "I love you, Shar. I want to spend the rest of my life with you by my side." He pushed her face away just far enough to focus on her eyes. "Marry me. Right now. Today."

She gasped. "Cade! We can't—"

He gave her a quick silencing kiss. "Just hear me out. All our family is here. The minister is waiting. And your father gave us his blessing."

"Papa… knows about this? About you wanting to marry me *today*?"

He nodded.

Excitement jolted through her, but she scooted back, pressing him away. Needing to think. "Cade, I don't know. We need to be sure…."

"*I've* never been *more* sure of anything in all my life."

A breathy laugh of disbelief escaped. "Cade, we don't have a place to live."

He leaned close and kissed her again. Lingering this time over the task. "You act like I haven't been planning this for months now."

"Months! You never said a word to me!"

"You've been so sick. I just didn't want you to have to worry over anything."

She tilted him a glance. "Where are we going to live?"

A grin bloomed on his face. "Is that a yes?"

Laughter bubbled up. "Where?"

"I bought Sam Perry's place."

"Sam P—wait... you *bought* his ranch?"

He nodded. "He and Missy are going to move back east. I figured we could stay around here for awhile. But if you want to move back to Shiloh, I can find someone to manage the place for us. However, the school board was so happy with the job you've done, they've agreed to let you stay on as the teacher for as long as you'd like, married, or not."

She leaned forward and lowered her voice. "Do you promise to come to my rescue the next time Brandon McBride puts a spider in my lunch?"

Cade's thumb traced a hot trail along her jaw line. "Every time."

"And what about when outlaws break in and steal me away?"

"They'll have a harder time with that now that Pa has stepped in as Sheriff."

She pulled back. "He did? I hadn't heard that."

"Shar...?"

She could hear the need for an answer in his tone. But she wanted to savor this moment. Tipping her face up she closed her eyes. A bee droned in the distance. Above them, a bird chirruped its happiness. One of the horses shook its head, jangling bit and harness.

She parted her lids and studied him. Blue eyes lined with black lashes, waiting for an answer with barely disguised impatience. Clean shaven jaw, shadowed with tomorrow morning's stubble. Black curls that begged for her fingers to run through them.

She gave in to the begging. "Ask me again."

He grasped her forearms and pressed his forehead to hers. "Marry me?"

"Yes." She grinned, then allowed a full out laugh. "Yes. Yes. Yes!"

"Thank you, God!" He crushed her to him and breathed, "I thought you'd never say it."

And as she lifted her lips to receive one more kiss, she knew she would never in her life forget this sanctuary, this holy place canopied in cherry blossoms and carpeted with crocuses and fresh spring grass, this place where the Lord had finally granted her the fullness of His goodness and mercy – true love.

Don't Miss…

THE SHEPHERD'S HEART - BOOK 1

ROCKY MOUNTAIN Oasis

He's different from any man she's ever known.
However, she's sworn never to risk her heart again.

Idaho Territory,

Brooke Baker, sold as a mail-order bride, looks to her future with dread but firm resolve. If she survived Uncle Jackson, she can survive anyone.

When Sky Jordan hears that his nefarious cousin has sent for a mail-order bride, he knows he has to prevent the marriage. No woman deserves to be left to that fate. Still, he's as surprised as anyone to find himself standing next to her before the minister.

Brooke's new husband turns out to be kinder than any man has ever been. But then the unthinkable happens and she holds the key that might save innocent lives but destroy Sky all in one fell swoop. It's a choice too unbearable to contemplate…but a choice that must be made.

A thirsty soul. Alluring hope. An Oasis of love.
Step into a day when outlaws ran free, the land was wild, and
guns blazed at the drop of a hat.

Find out more at: www.lynnettebonner.com

Also Available…

THE SHEPHERD'S HEART - BOOK 2

HIGH DESERT Haven

Is Jason Jordan really who he says he is?
Everything in Nicki's life depends on the answer.

Oregon Territory, 1887

When her husband dies in a mysterious riding accident, Nicki Trent is left with a toddler and a rundown ranch. Determined to bring her ranch back from the brink of death, Nicki hires handsome Jason Jordan to help. But when William, her neighbor, starts pressing for her hand in marriage, the bank calls in a loan she didn't even know about, bullets start flying, and a burlap dummy with a knife in its chest shows up on her doorstep, Nicki wonders if this ranch is worth all the trouble.

To make matters worse, terrible things keep happening to her neighbors. When her friend's homestead is burned to the ground and William lays the blame at Jason's feet, Nicki wonders how well she knows her new hand…and her own heart.

A desperate need. Malicious adversaries. Enticing love.
Step into a day when outlaws ran free, the land was wild, and guns blazed at the drop of a hat.

Also Available…

THE SHEPHERD'S HEART BOOK 3

FAIR VALLEY Refuge

She's loved him for as long as she can remember.
But can she trust her heart to a man haunted by constant danger?

Shiloh, Oregon, April 1887

Victoria Snyder, adopted when she was only days old, pastes on a smile for her mama's wedding day, but inside she's all atremble. Lawman Rocky Jordan is back home. And this time he's got a bullet hole in his shoulder and enough audacity to come calling. Since tragedy seems to strike those she cares for with uncanny frequency, she wants nothing to do with a man who could be killed in the line of duty like her father.

But when an orphan-train arrives at the Salem depot, Victoria is irresistibly drawn toward the three remaining "unlovable" children…and stunned by a proposal that will change all of their lives forever.

Can she risk her heart, and her future happiness, on someone she might lose at a moment's notice?

Two stubborn hearts. A most unusual proposal. Persevering love.
Step into a day when outlaws ran free, the land was wild, and
guns blazed at the drop of a hat.

Contemporary Romantic Suspense
Now Available from Lynnette Bonner...

The Unrelenting Tide
Islands of Intrigue, Book 1

She's been living a lie that could just get her killed...

Widowed former Hollywood actress Devynne Lang has been living a quiet life in the San Juan Islands of the Pacific Northwest. For years, she's hoped her fabricated death would keep her identity safe from the public, and more to the point, from the stalker who forced her into hiding. But strange things have been happening around her place and this time, with a daughter to protect, she can't afford one mistake – even if it means letting Carson Lang help.

Carson would do anything to protect his brother's widow and her daughter. So when he discovers Devynne may be in danger, he vows to find the man responsible.

The problem is, the danger just might be closer than they think – even as close as their hearts.

The Unrelenting Tide
AN EXCERPT

CHAPTER ONE

A scream gargled at the back of Devynne Lang's throat, jolting her from terrorized slumber. With a whimper she kicked back covers tangled against damp legs, yanked open the nightstand drawer, and fumbled for the familiar feel of her .38 special.

The rubberized, laser-trigger grip cool against her palm, she gave it a firm squeeze. The red laser light pierced the darkness beside the balcony curtains. Through the bathroom door. Into the black maw of her closet. Her gaze jerked from corner to corner, scrutinizing each shadow, each waver of light.

Nothing.

Her own ragged breathing registered and she blinked slowly. Pulled in a long full inhale, then released it along with some tension.

No one was here. It was the nightmare.

Again.

Running a hand back through her hair, she glanced down. She knelt in the middle of her bed, t-shirt and shorts plastered with sweat, knees denting sheets so jumbled it seemed a wrestling match had taken place. The angry red numbers of the clock on the nightstand read 4:30am.

If Marissa stayed true to form she would be up in a couple of hours begging to watch *Nick Jr.* while she ate her breakfast.

Devynne sank back against her ankles. Best she get on with her day. She took one more calming breath, then forced her legs over the edge of the bed.

She pulled back the floor length curtains and peered out onto the deck, giving the slider a tug to make sure it was still locked. The faint gleam of morning, just beginning to peek above the islands across the way, tinged the water gray and outlined the evergreen trees in the back yard stark black against the sky. All was as it should be.

Still, to be safe she padded across the hall and checked Marissa's room. No one behind the door. No one in the closet – the light was still on, just as she'd left it the night before when she tucked Marissa in. The only sound was the soft sonorous breaths the four year old made from under her Disney princess blanket on the canopied bed.

She crept down the stairs from the top level of her tri-story. Checked the kitchen, guest bath, living room and deck in the same way she'd done upstairs. No one on the middle level and the back door was still locked too.

A quick flip of the light switch in the sewing room on the bottom floor, revealed it was also empty.

Relief eased a little more of the strain – what she needed now was a hot shower to wash away the last vestiges.

Back in her room, she returned the Smith & Wesson Centennial 642CT Airweight to the nightstand, locked the drawer and took the key into the bathroom with her, hanging it high on the corner of the mirror like she did every morning.

She slapped on the hot water and let it run as she thought over her day.

Carson was coming this morning to take Marissa to his team's basketball game. He had mentioned the game several times this week and she knew he was a bit nervous for his varsity boys, even though he wouldn't have admitted it for anything.

Devynne pulled the shower curtain shut and stepped under the hot spray.

She would need to get Mrs. Abernathy's quilt finished soon. She'd better concentrate on that one today. One little misstep on that project and Mrs. Abernathy would be sure to let the world know what a disaster her dealings with *The Healing Quilt* had been. Devynne couldn't afford the bad publicity.

The Seattle Quilters' Guild had called yesterday and left a message to see if she could machine quilt three king size, a queen, and two double quilts in the next couple weeks.

Thank you God for the extra work. The bills had been piling up for awhile now.

She rinsed the shampoo out of her hair and thought of the account she hadn't touched since she'd fled California six years ago. How much money would be in it now?

Don't go there.

Marissa's safety was too important to ever go back for that money. Shania Hane, romantic-comedy actress, had died on a cold February day six years ago – at least that was the story her agent had been paid to tell – and needed to remain dead.

For now.

Marissa would need a good college education someday. Maybe then they would go back for the money. Maybe.

So, even though it would mean several late nights over the days to come, she would call the guild today and agree to take on the pieces.

She cranked the shower head to the massage setting and rolled her neck through the pounding water letting it beat away the last of the tension and adrenaline. She could have stood there all day, but the scent of freshly brewed coffee from her programmable pot lured her back to reality, and she shut off the tap.

The towel soft against her skin, she dried off, wrapped up, and stepped out into her room to grab her jeans and a t-shirt.

She froze.

Her night stand drawer stood cracked open, the key hanging from the lock in the front face.

The room's lights were on now and a quick scan proved she was alone. Hadn't she just put her gun in there, locked it, and hung the key in the bathroom?

Marissa!

She rushed to the drawer half expecting to find it empty, but the gun lay right where she always left it. Hurrying to snatch it up, she knocked it against the drawer. It tumbled from her grasp and landed on her foot.

She grunted but grabbed it up again and raced across the

hallway to Marissa's room, checking the loads as she went. All chambers held rounds.

Heart thudding so hard she could feel the beat of it in her chest, she pushed open Marissa's door with one foot and stepped into the room gun at the ready.

Nothing ahead. Nothing left, or right. The closet light still cast golden illumination across the Sleeping Beauty castle-shaped rug. Deep, undisturbed breathing still resonated.

Devynne slumped against the wall and leaned her head back. *Thank you, Jesus!*

Just that quickly she resumed her vigil. Someone could still be here.

No one was under the bed – she'd purposely gotten Marissa a high bed, and insisted she not store any toys underneath for times just like this – and the morning light streaming in from the window gleamed unbroken beneath it now. There was nowhere else to hide.

No one was here. *Please God, let that be true.*

A quick check through the rest of the levels revealed she and Marissa were the only ones there. And all the doors and windows were still locked.

Back in her room, she collapsed onto the edge of the bed and scooped damp hair away from her face with a trembling hand.

She was losing her mind.

She glanced down at the nightstand. There was no explanation other than she'd only *thought* she put the gun away and locked the drawer.

If Marissa had woken while she was in the shower and found the gun…

Her whole body shook at that thought. How could she have been so careless?

Tears pricked her eyes and exhaustion washed over her. She wanted nothing more than to flop over, pull the covers up to her neck, and not get up for another eight hours. The unending string of long days and late nights had been weighing heavy for the past few weeks.

She blinked hard. *Get a grip!*

She could do this. She *had* to do this. There was a little girl out there who needed her mommy to be strong, keep her fed, and keep a roof over her head. And Mommy wasn't going to let her down. Not in a million years.

She laid the gun back into the drawer. Shut it and locked it. Tested the drawer to make sure it wouldn't open. Then pulled on it one more time, for good measure. Satisfied that she had indeed locked the gun away this time, she stood.

Pain knifed through her right foot. She gasped and looked down.

A gash across the top of her foot seeped blood. She grimaced. *Great start to the day, Devynne. Just great.*

The Unrelenting Tide, Now Available.

ABOUT THE AUTHOR

Born and raised in Malawi, Africa. Lynnette Bonner spent the first years of her life reveling in warm equatorial sunshine and the late evening duets of cicadas and hyenas. The year she turned eight she was off to Rift Valley Academy, a boarding school in Kenya where she spent many joy-filled years, and graduated in 1990.

That fall, she traded to a new duet—one of traffic and rain—when she moved to Kirkland, Washington to attend Northwest University. It was there that she met her husband and a few years later they moved to the small town of Pierce, Idaho.

During the time they lived in Idaho, while studying the history of their little town, Lynnette was inspired to begin the Shepherd's Heart Series with Rocky Mountain Oasis.

Marty and Lynnette have four children, and currently live in Washington where Marty pastors a church.

Made in the USA
Coppell, TX
13 September 2020